PART I

1

HE IS STANDING LOOKING out over an alien landscape, red and dry and hot. He is alone, but he knows there are people out there somewhere, unseen. He thinks that they will remember he is there and come back for him, but he isn't certain. He knows he can't survive on his own. He shouldn't be there at all.

With a shock, he realises that he has forgotten to wear his suit. He has no breathing apparatus. He coughs, gasps, convulses, finds himself not on an alien planet but in a bright, white place where lots of people are looking after him.

SEVERAL TIMES ELLIOT makes temporary returns to consciousness. Some of his earliest thoughts are numinous. They are eureka moments, accompanied by sensations of sheer joy. It will be the saving of the human race when they understand that people are really animals with their skins on inside out. He can feel the fur in his viscera, soft and luxurious, but the problem is it creates hairballs, and they make him cough, and he is coughing and struggling for air in a blinding light and people in white are running. They are saying his name, doing things with tubes and noisy machinery. He is helpless; he seems to have no control over anything, not even his own body and, during those short spells of consciousness, he is absolutely terrified.

HE RETURNS to the red landscape again. Figures are approaching. They are walking out of a mirage-lake. Everything shimmers and ripples. Elliot thinks the figures must be wearing space suits, but as they come closer he sees they are not. One wears a stockman's hat. One wears a baseball cap. The third has a head of golden curls, like Harpo Marx.

2

THERE IS a young woman who comes to speak to him. She asks him if he remembers his name and he nods, with difficulty, and says 'Elliot,' in a slow, muddy kind of way. She asks him if he knows why he is in hospital, but he doesn't. He knows he was born in London but not what day it is, or what month, or what year. There are things coming to him that look like memories but might be dreams and things that look like dreams that might be memories. He has no facility for telling them apart. There is a pool of water in a red basin, and there is a deep hole in one end of it; its round, dark mouth beneath the water. There is something incalculably valuable at the bottom of the hole, but it is all filled up with mud and no one can get in there to clean it out.

The woman says, 'Do you remember anything about your life? What you do for a living? Do you remember working as a doctor?'

He finds that he does. He remembers working as a doctor in London, and in Dublin, and in Melbourne, and now, unlikely as it seems to him, he remembers working in remote communities in the central desert of Australia. He can't come anywhere near fitting his mouth around 'Central Australian', but he manages 'Health S-serv...,' and she nods and gives his hand a squeeze.

'You're going to be OK, Elliot. You've had a nasty head injury, but I think your mind is OK. Your memory will come back, bit by bit.'

IT DOES, exactly like that, bit by bit, and many of the bits are random and unrelated. Little shorts, or trailers, bubble up from nowhere. A first kiss, accompanied by all its sexual excitement, outside the gates of the Melbourne Zoo in the early, early hours. His father breaking down the door of his brother's bedroom and barging in, his mother's frame blocking the door, grunting and wrestling going on in there that he can't see. His mother bringing the family cat to a funeral. He remembers the name of the cat but not the name of the person in the coffin. Behind everything is a sense of movement, of travelling through unknown and surreal landscapes, of having to endure a relentless motion sickness.

A voice says, 'Elliot?' He wakes with a gasp and sees a nurse. He isn't sure whether he has seen her before or not.

'You have a visitor,' she says, but Elliot can't see anyone. He turns his head. There is a woman sitting beside his bed, and she confirms his worst fears. He doesn't know her. He is afraid that he has lost the ability to recognise faces, and that his world from now on will be full of strangers. But his visitor says,

'You don't know me, Elliot. I'm Sandra's sister. Remember Sandra?'

He almost does. He strains to remember Sandra.

Her sister says, 'From Nyaru?'

Yes. Nyaru creates a confluence of images. Lanky stockmen sitting around a table outside a community store. An old woman wearing a beanie, handing him something. Children and dogs running together along the street. A computer that never works. He can't think of any reason why he would have been in such a place. He isn't entirely sure he ever was.

But now he remembers Sandra. He sees her at the wheel of a white troop-carrier, dusty and tired.

'She'll come when she can get cover,' her sister says. 'We're going to deputise until she gets here.'

He drifts again, sinking away from the light. He hears explosions, feels them reverberate through his body, sees red smoke swirling. And then he is playing cricket for England, on the team at last, and he understands with a flash of insight that England can never win the match as long as his left leg is playing for Australia. When he wakes up, he wants to explain it to someone, anyone, but he can't speak properly. His tongue won't obey his orders. He is a prisoner in a body that has stopped working.

There was somebody there, but she has gone now. He talks himself through it. Sandra's sister. Sandra, who was the community nurse in Nyaru. If her sister has come to see him, Sandra must be someone important in his life. He finds her again, that same image in his memory; a thin woman, probably nearing middle-age, sitting behind the wheel of the clinic troopy.

3

SHE MET him at the airstrip when he landed that first day and ran through some of the need-to-know details as she drove him to the medical centre. He had completed his first clinics in two other communities and was already exhausted by the heat, by the stress of learning to operate new systems, by culture shock. He was met at the clinic by two men who formally introduced themselves as the community council. The older of the two, whose name Elliot couldn't remember, died of a stroke very soon afterwards. The younger, a man of around fifty, was Luke O'Neill.

HE WAS BARELY inside the clinic, which Sandra unlocked for him, before half the waiting room spilled in.

He said, 'Can we have people one at a time, please?' His voice was high and stiff with tension.

Sandra, said, 'It is just one. Just Doris.'

Elliot looked around. There was an old woman, a young woman with a baby on her hip and a toddler clinging to her skirt.

'Doris is your patient,' Sandra said. 'Linda is her granddaughter.'

Elliot nodded. He knew that people out here often brought someone else along for moral support. He had already come across it in the other clinics.

He said, 'And the children?'

'Linda's.'

'Do they all have to be in here?

Sandra said, 'Where would you like them to be?' She was talking with half her attention, the other half directed towards the computer, which appeared to be frozen on the clinic's home page and wasn't responding to any of her prompts. 'Bloody thing has crashed again,' she said, turning it off at the mains. 'I'll have to get you the paper files.'

She turned the power on again, and went out, leaving the computer to boot up. Elliot was beginning to believe that he wasn't cut out for working under these conditions. The baby was wriggling and dragging at her mother and the older child had a runny nose. All four of them, like Sandra, were covered in a thin film of pink dust.

Linda said, 'Doris got a cough. All the time coughing.'

Elliot dragged his attention away from the children and turned to the old woman. She was stick-thin, dressed in a light floral-patterned skirt and a loose blue tee-shirt. Curls of white hair emerged from a beanie with an AFL logo. Elliot said, 'What kind of cough do you have, Doris?'

For answer, Doris took a deep, rattling breath and gave a phlegmy cough.

Elliot nodded. He said, 'How long have you had it?'

Doris glanced at Linda. 'Few weeks, might be?'

Linda nodded. 'Yeah. About two weeks.'

Sandra had gone. A pair of teenaged girls were standing at the doorway and were leaning in, listening to the conversation. Behind them Elliot could see three more people in the waiting room, two men and a woman, all seriously overweight.

He said, 'Can you close the door, please?'

The girls seemed perplexed, not so much by what he had said, as by whether he wanted them to close it from the outside or the inside. Linda clarified with a small hand gesture. They went out. They closed the door.

Doris said, 'What you come to Nyaru for?'

Elliot sighed. New to remote community life, he had no idea how unusual it was for one of his patients to take any kind of personal interest in him. It would be a long, long time before anyone else asked him anything along the same lines. He shrugged and attempted to be light-hearted.

'It's not really up to me. They just put me on a plane and sent me here.' It went down like a lead balloon. Both women were silent, expecting more, or better. Elliot had undergone a thorough induction and read all the literature. He was aware of the need to give people time to get comfortable with him, but he had worked for far too long in time-poor regimes: he was habitually pressurised and impatient.

He said, 'Shall we talk about your cough, Doris?'

There was that hesitation again, which Elliot later came to understand was not due to lack of confidence, but a space for deliberation.

'Yuwayi,' she said. 'But where you from?'

Elliot worked hard at keeping his cool. 'Never mind about me. We're here to look after you, aren't we?'

As if she hadn't heard, Doris went on, 'You from Sydney?'

Linda said, 'She wants to know where your country is.'

Elliot sighed again. 'England,' he said. 'I've been living in Melbourne for years, but I was born in England.'

Doris nodded, slowly. 'I know about England. My husband been there. Over there in your country, long time ago. He met the queen that time.'

Elliot glanced at Linda. He expected her to confirm his assumption that her grandmother was losing her marbles, but Linda met his eye, just momentarily, and there was no complicity in her expression. What had it held, that glance? Hostility? Indifference? Contempt?

4

IT CREATES no charge in him now, in the white room in the hospital in Adelaide, but it did then. He thinks it did then. Or perhaps it was later that the charge came. The desire. He looks around him, surprised to find everything so normal and rational after all the rushing, the pain, the dreadful bubbling sounds of his lungs beings cleared. There is a slight creaking noise now, but whether it is from his lungs or crepitus from broken bones he can't tell from the inside. The important thing is that he is breathing. He is conscious. He is aware for the first time that he has survived something monumental, something of colossal, explosive force, but he isn't sure what. He wonders why no one has told him, and then he wonders whether someone has told him and he has forgotten. Anything is possible. He is calm, and he is connected, through his steady, creaky breathing, to his body. There are still dreams and imaginings hovering in his mental peripheries, but he likes what he feels when he remembers Linda. It is solid ground.

5

ELLIOT PUT the stethoscope into his ears and Doris stopped talking, allowed him to listen to the fluid on her lungs, pretty uniform across both sides. There was a pronounced wheeze there as well.

'Do you smoke, Doris?'

She said, 'No.'

'No cigarettes?'

'No, I don't smoke.'

Sandra returned and handed Elliot a thin file with *Doris Banks Nampijinpa* written on the front. As she went out again a dog trotted in and was quickly removed by one of the gate-keeping teenagers. Elliot waited until the door was closed again and then opened the file. While he read, Doris and Linda had a quiet conversation in language. The cough was a recurring problem, according to the notes. Previous doctors had prescribed several courses of antibiotics over the last couple of years.

'She smoked one time,' Linda said when he looked up from the file. 'Back in the old days. She was working on a station, that place'—she pointed at the wall—'Kimberley way. All the people smoking that time. Men and women the same. She don't smoke no more.'

'I don't like it,' Doris said. 'I don't like smoking and I don't like grog.'

'And have you lost any weight, recently, do you think? Or were you always, you know…'

Doris laughed again. 'No. Always skinny one. Healthy one, that way.'

Elliot said, 'Except for this cough. I think we should get an x-ray and see what's going on. Could be you have some problem in your lungs. They can do that for you in Alice. Just a visit to the hospital, in and out.'

Doris shook her head and turned to Linda. Again, they spoke in Warlpiri. This time the discussion was more animated. Elliot began to write a note in Doris' file, but the pen stopped working, and he realised the sweat from his hand was making the paper damp. There was an air conditioner on the wall behind him and it was making a ferocious amount of noise but didn't appear to be having any effect on the temperature. There was a fridge magnet on the filing cabinet with a picture of a Flying Doctor plane and a little inbuilt thermometer, but it was stuck somewhere around twelve degrees. He caught the eye of the snotty toddler, who was watching him intently. He tried a smile, but he couldn't even get that to work properly that day.

Linda said, 'No, she won't go.'

Doris said, 'That other doctor, the one we had before you, she gave me medicine for this.'

Elliot had been warned that people who lived so far out in the bush were often reluctant to go to hospital. It wasn't difficult to understand why. Alice Springs was a long day's drive from home, and the hostels and the town camps where visitors usually stayed could be hard going. He looked at Linda. The baby was dragging at her football jersey, trying to stand up. The toddler was at her feet, taking off her sandals.

'Do you live with your grandmother?' he asked her.

'Some of the time,' she said.

Doris said, 'Some time she stopping with me. Some time she stopping with her husband down there in Hoppy's Camp.'

'You live in Alice?' said Elliot.

'Some of the time,' said Linda.

'So how long will you be here?' Elliot said. 'If I give Doris medicine for her cough, can you make sure she takes it?'

'She can take it,' Linda said, and there was an edge of irritation in her voice. 'She don't need me.'

Elliot sighed. 'Three times a day, Doris,' he said. 'Morning time when you get up. Middle of the day, when the sun is up there. Overhead? And night time when you go to bed. Can you do that?'

After the obligatory pause, Doris said. 'Yuwayi, no problem.'

'And finish the course? Keep going until the very end. Two weeks I'll give you.'

'OK,' Doris sang, somehow succeeding in imbuing that small pronouncement with relief, satisfaction and triumph.

Elliot wrote a note for the file then filled out a prescription and handed it to Doris.

'Sandra will get it for you. Remember it's good for you but bad for the children, OK? You have to make sure they don't get their hands on it. Do you understand?'

'She understands.' Linda said.

'Right. And you have to come back and see me next time I come, OK? In two weeks' time. We'll see how you're going then.'

Doris nodded. Linda bent to retrieve her shoes. Neither made any move to leave. Elliot approached the door with the intention of ushering them out.

Doris said, 'You must be very sad, so far away from your country.'

'Oh, I'm OK,' Elliot said, but Doris went on, 'You married? You got family here?'

Every cell in Elliot's being was urging Doris towards the door of the surgery. His body language was screaming at her, but she was impervious to hurry. This was a battle of wills, and she was winning it hands down. Elliot leaned against the desk.

He said, 'No. No family.'

Doris looked genuinely disappointed for him. 'Why then? Why you want to come all the way out here?'

Elliot, on the back foot, shrugged. 'I don't know. I like the desert.' While Doris thought about that he went on, 'I like your country.'

'My country?' Doris said. 'You seen my country?' She spoke a list of names, so alien to Elliot's ear that he couldn't even have repeated them. 'You been out there?'

Linda watched his response. The toddler had pulled one of her sandals off again and was making off towards the waiting room with it.

'Good country, out there,' Doris said.

'I'm sure it is,' said Elliot. 'I'd love to see it. I'm planning on getting a good car and making some trips. I'm sure I'll get out there someday.'

Doris nodded, sitting back, sinking into reflection as though the speaking of those place names had distanced her from the others. But Linda was glaring at him contemptuously, as though he had broken some important social convention.

6

WHICH HE HAD, of course, and he squirms with embarrassment in his private white hospital hell. As though it was up to him to decide whether or not to visit Doris' country, the way you might decide to take a trip to Norwich or Glasgow. As though all you needed was the right form of transport. A hot rage floods him and he can't tell whether it is aimed at himself or at his culture, with its blasé assumptions of entitlement. He had not been good at tuning in to the sensibilities of his patients, particularly at the beginning. Sandra was helpful, and the other communities where he worked had Aboriginal health workers who were brilliant at bridging the cultural divide. But all too often he failed to consult the experts and blundered into mistakes, moving too fast, neglecting to obtain proper permissions or pass on the right information to the right people.

He thinks that no one should be compelled to live in a place like Nyaru with its heat and its flies and its perpetually insufficient infrastructure, but he doesn't know who is responsible for the problems in those places. Government threw money at them, he knew that: twice as much per head as for the non-indigenous population. But what happened to it? Like water into sand, it seemed to vanish without trace. He doesn't know what to believe, and he never did.

7

THAT FIRST CLINIC WAS BUSY. It ran for most of the day, and just when Elliot thought it was finally over, he was persuaded by Sandra to make a couple of home visits to people who couldn't make it to the medical centre. They called on an old man at the edge of town who had been waiting all day for a nephew to come and collect him, and another one who ran when he saw them coming and hid behind a neighbour's house. Sandra went to talk to him, but she couldn't persuade him to come out, so she took Elliot back to the store to get something to eat. There had been some talk of lunch around midday, but it had never materialised. There was pressure in his head. In the store, he bought a two-litre bottle of water and a slab of oily lasagne and took them to the outdoor table. A couple of schoolboys in footy jumpers came and sat on the opposite bench, sharing a can of orange soft drink, watching him. Elliot knew he ought to make conversation with them, but he couldn't think of anything to say. He prodded the lasagne with a plastic fork but before he got any into his mouth, he felt the familiar hot trickle of his nose beginning to bleed. He swore, picked up the thin napkin that came with his meal, pinched his nose with it, and tipped back his head. The boys giggled, then asked if they could help him. He said he would be OK in a minute or two. A couple of young women, just shadows in the corner of his eye, stopped and hovered, then went on their way, laughing. Elliot took a chance on straightening his head. The boys shunted along the bench as a tall, broad-chested man sat down beside them. He said, 'You OK, doctor?'

Elliot nodded. He knew he had met the man before, but he had encountered too many new people that day and was at a loss.

'Luke O'Neill,' the man said. 'Community council.'

'I'm sorry,' Elliot said. 'You met me this morning. I remember now.'

Luke nodded. 'You get on OK? Somebody punch you in the face?'

Elliot's nosebleeds weren't serious, but they always left him feeling washed out, and he was in no mood to make social effort. He said,

'Just a nosebleed. Stopping now.'

Luke said, 'Reckon you can fix us all up?'

Elliot wasn't sure how to respond. He suspected there might be an element of sarcasm in Luke's words. He looked at his lasagne, sitting in its moat of grease. An effort had been made at salad, but it was blackening in the sun even as he watched. He decided to eat it first.

Luke said, 'Well. We got problems here. You can see it.'

Elliot said, 'I thought there were no councils any more. Since the intervention.'

'Not whitefella way, true. But we still have our council, yapa way. We still looking after our community.'

Elliot wiped his nose, carefully, glanced at the pink result on the back of his hand. He waited for Luke to continue and when he didn't, he said, 'Do you want to eat something? Can I buy you some of this? Cup of coffee maybe?'

Luke shook his head and lifted the bottle of cola at his side. It looked warm and flat.

Before he could stop himself, Elliot said, 'You know you shouldn't drink that stuff. It will make you diabetic.'

There was a pause, and Elliot could sense Luke's annoyance. He said,

'Sorry. I'm sure you know that.'

One of the boys asked a question in language, and there was a short conversation, of which Elliot understood not one word.

'He says I should drink diet coke,' Luke explained.

'Oh,' Elliot said. 'Well, he's probably right.'

That was when Luke produced a folder from a dusty black backpack beside his feet. 'Will you sign this for us? It's a petition. Still the intervention, you know? We want our communities back. We are not children. We can run our own lives.'

8

THE MEMORY of Luke is setting off depth charges in Elliot's damaged brain. Luke is important. Luke is somehow connected with him being there in hospital, he is sure of it. He tries to find more memories of him, anything that might give him an idea of why the two of them are connected, but nothing comes. Other images of Luke come and go on the peripheries of his imagination, but they are out of context and untrustworthy.

A NURSE COMES to check his vital signs and change his drip. He is resentful at the disturbance and tries to hold on to his little narrative, which is slipping away like a lizard into a hole, and he keeps trying to grab at its tail, but his hands won't grip properly, and the lizard is kicking up dust with its back feet, making him cough, choking him, and the nurse is calling out for assistance to get his lungs cleared again, and he sacrifices some section of his consciousness to the process, like a little blackout which saves him from the worst of the discomfort.

· · ·

HE DREAMS, or perhaps he remembers, his father mid-lecture. They are at the kitchen table. His mother, who is twenty years younger than his father, prefers evasion to confrontation and has done what she always does on these occasions, which is to get up and busy herself elsewhere. Elliot dare not leave, even though the rant, like most of them, is aimed primarily at his older brother, Matty. Elliot has learned not to offer opinions within earshot of his father, but Matty insists on airing his. He won't put up with the consequences, either, but will finish his pudding and slip out of his chair or begin talking to one of the cats, ignoring their father's objections and thus ramping up his indignation, and leaving Elliot as the sole target.

What was it about? He cannot make out any words in the memory. It is just tones, just emotions. The stress it creates is acting like a chemical in his body. He wants to get up and walk around, leave it behind, but he knows he can't, and he hasn't the courage to try. He is afraid to revisit the experience of his body's unresponsiveness. He suspects something terrible has happened to him. For the time being, for as long as possible, he prefers to remain in a state of ignorance.

His mind is full of locked doors, but he finds an open one; finds himself back with Luke and the petition outside the store in Nyaru, finds that what happened there is not unrelated to this other remembered scene. It is why he made no response to Luke's petition. His disinclination to express opinions had developed into a life philosophy and had served him well enough over the years. His father would have backed John Howard: he would say it was clear that Aboriginal people were incapable of running their own affairs and that the government was completely justified in taking over the communities and stopping the rot. Matty would have been opposed. He would have seen the action as completely opportunistic, the report on sexual abuse of children a gift for media manipulation while the government moved in and took back rights that had taken indigenous people generations to acquire. He would say it was all about power, and control, and access to resources. He would say that it confirmed the continuance of a programme of assimilation. Elliot occupied the comfortable limbo in between. He liked to think of himself as the Médecins sans Frontières type, above or outside of politics, but it was to become clear to him soon enough that this was not a recognisable position in that part of the world.

9

LUKE HANDED the petition to Elliot, who took it and read the heading:

'Indigenous peoples have the right of self-determination. By virtue of that right they freely determine their political status and freely pursue their economic, social and cultural development'. - UN Declaration on the Rights of Indigenous Peoples

A LETTER in Warlpiri followed it, several paragraphs long. On the next page, it was translated into English. Elliot scanned it briefly, taking in very little. At the back were more pages filled with signatures, many of them extremely shaky, but beside each one was a printed name with the community and profession or tribal position. There were many senior men and women, he noticed, describing themselves as 'elder.' Sandra had signed, and the store owner, several teachers and teacher's assistants. Luke slid a biro towards him. Elliot held up his fork in self-defence and closed the document, ashamed to see that he had left a bloody thumbprint on the front page.

'I have more copies,' Luke said. 'Might be you take one to Alice with you? Get some names on it that side?'

It was a let-out and Elliot took it. 'Sure. And I can get a proper read of it when I get home, too.'

Luke fished out a new copy, in its own clean green folder. 'Put in all your names and jobs, all the doctors, nurses, pilots, all them people. Kardiya names is good. You can send it to Canberra when it's filled up.' He pointed to the address on the top page. 'Before the end of this month, they need to go.'

Elliot put the folder on the bench beside him. A little mob of small children flew past, in pursuit of a bigger child on a bike. A skinny dog shot out from under the table and raced after them, and the two boys got up from the bench and followed. Elliot gave the folder a pat and returned to his lunch, but Luke was still with the petition.

'All of us mob were happy when he got elected, that Kevin Rudd. And he line us all up for the apology. But when he's up there on the stage saying sorry for our stolen generation, same time, behind our back, he supporting the intervention and carrying it on. How is that for duplicity, Elliot?'

Elliot's mouth was full. He wasn't entirely sure what duplicity was, and in any case, he was not going to be drawn into discussing politics. He patted the petition again and swallowed. 'I'll have a read of this.'

Luke turned away. An old man, long and gangly, appeared from around the side of the store and sat on the bench beside Luke, his feet facing away from the table, his back to Elliot. The two men spoke softly in language. Luke handed over a blue banknote. The old man stood up and went into the store. Elliot gave up on the lasagne and pushed it away. He took a long drink of his water.

Luke said, 'You got some connection out here? Must be some reason you want to work in a place like this, eh?'

Elliot gave a despairing shrug. There it was again. It seemed like an impossible question, particularly as, the way he was feeling just then, he definitely did not want to work out there ever again. But he remembered why it was that he had come.

'I was travelling with a friend,' he said. 'Back in the nineties. Early nineties, it was. We had a four-wheel drive. We drove up from Adelaide to Alice, then on up the Tanami road to Hall's Creek. I kind of fell in love with the desert country, you know? I've always wanted to come back and see more of it.'

10

IN THE BRIGHT room in Adelaide, Elliot tries to say, 'Luke,' but it doesn't come out right, and in any case, there is still no one there. He remembers Sandra's sister, but he can't think when it was that she visited. It might have been five minutes ago and it might have been yesterday. If she was actually there and wasn't just a character from his dream world. The memory of the meeting with Luke is contaminated with intrusive images that make no sense. Luke with his back against a car wheel, his chin on his chest. Luke coming over the brow of a dune looking like a butcher, his arms and torso glowing red. Elliot tries to make sense of the images, but he can't find any context for them. Instead, he thinks back to that first trip, begins to relive it, travels across the arid landscape. Travels above it, gliding on air, looking down at the amazing designs in the red landscape, knows he has to come down, and so he does. Finds himself in a car instead, a white troopy. He assumes he is driving, but he isn't. And when he looks for the driver, he finds it is an old woman with white hair, sitting cross-legged on the seat, making no contact with the pedals. What they are driving over is more like a map. Or maybe it's a painting. It goes on forever. The colours are insanely beautiful.

11

HE WANTS it to be just him and Miles, but when he tries to put Miles in
the driving seat instead of the old woman, he can't. He finds a hollow
place inside him and understands that Miles is not there any more. He
doesn't know what has become of him. He has to work, he has to dig,
but eventually Miles is there, and Elliot remembers the first day of
driving; the first few hours pleasant enough, through vineyards and
arable farms, all green and healthy at that time of year. Then there was
Port Augusta, and after that, something completely different. It was
like arriving on a different planet. Suddenly there was mile after mile
with no houses, no farms, no sign of any human occupation at all. His
mind had refused to believe it, remaining in a state of anticipation
certain that, around the next bend, there would be something. In the
UK, even in country places, there was almost always some sign of
people; if not a town or a village, then a farmhouse or a barn, or a side-
road with a sign for a Bed and Breakfast. Even in the remotest places,
in the hill country or the moorlands, there would be stone walls, fences,
telegraph poles. But out there, mile after mile after mile unravelled
beneath their wheels and the road itself was the only sign of human
existence.

What he doesn't remember so well is how and when the transformation came about in his mind, just when the empty landscape ceased to horrify him and began to get under his skin. In fact, quite a lot of the first part of that journey became lost in an alcoholic haze. He wasn't a safe drinker and had learned from bitter experience to avoid over-indulgence, but he was on the rebound from a broken relationship, working hard at being hard, driving faster than he wanted to, trying to prove something to no one in particular, except for Jyoti perhaps, who wasn't there to see it. Miles' role models, if he had any, would have been more along the line of Lawrence of Arabia, or perhaps the early African explorers, in whose image he wore lots of loose white cotton or linen; heavy fabric that worked beautifully on his long, lean frame but would never work the same way on Elliot, who was too short and would just look like a schoolboy cricketer who had forgotten his bat. It wasn't for him then, that Elliot secretly encouraged holes in the knees of his jeans and cut the collars off two of his best shirts and the sleeves off all of them, even his tee-shirts.

HE COUGHS A LITTLE, swallows something that tastes very bad. A nurse comes. She is gentle and solicitous, but he is OK. He doesn't need to cough any more or be cleared again. He wants to tell her something, though, because he is having a eureka moment about his behaviour on that trip. It was his father he was trying to get at. He was going through his teenage rebellion, about ten years late.

'My father...' The words are painfully extruded. They sound like something else. The nurse waits patiently. Elliot struggles for more but it is too hard; he has bitten off way more than he can chew. The struggle frustrates him; he begins to get angry. 'F-fuck him,' he finishes.

'I know,' said the nurse. 'I know.'

THEY MADE the obligatory detour to Coober Pedy, fossicked half-heart-edly for opals in the spoil heaps, visited an underground house, spent an evening drinking with a man whose job was to keep a stretch of the

Dog Fence in good repair. He had a whole philosophy built up around the fence, which ran for five thousand kilometres right across the continent, keeping the dingoes out of the rich sheep-farming country of the Southeast. It was along the 'two kinds of people' line, and Elliot got argumentative and said that there were indeed two kinds of people, those who believed that there were two kinds of people and those that knew there were a lot more than that, and Miles quietly extricated them both from the pub before damage occurred.

The roadhouse in Oodnadatta knocked some of the spikes off him. They were holed up there for three days waiting for the road train to come through with a part for their car, and Elliot flirted half-heartedly with a couple of tourists, and came off worst in an altercation with a local station hand. This resulted in a spectacular nosebleed, far more lengthy and prolific than his regular ones, and Miles moved the tent to a quiet patch of ground on the edge of town and parked him in it for the twenty-four hours it took him to recover. A little subdued by all that, Elliot laid off the beer for the remainder of the trip.

They chose the scenic route to Alice Springs, which took them out along the Old Andado road, past the edge of the Simpson desert, where the dunes were as red as delirium and where they came upon the first thing which had frightened them: a heap of freshly dead camels with no one around to have killed them. They reversed in their tracks, found the road they had inadvertently strayed from, and tore out of there. But after that, everything changed. That leg of the trip was the one that, if it didn't heal him, at least made Elliot forget that he was angry and hurt, and brought him to a place within himself that he had never been to before.

The land they passed through was like a beautiful drug; it both calmed and energised them. Miles referred to Australia as the 'New World', but it seemed very old to Elliot. As old and as strange as the moon, but not as indifferent. He did not know the place, but he could not shake off the ever-present awareness that the place knew him.

Those were days out of time. That journey took away the hurry from Elliot and stopped Miles from complaining about the heat and the flies. They saw hardly anyone; just the occasional station worker in a ute, a grader once, repairing a stretch of road, a little caravan of local people in an assortment of vehicles going in the opposite direction to them, emerging out of their own cloud of dust for as long as it took them to pass by, then vanishing back into it again. Miles and Elliot had intended to make it to Alice within three days but, in the end, they took a week, slowing down more each day, exploring lonely station tracks. They stopped to wander through rocky outcrops or along dry creeks, or through the bands of bush between the dunes, making up names for trees and plants they had no names for. To begin with, everything was mulga or ghost-gum or saltbush or spinifex, but they found things that weren't any of those, which they called 'that green one' or 'the needly one' or 'the big shaggy one' or 'the little red-leaf thing'. They noted bushes which carried berries or hard green fruits; they collected some which they were tempted to try and eat but, in the end, they decided against it, being days from the nearest medical centre and having no means of communication.

Which itself was a large part of the pleasure: to be beyond the reach of phones and pagers and radio and television, to be lost to their own world and entirely free. They took each day, each hour as it presented itself, almost entirely without plan or aspiration, allowing their stocks to run down and run out; first the bread, then the crackers, the tinned beans, the dried milk, until, in the end, they were eating corned beef and spaghetti at every meal, with bitter black tea, smoky from the tar-encrusted billy which they boiled on open fires. When their water containers were nearly empty and it looked as though they would have to proceed on to Alice with no more delays, they came upon or, as it seemed to them, were presented with, a reprieve. It was in a bend of a creek bed that looked, when they set out along it, as dry as all the others they had mooched along. They spent the day beside the deep pool, drinking the clear water, swimming in it, lying in the shade of the massive river gums, watching all kinds of birds coming and going. Lizards lounged beside them on the rocks. Miles took a wander and found some marks that he thought might be paintings, but he couldn't be sure they weren't made by natural variations in the colours of the rock layers. He said he was certain that people had been there in the past; he could sense ghosts hovering, but Elliot felt no presences beyond the curious butcher birds in the trees. It was obvious to him that people would make use of a water source in a dry country. It was as obvious as shopping. He could see nothing mysterious about it.

At dusk, there were other animals: wallabies and smaller, rodent-like things that neither of them could identify. Around the moment when the flies all switched themselves off, punctual as tiny robots, the mosquitos came out, making Elliot wish he hadn't cut the sleeves off his shirts. He turned to look down the creek and saw a dingo, barely twenty metres away, watching them, and he was struck by the realisation that it knew him, not personally but genetically. The dingo race knew the human race, and this one was sizing them up, working out whether they were threatening or neutral, whether they might have anything worth scavenging. Eventually, it trotted off up the bank of the creek, casually on its way, and Elliot was sorry to see it go.

Still, they couldn't bring themselves to leave. They could hear other creatures stirring in the dry grass, the tiny plink of droplets falling from dipped noses. They could hear the high sound of bats feeding on moths above the branches, and see their darting shapes cutting across the brilliant starscapes that appeared when the last pink flush of the sunset was gone. Eventually, they made their way back to the car and got into their swags. Soon after that, dingoes started howling. From two sides, thrillingly close, a whole pack of them opened up. Miles said, 'Jesus. Should we get in the car?' But Elliot wasn't afraid. He was energised by the sound, struck by the realisation that the man in Coober Pedy might have been right after all, and if he was, then Elliot might have found the place where he belonged, on the dingo side of the fence.

In the morning they drove the car down the creek and filled their containers with that good water, and it gave them two more days to dawdle on the road before their stock of spaghetti ran out and they had no choice but to complete the run into Alice.

12

ELLIOT COUGHS, swallows, opens his eyes and looks up at the ceiling. There is less light than there was, and he guesses it is night-time. He is aware of a restlessness in his body. He lifts his head, turns it, sees another bed in the room, with someone sleeping in it. The door is open and there is low light in the corridor. A shape crosses through it and is gone. Elliot feels that enough time has passed since the hospital staff last visited him. He wants some kind of action. He wants company. Most of all, he wants to be up and out of there, but he has a feeling it might be some time before that happens.

He would like to try out his voice again, but he doesn't want to disturb his room-mate. Instead, he tries moving each part of his body in turn. The results are mixed. Most things seem to work, but nothing works well. Everything is laboured and much too slow. He knows what this is. He has seen the results of head injuries before, and he wishes now that he hadn't.

13

In Nyaru, Luke questioned Elliot closely about the route he and Miles had taken and the places they had seen. He wasn't so interested in the country south of Alice and was disappointed that Elliot hadn't ventured into the Great Sandy Desert, into his own country.

'Someday soon I need to go out there,' he said. He indicated a smart Land Cruiser parked nose-in against the store fence, a relatively recent model, its bodywork good beneath the inevitable coating of red dust. 'You want to come?'

Elliot said, 'Definitely,' and meant it. He had taken a couple of side trips out of Alice, to national parks and tourist trails, but although they reminded him of his travels with Miles, it was not the same. These were tired, managed places, and bore little resemblance to the wild country that had affected him so deeply. He listened as Luke talked about the sacred places he knew: the waterholes and hills and rock formations, each with its own name and dreaming story.

'I never lived there,' he told Elliot. 'My mum and dad, they were working on a station, Kimberley way, you know? But when I was a kid, every year my father and my uncle take me there. Been show me all them places.'

He fell silent and allowed Elliot to retreat into his exhaustion for a while. Then he went on, 'My family all finish now. Only one or two. Mostly Katherine way, settled there. Nobody initiated, not proper way. No one left that time for ceremony.'

For Elliot, the word 'initiation' rang medical bells. *"Cicatrices uncommon now, except in the very old." "Circumcisions gone wrong occasionally turn up at the clinic." "Be prepared to treat such conditions in secret if you are asked to."*

'I know little bit, that law,' Luke went on. 'I can show you some real good country.'

They exchanged phone numbers. There was no mobile coverage in Nyaru, but there was a payphone that Luke could use to call Elliot, and he also had a mobile that he used when he went into town.

'You'll need to give me a bit of warning,' Elliot said. 'I might have to move things around a bit. But I can do that. I can fit in with pretty much anything if I have a few days' notice.'

They shook hands on it, and Elliot lived in hope over the weeks that followed. But Luke didn't phone.

14

ELLIOT THINKS he is the last of his people. There is no one left who
speaks his language and he can't make himself understood. Everything
is crumbling beneath him. He has no foundations. He wakes in a
wailing panic, weeping real tears, and is soon surrounded by people
like himself, all speaking his language. But it is true that he can't make
himself understood. There are words in his head, but they are backing
up behind his mouth. Sometimes they come out, but always too slowly,
always too late.

He has another visitor. It is a pilot in the RFDS who often flew
Elliot out to his remote clinics. He is the first person Elliot properly
recognises, and the relief is a physical flood that makes him well up,
and he is embarrassed. Everyone thinks he is worse than he is. He is
fine, he knows it, or he would be if he could just get his moving parts
to obey his directions. He is grateful to the pilot for talking, for telling
him the news of the other people he knows in healthcare. He says that
Luke will be going back up with him on the next flight, and after that,
all Elliot can think is that he wants to see Luke, but 'L' is a brick wall
that he can't get over. He can say 'Mike,' which is the name of the pilot,
and he can say 'Sandra', or something like it. Maybe 'Sanja'. But 'Luke'
requires an articulation of the tongue that won't happen for him. In

despair he says, 'Ooook,' but Mike has already gone by then, and the nurse who is there pats him on the hand in a condescending manner and brings him a drink of water with a straw.

But he thinks Luke has been there to see him. He can visualise him now, looking down on the bed, sad to see Elliot in such a state. He thinks Luke might have been there many times, and he finds he can adopt his presence quite easily, like a guardian angel beside the bed whenever he closes his eyes. To the nurses, his efforts sound like burbling, but they are his first attempts at rehabilitation. 'W's are difficult too, so not even 'Wuke' will work properly. He says it over and over. 'Oook, Yook. Oook.'

15

ELLIOT AND MILES were like a pair of mariners who had been adrift on a raft. It was only a week since they had left Oodnadatta, but it felt to them as though they hadn't seen civilisation for months. The people and the noise in Alice Springs were irritating, the shops and cafes too cold and the light inside them stark and artificial. Elliot wanted to stay in a place on the edge of town where the rooms looked out on to the hillside and they would have use of a swimming pool, but Miles said it was too expensive, and instead they booked a room in a motel in the centre of town where all the sheets and towels, though they had clearly been laundered, had faint pink smudges. There were letters for both of them waiting at the post office, bringing reminders, mostly unwelcome, that they had lives in another hemisphere. There was nothing for Elliot from Jyoti, which created a significant after-shock to his already damaged self-esteem, and it took him at least twenty-four hours to land properly and to begin to get culturally acclimatised to Alice Springs.

He had never seen it before, and suddenly it was everywhere. Every cafe and restaurant, even their hotel room, had its own little collection of Aboriginal art. The main strip, Todd Mall, was ablaze with it; every second commercial unit was either a gallery or a souvenir shop that also sold paintings. Walls and windows were crowded with stretched canvases; unstretched ones hung on swinging racks like rugs or carpet samples. Tourists and collectors browsed, languid in the heat, becoming animated only when it became necessary to evade an artist who, deciding to dispense with the middleman, made a direct approach.

The authors of this gold rush were everywhere. Mostly, as far as Elliot could see, they were getting on with their lives, piling their shopping and their kids into cars, going places, calling out to their mates in the street or just killing time; sitting around outside the pubs or in the dry riverbed which ran through the centre of town. But there were hustlers as well, trying to sell confused sob stories or just asking for cash. Police cars crawled continually around the tourist drag, like a constant reminder to visitors that they weren't safe, and Elliot saw a thing he had never come across before: petrol sniffers, their cans suspended on strings around their necks. Miles said there was a kind of apartheid system in operation; he pointed out the signs about dress code on the doors of many of the pubs and restaurants, *no bare feet, no singlets,* designed, so he said, to keep Aboriginal people out. And did Elliot notice how none of the blacks would make eye contact? It was, he said, because they were all downtrodden and oppressed.

16

HAD MILES REALLY CALLED THEM 'BLACKS', or is he misremembering? Has he layered the word on, to fit with the loose white clothes and what little he knows of Miles' privileged lineage?

He sees Miles in an elegant suit, crossing a road in Knightsbridge, just a glimpse. Where did that come from? He sees him sitting in their tent, trapping flies against the gauze shell and squashing them. It seems so unlikely that the two of them would ever have been friends, or at least, that they would have remained friends after Miles dropped out of first-year medicine.

Elliot's mind swims. Perhaps he sleeps again. He sees himself walking down the street where all the galleries are in Alice Springs. It is full of Aboriginal people and they are all watching him. He is carrying something over his shoulder. It is long and unwieldy. A bazooka? A rocket launcher?

17

'IS THIS COLONIALISM,' Miles had asked, 'or is it post-colonialism? It gives me the heebie-jeebies.'

It had taken Elliot a moment or two to realise he wasn't joking. Out of loyalty to Miles, and in an attempt to understand what he was saying, he tried to imagine himself into experiencing post-colonial heebie-jeebies, but he couldn't do it. He had no idea what it was about. He was reminded of a thing Jyoti had once said to him.

'One of the reasons I like being with you is you don't feel guilty about India.'

Elliot was genuinely perplexed. 'Why on earth should I feel guilty about India?'

'Because you are a member of the oppressor's race. Whether you like it or not. Your people occupied my country for hundreds of years.'

'It was nothing to do with me.'

Jyoti said, 'That's what I mean.'

They had probed it a bit from time to time, and it had come up in other kinds of conversation, complaints really, about how certain types of intellectual were ultra-nice to Jyoti and her compatriots; over-friendly, over-compensating for being English and thus proving themselves to be as racist as the drunks on the bus who called her 'Paki scum' one night and told her to go home. 'Those people are so fucked up,' she said. 'The men don't know how to be men and the women don't know how to be women.'

Elliot said, 'I don't know who they are, these over-compensators you're talking about.'

'They are the Islington set and the Archway set and the ones who are slumming it all over London so they can save on rent while they wait for their inheritances to arrive.'

Elliot thought he didn't know any people like that, but Jyoti said, 'You do. Some of them have been here for dinner.'

'Like who?'

'I'm not going to name names.'

'Is Miles one of them?' Elliot said.

'Don't be ridiculous. Miles doesn't qualify on any count.'

'Why not? I've met relatives of his who were born in India. Colonial to the bone I would have thought.'

'Yes, but it's different.'

'Why?'

'Because Miles knows where he fits in. He doesn't try to compensate.'

Elliot said, 'Hmm. So it doesn't matter what you do as long as you don't apologise for it.'

Jyoti said, 'No. It's just different. Miles is who he is. He doesn't try to hide anything.'

Elliot had a sudden insight. The thing that Miles and Jyoti shared was an inherited and deeply entrenched sense of entitlement. He said, 'He's like you.'

Jyoti said, 'No, he's not like me.'

'I think he is. I think you both belong to the ruling class.'

Jyoti said, 'Actually, it's possibly true that there are some things in the past. But that's a different story. Do you want to get into an examination of who was oppressed by my family and who was oppressed by Miles's family?'

'Well, no—'

'Maybe you were,' Jyoti said. 'Maybe your ancestors were oppressed by Miles's ancestors.'

But Elliot had no idea who his ancestors were and didn't much care. He had only known one grandparent, his mother's mother, and she had lived in a village in rural Kent which they visited for a week or two each summer and for alternate Christmases. She had a fantastic garden where she grew enormous flowers and small, crooked vegetables and lettuces that were always full of slugs. His parents built an extension for her with a kitchenette and a bedroom with its own bathroom, so she could move in with them in London when she got too old to look after herself, but she didn't like Elliot's dad, Ron. She called him 'that old squaddie' and once told Elliot in confidence that she would never come and live with them; she would top herself before she would stay under the same roof as 'that boring old fart.'

He said to Jyoti, 'Well, what if they were? Is it better if Miles feels guilty about it or is it worse? I don't really know what you're talking about.'

18

It's a length of water pipe, the thing he is carrying on his shoulder. PVC. White. Whatever is inside it has been stolen from the people who are watching him. Elliot can't remember what it is. He thinks, if he tips it on end, water might come out, or maybe red sand, or dots. He knows that what he is carrying in the pipe is country, but that makes no sense to him. How he could be carrying country in a water pipe?

19

MILES WAS LOOKING into the window of a stockman's outfitter, at a big display of waxed coats and jackets, and the sunlight was streaming through the hole in the ozone and stinging their skin and Miles was being obtuse about colonialism.

Elliot said, 'Was your family involved? In...you know...the Aboriginal stuff.'

'Not the ones in Adelaide who lent us the car,' Miles said. 'They came later. But Mummy's family were everywhere. Absolutely everywhere. We still have some land here somewhere. Some other cousins have.'

'Are we going to visit them?'

'They don't live on it,' Miles said, and his tone suggested the idea was absurd. 'It's...I don't know...cattle stations and rain forest and bush and stuff. Leasehold property.' He fell silent, staring at the waxed jackets.

Elliot said, 'You don't need a coat.'

Miles said, 'I'd like one, though.' He grinned and emerged from his uncharacteristic gloom. 'Thing is, I promised an uncle... well, he's more of a second or third cousin really, on Daddy's side, he's a bit of a family favourite actually, comes home every Christmas. Did you meet him, I wonder? Roly we call him.' He paused for just long enough for Elliot to shake his head, then went on, 'Well, he's a bit of a collector. Got a knack for it. Uncanny really. Keeps his ear to the ground and stays ahead of the pack. He wants me to pick up a few paintings for him. Since we're in the area anyway.'

Elliot felt his heart sink, but it was a moment or two before he realised why. Had this been Miles' plan all along, and if so, why hadn't he told him? He didn't know why it should matter so much but it did.

Miles said, 'Do you mind?'

Elliot shrugged. 'Why should I?'

'It might mean hanging around here for a few days. I might have to engage in a bit of negotiation.'

Elliot couldn't imagine what he could possibly do in Alice Springs for a few days, but he didn't feel he could refuse. 'Fine by me.'

Miles went into the shop, but Elliot didn't follow. He wandered along the street and examined, from a distance, some paintings spread on a little grass mound at the side of the street. The two women who were displaying them there looked bored. He turned away from them and wandered over to the gallery opposite. There was more of the same kind of thing in its window: dots on canvas in bright colours, most of it sloppily done. It baffled him. It all looked the same, just dots and more dots. Why on earth would Miles' uncle want to buy it?

He looked back towards the door of the shop, but Miles hadn't come out yet, and he found himself wondering why it was that the richest people he knew were the ones who most often complained about having no money. Over the years he had been hanging round with Miles, he had learned that it could mean any number of different things, from no money in the current account, necessitating the transfer of funds from some other source or the liquidation of an asset or two, to no money for an idea of Elliot's as opposed to an idea of Miles's, to plenty of money but all of it earmarked for other things. There was always enough, though; the credit card would appear for a meal out if it was too late to cook, or a ten-pound note for a taxi fare if it was raining or if he couldn't be bothered to walk. There hadn't been enough money to stay in the nice place on the edge of town that Elliot wanted, but Miles would probably come out of that shop with the best waxed coat money could buy, then drive over it in the troopy a few times to take the new look off it.

20

ELLIOT REMEMBERS he has a bladder but doesn't remember when he last emptied it. He is pretty sure he has been lying in the hospital bed for days and not hours. He must have a catheter. He wants to ask someone, but no one is there. Elliot never thought he would need to have a catheter. It never occurred to him that any kind of intensive treatment would happen to him. It hadn't been part of his life plan. He hears his father's words, booming and echoing like the voice of God : *Yes well you always thought you were immortal you never could take anyone's advice you are like all young people you think you know it all and you wouldn't know good advice if you fell over it and you shouldn't have been...you shouldn't have been...*

What? What or where should he not have been? Is it his own fault that he's here? The memory of what happened must be inside his head somewhere, but he can't find it.

21

HE WENT with Miles across the dry bed of the Todd and out to the far edge of the Eastern suburbs to have a look at the paintings that interested Uncle Roly. There were three of them, leaning against the wall in a big shed with sliding doors at the back of an old brick-built house. Their owner, a short, thin man with enormous joints, introduced himself as Charlie Molloy, then dragged the paintings out from beneath a tarpaulin covered in sparrow-shit. He dislodged at least one red-back spider, then tried, ineffectually, to brush away the dust and cobwebs using an old tee-shirt, stiffened by its previous use as a paint-rag. He said,

'There you are. You're looking at some of the first Aboriginal artworks ever made.'

Elliot and Miles looked at them. They were done on composite board of some kind, roughly cut, the edges unstable. One of them was damaged in one corner, but the artist had continued on over the disintegrating surface. The paint, which looked to Elliot like household gloss, was holding it all together. One had some tiny figures and animal tracks. Another had waving lines and long oval shapes. All of them had dots, in varying quantities.

The man went on, 'Not the first Aboriginal art, I'm saying. That's on rock walls and caves and shit, all over Australia. Goes back thirty or forty thousand years, some of it. So they say, anyway. You know all this stuff, I suppose?' He was watching Miles closely, alert to any response, but Miles was poker-faced, examining the paintings in silence. 'But these ones are from Papunya. You know about Papunya, don't you?' Still Miles said nothing, and even Elliot couldn't interpret his silence. Did Papunya mean anything to him? It certainly meant nothing to Elliot. He met the thin man's eye and shrugged.

'There was a government settlement there where they were looking after the blackfellas who came in out of the desert. Back in the seventies, this was. There was a schoolteacher there who had this idea of getting the men to paint a mural on the wall of the schoolhouse, and then he set up a workshop where they could go and paint and they started doing these.' He nudged the nearest board with his foot. 'Some of those men made a lot of money out of painting. That Clifford Possum. Ever hear of him?'

Miles shook his head and broke his silence at last, explained that he was there on behalf of his uncle who collected ethnographic stuff from all over the world and that he himself was completely out of his depth and had no idea what he was looking at.

The man rubbed at a swollen elbow with swollen fingers, then said, 'Well, if you're not interested.'

Miles said, 'Oh no. We are interested. My uncle is, anyway.' He turned his big, goofy smile on Molloy, who was instantly won over. He said,

'My dad picked them up. He used to go out to all those communities looking after the electrics. Generators and stuff. That's what he did.' He gestured towards a lean-to further away from the house: open-fronted, double-bayed, every inch filled with banked-up equipment, wires and wheels and handles and dials everywhere, not one thing amongst it all that Elliot could readily identify. 'He loved those black-fellas, my dad did. Often picked up paintings and craft stuff when he was out there working. I have loads of Hermannsburg paintings inside, but my wife likes those. She wants to hold on to them.' He waited for some hint of recognition and, getting none, continued. 'She wouldn't have these ones up on the wall. Says they're too daggy.'

Miles nodded. 'They are a bit daggy.'

'They're the real thing, though. That nearly proves it. Dad met a lot of these artists, you know. They were tribal people, straight out of the desert, some of them. He said they were like people from another planet. They didn't think the same way as we did. That's what makes these ones so collectable, you see. There will never be people like that again.'

Miles nodded. 'So did he buy these directly from the artists?'

The man shook his head. 'Not these ones. I don't know why, but he bought them from a woman who had a bit of a gallery on the edge of town. First one in Alice, it was. They got stuff on the back. Numbers and shit.' He tilted the biggest of the three boards, the one with the little figures. 'Tim...Tim Leura it looks like.'

Miles leaned over to inspect the label and agreed. The next one was by Johnny someone; they couldn't read it, and the label on the third was missing.

'It might be on a paper in the house,' he said. 'There's a lot of papers in there that Dad kept. Do you want me to ask my wife? She looks after all the paperwork. She probably knows where they are.'

Miles said, 'Maybe. But maybe we should talk basics first. Like, how much are you asking for them?'

Molloy said, 'Well, it's not easy to put a value on them, really. They are a finite resource, see? There are thousands of paintings for sale in Alice, but you won't find many like these.'

'I'm sure it's true,' Miles said, oozing sincerity.

'There were only a few hundred painted this way,' Molloy said. 'They were cheap when Dad bought them but they're worth a lot these days. And they'll only get more valuable, things like that.'

Miles nodded. 'So what do you think they are worth?'

Molloy shrugged. 'You might have an idea yourself. Want to make me an offer?'

Elliot sighed and turned to look out of the wide doorway. He wasn't particularly interested in being a witness to negotiations. It was blisteringly hot in there beneath the tin roof, but it looked even hotter in the dry yard outside. A blue heeler on a chain was curled up against the trunk of a big old eucalypt, which was providing the only patch of shade he could see. He could go back to the car, but it would be like an oven. He sat down on a pink plastic crate just inside the shed doors.

Miles was saying, 'I'm afraid not. And to be perfectly honest with you, there is only one way to proceed with this, and that is for you to give me a price and for me to go back with it to my uncle and see what he thinks.'

Molloy said, 'What, back to England?'

'No, no. I'll phone him. From the hotel. Describe what I've seen and let you know what he says. But we need a starting price.'

Molloy said. 'Fuck. Hard fucking way to do business, with some bloke ten thousand miles away.'

'I know,' Miles said. 'It's not ideal.'

Molloy said, 'I don't really want to sell them at all. Dad loved them. But I can't work no more.' He indicated his swollen knees and knuckles. 'I need the money.'

From the doorway, Elliot examined the inflamed joints with a professional eye. Miles nodded in sympathy and waited.

Molloy said, 'Fuck.' He looked at the paintings, turned away from them, looked towards the house where, it occurred to Elliot, his wife might well have been waiting, as anxious as he was. He tilted the Tim Leura again, then dropped it back against the wall. 'Twenty grand,' he said, breathless with anxiety. 'I won't take less than twenty for that one.'

Elliot turned his face away, grinned at the concrete floor between his feet. The man's neck was laughable. Molloy went on, 'And twelve for this one. And…I don't know…Shit. Eight for the smaller one.'

Elliot straightened his face and glanced over at the others. Miles, pokerfaced again, was scrutinising the three boards. Molloy was saying, 'I have to get that for them, mate. I can't sell them for less. They're my pension. They'll be an investment for your uncle, but I can't hold onto them, see? I need the money to live on.'

Still Miles said nothing; gave nothing away.

'I've definitely got the papers for those. Receipts.' Molloy waved towards the house. 'My wife will get them. You can have a look. Make sure everything's in order.'

Miles said, 'Maybe later. Best thing is if I go back and talk to my uncle and see what he thinks.'

Molloy said, 'Alright, alright. But that's the best I can do. Sorry about that. I'll dig out those papers while you're gone. You can see them if you come back later.'

Miles said, 'Fine. I'll phone you either way. To let you know.'

'Right-oh.' Molloy could not conceal his anxiety. 'I'll hear from you then. In an hour or two?'

'Depends,' Miles said. 'What with the time difference and everything, it might be tomorrow.'

'Tomorrow?' said Molloy. 'There's someone else interested, you know. He's coming out this afternoon.'

'What a coincidence!' Miles concealed his sarcasm behind a bright, charming smile that for an instant made Elliot turn away in shame. 'Do go ahead and sell them if you get an offer you like. I just have no idea what my uncle's response will be. I'm sure you understand.'

Molloy looked resigned. 'Right-oh,' he said again. 'Yeah. Well. I suppose. If he was to take all three of them. Thirty-five, I suppose. For all three. Thirty-five K.'

A woman emerged from the house amid an eruption of small dogs, which raced up to the troopy and took turns to piss on the wheels. She looked much younger than her husband, and maybe she was, but it could have been that Molloy's illness had aged him. She carried a manila folder that contained a thick sheaf of papers.

'Receipts,' she said, leafing through them, finding the ones belonging to the Papunya boards at the very bottom. Miles took them from her and, on the back of a till receipt he found in his pocket, wrote down the names of the artists.

Molloy said, 'Thirty-five K. For the three.'

Miles tossed his keys and started for the car. 'I'll put it to him.'

Elliot hung back and shook Molloy's hand gently. 'Is it rheumatoid arthritis?' he asked.

Molloy said, 'Yeah. Fucking right. Are you a doctor?' Elliot nodded and Molloy went on, 'What would you give me for it?'

Elliot said, 'Same as your own doctor, I'm sure. Just keep moving. That's the main thing.'

22

ANOTHER PERSON COMES to see Elliot in hospital, another sibling of Sandra's. His name is Alan, and he never stops talking. He says Sandra will be home on leave very soon and will come in and see him herself. Until then, her family is deputising for her. Elliot remembers the sister saying that. He likes the word. He likes the sentiment, even though he doesn't really know what to do with visitors yet. Alan says his mum will be in tomorrow, and his little sister Margie, the one in the wheel-chair, will be in again soon as well, and if there's anything he wants they will get it. Anything at all. A slab maybe? A couple of casks? Smokes? Elliot knows these are jokes, but he can't yet raise a smile, let alone a laugh.

'I know what you want,' Alan says. 'Audiobooks. I'll send some in with mum. I can get millions of them from the library.'

Elliot remembers the sister but not the wheelchair. He supposes the brother probably knows better than him. He tries to think of something he wants, but there isn't anything. To be better, maybe; to be out of there, but Alan and his family can't deliver that.

23

IN THE CAR, Miles said nothing until they were back on the main road. Then he cracked a conspiratorial smile. He said, 'If they are what he says they are, Uncle Roly will pay twice that for them. We'll let him sweat for a few hours then knock him down another couple of thousand or so.'

Elliot said, 'Your uncle is barking. They're just building offcuts with bits of old house paint slapped on them.'

Miles said, 'Both those statements are undoubtedly true.' He was driving too fast, pumped with the thrill of the chase. 'But mad as he might be, Roly is seldom wrong about these things. He has a nose for a ripening market, and it's pretty much infallible.'

Back in the hotel room, Miles picked up the phone before even taking his hat off.

Elliot said, 'Isn't it the middle of the night there?'

'Roly doesn't go by the clock,' Miles said. 'Not when the hounds are running, anyway. He has a phone beside his bed.'

Sure enough, the call was answered within a few seconds and Miles began to describe what they had seen, reading out the names and other details he had taken from the receipts.

Elliot left him and took a shower, his second of the day, more for the sake of cooling down than getting clean. When he came out, the phone call was finished. Miles looked pleased. He said, 'He's sending the thirty-five K. We can collect it from the bank in an hour or two.' He checked his watch. 'And we can keep any change we get out of it.'

Elliot shook his head. 'I don't get it. If you are going to buy them, at least give old Molloy what he's asking. He needs the money more than Roly does. That's a brutal illness he has.'

Miles shook his head. 'It doesn't work like that. If we give him what he's asking, he'll be disappointed that he didn't ask for more. That's how the game works. If we knock him down a bit, he'll think he drove a hard bargain. He's only expecting to get twenty grand for them, max. He'll be thrilled to get twenty-five.'

'Well, I don't want anything out of it,' Elliot said. 'I think the whole business is insane. All that money for splotches on chipboard.'

Miles said, 'It's ethnography. It's a bit of cultural history. Those men painted their tribal stories and ceremonial traditions on those boards, fresh from forty thousand years of uninterrupted isolation here.'

Elliot said, 'Yesterday you said you were uncomfortable about all that colonialism and stuff. Now you seem happy to make money out of it.'

Miles said, 'It isn't colonialism that bothers me, not really. It's this weird hinterland here, you know? Where nothing is quite clear.' Elliot said nothing, and after a while Miles went on, 'Anyway, this is different. Buying this stuff isn't exploiting anybody. This is just buying some bits of art.'

That night there was thirty-five thousand Australian dollars in cash in the room with them. It was considerably more than Elliot earned in a year. He had never seen so much money in cash before and it made him jittery.

Miles said, 'Were you afraid of being robbed yesterday?'

'No.'

'So why are we more likely to be robbed today?'

'Because we were in the bank. We got handed a large envelope stuffed with cash. People will have seen it.'

Miles turned over and switched off the light beside his bed. He said, 'Don't worry about it. It won't happen.'

Elliot thought that it probably wouldn't, but all the same a drunken argument in the street outside the hotel set his heart racing. Miles snored through it, and sometime in the small hours Elliot came to the realisation that he was more concerned about Miles's money than Miles was, and it annoyed him that Miles could sleep so soundly while he lay awake and worried about it. It was clear that it wouldn't be such a big deal to Miles if he lost that huge sum of money. There were other thirty-five thousands where that came from, and there always would be. He didn't remember ever feeling angry with Miles before, and he wished it would go away, but he was haunted by the memory of Molloy and his painful joints, and something else as well: Miles's delight at the prospect of getting the paintings. It wasn't personal greed, he knew that, but there was something ugly about it all the same, a kind of glee in acquisition.

Later, he wondered whether his mood might have had more to do with being in Alice Springs, which seemed to have its own micro-climate of human behaviour, where tempers frayed easily, and all-out fury erupted at night. In the morning his head was stuffy, and he was cranky. He told Miles he wanted no more to do with the art deal, and he stayed in the motel when Miles set off with the money and the car. Unable to face the centre of town again, he walked along beside the riverbed and was surprised by how quickly he reached the edge of town, and how wild it felt to him when he could no longer see houses and cars. Even so close to town he was enthralled by the power of the place, the massive river gums, the line of brittle hills along the southern edge of town. Before long the path vanished into thick buffel grass and, since he was wearing only light trainers, he began to worry about snakes. Soon afterwards he broke, with the bridge of his nose, a spider web strung across the path, so strong and tight it felt like piano wire, and he took it as a sign to turn back. Then, once he was again nearing the centre of town, he turned away from the river and began to explore the streets. There wasn't much to see: tired bungalows, bland commercial buildings, a tourist hostel with a trendy name, a petrol station. He longed for the open country they had travelled through on their way there.

The heat was rising steadily. Elliot turned back in the direction of the hotel and found himself passing the hospital. On the grass at the front of it, families were sitting around, one or two with patients among them, wearing hospital gowns. One young woman was in a wheelchair, her head lolling on her chest. A middle-aged man, also in a wheelchair, was making short work of a cigarette while two children, leaning close together, made drawings on the freshly bandaged stump of his left leg. Aware that he, too, was staring at it, Elliot turned away and went on. He found himself thinking that he could work in that hospital and that the idea held an attraction for him that he couldn't account for. He felt no particular affinity for the local people. The building looked small and shabby and unappealing and, although he could usually handle the heat, he didn't like it, particularly on days like this when he expected a nosebleed at any moment. All the same, a seed had lodged itself in his imagination. Over time it would germinate and grow, and become an idea, and then a plan, and then an action. All without having a clear idea of why, except that the country, the place that the whole of Alice Springs was parked on, held a fascination for him that he felt compelled to explore.

Back at the hotel, he found the three Papunya boards leaning against his bed. Despite the wipe their previous owner had given them with the painting rag, they were still covered in grime and cobwebs and were transferring dirt to his bedclothes. Irritated, he moved them over to Miles's bed and brushed away the marks as well as he could. They were of no significance. There were worse marks all over the room, from the red dust they had brought in from their travels. But still, that particular smudge on his sheets infuriated Elliot. It was petty, beyond absurd for him to mind where Miles put his things and he knew, even as he raged, that it wasn't about a bit of dust on his sheets. It was the greater problem that it symbolised, the hijacking of their trip for a private, financial purpose.

He turned on the air-conditioner and made himself a fresh lime soda, adding salt as well as sugar, the way Jyoti made them on hot summer days in London. Something about the combination made them irresistible and he drank down the first one and made a second, then sat in the only armchair, making that one last. He heard Miles on the stairs, clumping up, clattering something against the iron railings then breathing hard outside the room, searching for his key. Forty-eight hours ago, Elliot would have jumped up to open the door for him, but today he wouldn't, even though it felt uncomfortable to stay where he was. Eventually, Miles got it open and came in sideways, dragging an enormous cardboard box and several plastic bags with the logo of the stockman's outfitters. The whole lot was dumped at the end of the space between the two beds, too close to Elliot's side of the room for his liking and blocking his passage to the fridge.

Miles said, 'Oof,' and went straight to the bathroom for a shower. Elliot got up and moved the box and the bags, which were heavy, up against the foot of Miles' bed. Inside the box was a bundle of old news-papers and a roll of parcel tape.

When Miles emerged from the bathroom, still wet, a towel around his waist, he said, 'I gave him twenty-nine.' He turned off the air condi-tioning and Elliot erupted.

'For fuck's sake! I just turned that on!'

'But it's cold,' Miles said.

'It's not cold. You're wet. You'll be sweating again in a minute.'

Miles turned the air-con on again and towelled himself off. He opened the nearest bag and pulled out a huge, full-length waxed coat with shoulder-flaps and a hood. Smaller things were dragged out in its wake; a pair of cowboy shirts with pearl press-studs, a roll of cotton singlets in desert fatigue colours. 'What do you think?'

Elliot shrugged.

Miles said, 'Don't you like it?'

Elliot said, 'Not particularly, no.'

'That's a shame,' Miles said. 'I got one for you as well.'

Elliot's spirits rose momentarily, then fell again. He was pleased with the gesture, but he would never wear a thing like that. 'Not for me.'

'Really?'

'No, honestly. I wouldn't wear it.'

Miles said, 'It's OK, never mind. I'm sure they'll give us the money back. Or change it for something else. Is there anything else you'd like from there?'

'I don't like that clobber,' Elliot said. 'It's not me. It's not you, either, Miles. Can't you see that?' After a moment, and with an enormous effort, he added, 'Thanks anyway.'

Miles finished dressing, then said, 'Do you mind if we stay another day or two?'

'Why?'

'Roly has some other artists he wants me to look at. Contemporary ones. And I thought I might have a look around on my own account. Spend some of my ill-gotten gains. Invest in a few bits and pieces myself.'

Elliot shrugged, still battling with that unnameable rage. 'Whatever you like. But I think you're mad.'

'Maybe. But he's usually right, Roly is.' He sat on the bed and examined the loot in the bags. 'You're due a cut of this,' he said. 'If you wanted to buy a painting yourself. As an investment.'

Elliot said, 'It's junk, Miles. Can't you see that?'

'Not all of it,' Miles said. 'There's really good stuff as well.' Elliot said nothing, and he went on, 'Or if you wanted something in cash.'

'You can pay for the room,' Elliot said. 'And I want the car.'

Miles was shocked.

'While you're hanging around town looking at paintings.' Elliot pointed in a random direction. 'I want to go back out there.'

'But I might need...'

'You can get a cab around town. Or rent a car if you want. I'm not interested in traipsing around looking at spots and splashes. I've seen enough of them to last me a lifetime. I want to see the Milky Way again. I'll come back for you whenever you want.'

While Miles packed up the Papunya boards for the courier, Elliot gathered what he would need for the trip and packed it in the car. Then he dropped Miles and the box at the post office, filled up with diesel and set out. Instinctively, he headed out of town the way they had come in, unable to imagine that there was any more beautiful country than what they had already seen. He failed to find the waterhole again, but ended up in another creek just as beautiful, slept in a swag under the stars and woke, with a mild nosebleed, at dawn. For the next two days he stayed there, following the shade of the big gums which sloughed off their bark in great strips, revealing fresh new skins underneath; white and sage green and pink, looking as smooth and soft as the skin of a newborn. Even without water, it was a busy place, full of insects and lizards. He had learned to identify the footprints of kangaroos and dingoes but not the many smaller ones that criss-crossed the deep sand. Once a flock of red-tailed black cockatoos came sailing in and stopped for a conference in the branches above him. He watched and listened, and as they lifted off to continue on their way, a single tail-feather drifted down and landed at his feet: soot black with a crimson band. Elliot thought that if he were of a mystical bent, he would see it as a gift from the bird, or from the land, and would attach deep significance to it. As it was, he merely kept it, pushing it through the vent holes in his white hat and then, later, carefully parking it between the pages of a medical journal he had intended to read but which hadn't yet emerged from the bottom of his suitcase.

And when he found it again, he thought that, had he been of a mystical bent, he would have seen it as a message, inviting him back to that country. It fell out of the journal when he was packing up to move out of the flat where he and Jyoti had made another attempt at living together, which had lasted for nearly three years. It reminded him that there were other possibilities, not just outside London but also outside Europe. By then he had already signed a two-year contract to work in Dublin, but he didn't forget about Australia this time, and well before his Dublin contract was up, he had lined up a position in Melbourne to work as a GP.

He rang in the Millennium there, twelve hours ahead of his friends and family in the UK.

24

THE TALKATIVE BROTHER is as good as his word. He brings in a metre-high stack of audiobooks on CD, which the nurses put on for Elliot in the evenings to help him sleep. It is nice, having those soothing voices read to him, but they add to his confusion. Did Ned Kelly's mother really shack up with a policeman? Is there someone called Angel Day who lives in a place called Desperance? Has he been there? Does he know her? They walk into his dreams, some of them. They mingle with the people that he remembers, get confused with them sometimes. Mort Blacksmith is someone he is sure he knows. Elliot has been on a trip with him, hasn't he? Or a flight to Adelaide, perhaps.

But who took who to the hospital? There are times when he thinks the whole Central Australian part of his life is a dream or an audiobook. How can it have been otherwise? Do places like that and people like that really exist?

25

ELLIOT CHOSE to apply for the job in Melbourne because it suited him in many ways, and he was well qualified for it. The mistake he made, and it was a common one among Europeans, was to underestimate the size of Australia. Even though he had been there before, his perception of the distances had been compromised by the passage of time; he hadn't taken time to think out what would be involved in getting to those parts of the country that he wanted to see again. It was the same country, and that was as far as his thoughts went. It wasn't until he arrived and got stuck into the job that the truth of his situation came home to him. He had somehow forgotten that extraordinary experience of driving up through South Australia: all the miles, all the hours, the days and nights passing.

And in any case, getting himself set up in Melbourne took all the spare money and energy he had. He wanted his own place, where he could finally have a cat, and no one could complain or be allergic to it, so he bought a small house with a big garden in the inner suburbs. His savings covered the deposit and his mortgage repayments were less than he would have paid in rent. It was a decision he was never to regret. Over the next few years, his life in the city expanded, and he and his flea-bitten rescue cat got well settled in. He liked the people and made friends quickly, entering into a new relationship with a woman from Ireland who was working at the zoo. The small practice where he worked was in a part of North Melbourne that was becoming trendy; house prices were rising, there were new developments of apartments going up, the population was increasing and so was their traffic. His boss asked him if he would be interested in going into part-nership with her and moving to bigger premises where they could engage another GP or two. It involved taking out a business loan, but the economy was good, the banks were willing, and Elliot moved from being an employee to being an employer. Their client list continued to grow. Life was busy and fulfilling. He loved Melbourne, but he didn't forget the real reason he came to Australia. He was always aware of the pull of the red centre, and eventually, it became too strong to resist.

26

ELLIOT PRACTICES SMILING. As far as he knows, he has nothing in particular to smile about, but he knows it is an essential skill in human interaction and a thing he will need. At first, nothing much happens at all, but he keeps at it. Gradually his face begins to respond to his commands. He suspects that the early results are not pretty, but he tries them out on the nurses, and they are pleased. He tries them out on the consultant who comes to examine him every morning. She asks him if he is in pain. He doesn't give up. He is determined to learn to smile again.

27

THE JOB he took with the Central Australian Health Service had him based in Alice Springs. When he first arrived, he experienced a charge of excitement at being there again. The town was pretty much as he remembered it from all those years ago, although it seemed to him that some parts had been smartened up, and there were even more galleries along Todd Mall.

A colleague, a long-serving, long-suffering doctor called Drew Saunders, supervised an induction session for new recruits. There was a lot of information about cultural differences and ways of behaving in Aboriginal communities, and a lot more on the particular kinds of problems doctors were most likely to encounter. Towards the end he offered an unexpected piece of advice:

'They say that everyone who works in Aboriginal communities is either a missionary, a mercenary or a misfit. I'm not asking you to identify yourselves here and now, but it can be a good idea to have a think about it. Understand what motivates you, what you're expecting to get out of working out there. It can help you avoid misunderstandings and disappointments.'

Elliot did his best, but he couldn't see himself fitting into any of those categories.

28

HE SEES red smoke swirling across the surface of the plain. He is above it, looking down, and now he sees it isn't smoke but sediment in water, responding to the lightest of touches, lifting from the bottom of a clay-pan, spreading like smoke, dispersing. It is moving around the edges of the wide mouth, the clogged funnel that haunts him. Breath, he thinks. The drowned mouth is breathing.

29

A SMALL TEAM of physiotherapists come to chat to him and to move his limbs.

'Don't do anything,' one of them tells him. 'Just relax and let us do all the work.'

They bend and stretch his arms and legs, and sit him up in bed, get him to cough up some gunk, turn his head gently this way and that. He likes the feeling of hands on his body, but he is increasingly terrified by the situation he is in. He has seen brain-damaged people plenty of times and is in possession of too much information. The knowledge of what might be ahead of him, what his future life might consist of, is a black despair waiting to engulf him. He doesn't know how long he can continue to avoid it.

So he keeps on thinking, moving pieces of memory around in his mind, creating episodes, telling himself stories. He doesn't mind if things don't return in order. The sound of something dropped in the corridor reminds him of a woman having a meltdown in his local IGA, throwing down tins and bottles by the shelf-load. The smell of rainfall on parched earth that made its way into his room one day set off a whole chain of memories. A nurse's mention of a new puppy brings memories of nights in Nyaru, planned or unplanned, and the dogs there that invariably kept him awake. He learned to pack earplugs and later headphones as well, but nothing could keep out the noise they made. It was as though they took over the entire place once the people got too tired to exert their authority. Sometimes there were reasons that he could hear and understand: a family argument slamming its way across town, a mob of horses or camels wandering through, looking for water. Sometimes dingoes set them off, howling out in the bush. But as often as not there was no reason for the noise that Elliot could discern. It was just on-going, barking and howling that sometimes stopped for just long enough for him to give him hope, then started up all over again. Sandra told him she had no problem sleeping through it and that he wouldn't either if he was tired enough. He saw an implied criticism in her words and didn't mention it again. No matter how tired he was; he never succeeded in sleeping a full night in Nyaru.

30

He is physically but not emotionally inert. A hurricane of anguish and panic threatens to make landfall at any time. He has to apply phenomenal amounts of energy to keep himself under control, and a lot of what he remembers is not the kind of upbeat stuff he knows would be good for him. He thinks about Eileen, the zookeeper: how she was insanely sentimental about animals but perpetually furious with him. He remembers how their relationship went sour: the physical violence he endured at her hands and how it had diminished him, how he had been diminished before he even started work in the Northern Territory. It was 2010, and there were revolutionary diets and exercise programmes springing up every week. Headlines on health magazines and pop-up ads on browsers promised the benefits of the new miracle diet. In the world of white people, the latest fad was that the diet of their hunter-gatherer ancestors was optimal for human health, and the overweight wealthy were adopting it at enormous expense. Meanwhile, people who had been forcibly displaced from their hunter-gatherer way of life were suffering and dying from the effects of processed foods. Elliot tried to find the humour in it but failed. The entire experience in those early days was utterly dispiriting, and at times he suspected that, at forty-two, he was too old to adjust; that he might be one of the many who failed out there because they didn't have the emotional stamina.

But his life was not without its compensations. Doris was in the waiting room again when he arrived in Nyaru for his second clinic a fortnight later, and Linda was there with the baby and a little boy of about six. Elliot's new-job exhaustion was at its worst; from then on he would begin to acclimatise to the conditions and see a return to his former energy levels, but on that day he was leaden and miserable, and surprised to find that the sight of Doris and Linda lifted his spirits. They were the first people in the whole crazy circus that he recognised, and there was reassurance in that; in the fact that it would happen again, and that not every encounter would be a brand new one.

When they came into the surgery, he said, 'Hello again.' He didn't remember Doris' name, but he remembered Linda's. He said it aloud. 'How are you?'

The computer was still not working. Elliot looked at Sandra's list on the pile of files on his desk, hoping her name would be at the top. It wasn't. He said, 'Um, and how are you feeling today? Any better?'

'Little bit,' Doris said.

He remembered now, the cough, the antibiotics. He dug through the pile and found her file.

'Doris,' he said. 'Did you finish your medicine?'

'Yuwayi.'

'Let me have a listen to your chest.' He put the stethoscope to his ears, listened to her lungs through the thin fabric of her tee-shirt. He checked the notes. There was a big improvement since the last time. He said,

'It sounds much better, but there's still a bit of noise in your chest.'

There was that little pause again before she spoke. 'I can sleep now.'

'That's good. But it might come back again if it hasn't completely gone away. Will you take more medicine if I give it to you?'

She nodded. 'I can take it. No problem.'

Elliot found another file attached to Doris's one with a paperclip and was thankful for Sandra's efficiency. The file was for a child, a boy called Stan, the latest notes concerning a foot injury. He said,

'Is that Stan?' and Linda pulled him out from behind her chair.

'Sandra gave me cream for it,' Linda said, producing a greasy tube, half empty. 'No good.' He took the tube, a basic antiseptic cream, about as much use on a puncture wound out here as spitting on it. He didn't blame Sandra. She had worked in Nyaru for years and was as skilled in that situation as any doctor, but she still wasn't allowed to prescribe and had to make decisions every day about whether or not to phone him and get him to do it over the phone. On this occasion, she had decided to wait and let him see for himself. Stan, according to his file, was just six. He had trodden on a nail while he was playing in the street and now, a few days later, his foot was swollen like a mango. He giggled and kicked when Elliot tried to get a closer look at it, then wailed at the pain.

Elliot said, 'If I give you a bottle for Stan, will you make sure he takes it three times every day? And it's only for him. Not for any of the others.'

Linda nodded.

'Very bad for the other children,' he said.

'I know that,' Linda said. 'I understand how it works.'

While Elliot was writing out their prescriptions, Doris said, 'Do they know about us, in England? Your people?'

Elliot said, 'Of course they do, Doris.'

He handed the scripts to Linda, then crossed the room and opened the door. Linda passed him, holding Stan by the hand. She didn't look up.

'I want to see him again next time,' he said. 'And you too, Doris. I want to keep an eye on that chest.'

Reluctantly, Doris got up from the chair. As she passed him, she said,

'Do they know about our culture, though? Do they care about what happens to us?'

Elliot said, 'Well...I'm not...' He stepped back to allow a man in a wheelchair to come through, then went on, 'Can we talk about this some other time, Doris?

The clinic was a short one that day, and afterwards, Elliot went with Sandra in the centre's troopy to try and round up more patients. Nyaru had started life as an outstation during the 1980s, one of many in the surrounding area, out on the far Western edge of the Tanami desert, where Warlpiri country bordered Ngarti. Over the years a lot of the outstations failed, and their residents concentrated in Nyaru. The population remained largely Warlpiri, but there were some Ngarti people as well, and a few Pintupi and Kukatja, arriving there mainly through inter-marriage. By the time Elliot began working there, the population had risen to around two hundred and fifty, but it was an unstable figure. People moved around, married, separated, went to other states to look after family members or to be looked after by them. People who wanted to drink moved into one or other of the bigger towns, and those who stopped drinking moved back. Families moved in and out of the remaining outstations, depending on the season or the school terms. Sorry business and its associated obligations could halve the number of people in town, and just as easily double it. At times Elliot's waiting room could be practically empty, making him wonder whether it had been worth coming, and at other times it could be bursting at the seams with out-of-towners, many of whom had their medical records in another place.

On that particular day there was red ochre business going on at one of the nearby sites, Sandra told him, and most of the men and older boys would be gone for a few days. The town was quiet, and there was a sense of dereliction about parts of it. A dying horse was standing on a corner block, too close to its end to bother leaving town. The art centre, which had been the thriving heart of the community until the crash of 2008, was silent now, its large studio space used only for the occasional youth disco, its faded dreaming murals obscured by graffiti. The old council yard's fence had been plundered for makeshift housing repairs. The yard contained nothing now except the stripped carcass of a grader and a few broken plastic barrels. At times, the only animate thing was the wind, which passed through in irregular gusts, or stood up and strode through town in the form of a willy-willy, redistributing the litter as it went.

They ran through Sandra's list methodically, crossing each person off as they learnt of their whereabouts, tracking down those they could. One child was at school, feeling better, finishing a project. Another had moved with her mother to a community in WA. They passed Doris' house and Sandra pointed it out to him. It was the last of the old houses on the road and would have been the edge of town in the recent past. Now there was a new road against her western boundary, and on the other side of it, a block of units was being built, to house the growing numbers of teachers and social workers being sent out there. There were builders working on it now, but there was no one to be seen at Doris' place. A half-finished painting was laid out on the ground in front of the verandah, paint pots and dipping sticks beside it, waiting for the return of the artist.

'Who's the painter?' Elliot asked.

Sandra said, 'Doris is. She's a fairly well-known artist, you know.'

'Is she?'

'When we get the art centre open again, she should do a lot better. It's difficult for the artists without one. They are at the mercy of the dealers, you know? It can all be a bit hit and miss.'

Elliot looked at the painting. He wanted to understand, wished he could see what other people saw in circles and half-moons and stripes. He still couldn't though. It was still just dots. Sandra engaged first gear but didn't move off.

'Main thing about this place, though, you need to know it's a jilimi.'

'Is that a women's place?' Elliot had come across it in his induction notes.

'You can't go in there at all, and you won't be invited. If you need to see someone in there, just wait at the fence-line until they come out.'

'Fair enough.'

As they drove on, Sandra said, 'Actually, it's a bit more than a jilimi. Doris and Linda are trying to make it a culture centre where women can go and learn ceremony and law.'

'I thought there was a women's centre already?'

'There is, but it's not the same. The women's centre runs programmes around domestic violence, kids' nutrition, they've got a little laundry going and there are plans for putting up a safe house, that kind of thing. They make trips out on country sometimes, but it's haphazard, requires endless negotiation about the use of the vehicle and then there are forms to fill in and reports to be written. Those trips tend to turn into picnic outings for the mothers and little kids, mostly. Doris has a different idea. She wants a place that only looks after culture.'

The builders were packing up for the day, loading tools into their company utes. Those new units were just being started when Elliot saw them that day. By the time Doris came to him looking for help, they were completed and fully occupied.

31

THE FRIENDLY CONSULTANT visits Elliot again, with an assistant. It seems as though another day has passed, though Elliot can't properly account for it. They shift him up in the bed a bit, so he is half-sitting, and then they put him through his paces. He is asked to raise each arm and each foot, one at a time, and to bend his knees and his good elbow, and to turn his head to one side and then the other. He is asked to touch his ears and his nose with his right hand. He is asked a number of questions about his name and history. Although he has very limited success in any these tasks, there are signs that please the consultant, and she tells him again that she expects him to recover reasonably well. She will send a speech and language therapist as well as the physios, and they will start him on some programmes as soon as possible because the sooner he starts his rehabilitation, the more successful the outcome will be.

They leave him in that position, with his trunk slightly raised. She tells him it will make it easier for him to cough, and she is right, though it doesn't prevent the broken ribs from hurting when he does. For a while, he tries to keep his eyes open and his attention on the world out there, but when the people are gone, there is nothing left to see. The other bed is empty and freshly made up. Someone has come and gone without him ever knowing who it was.

He closes his eyes again, waits to see what comes. He sees a horse, red-coloured and red-stained, running down the street. The community is without a name. It might have been any of them. The horse has a makeshift bridle, rigged out of a nylon halter, rope used as a bit, more rope attached as reins, but dragging in the dust, so the horse stands on them every few strides and gets a jab in the mouth. Elliot is in a car, on a round of home visits, perhaps. The horse stops and turns to look back the way it has come, its great ribs heaving, its ears scanning for sound. Red dust is crusting on its neck and shoulders, red drops of sweat run down its forelegs and its face. It turns, sees Elliot in the car, starts, sets out again. It whinnies, long and hard, listens for an answer that doesn't come. Elliot has no idea where it has come from and he watches its hesitant progress, looking into each yard and down each side-street it passes. Three teenage boys arrive in pursuit, one on a bicycle. They ask Elliot for a lift to help them catch the horse, but he is going in the opposite direction. They hop up on top of the car anyway, arrange themselves on the roof rack, yell at him to go faster, faster, faster.

32

DORIS DIDN'T COME to surgery the following fortnight, and nor did Linda. It surprised Elliot to realise he had been expecting to see them; looking forward to it even, and he was disappointed when they didn't turn up. Was he already smitten by then? He can't remember. Nor can he work out why he would have latched his libido onto someone so completely unsuitable in every way. Linda was at least 15 years younger than him, involved in a complicated marriage with four kids, and living most of the time in a desert community about as far from mainstream life as it was possible to get. But he couldn't deny his infatuation and he couldn't escape from it. His visits to Nyaru took on an entirely different character to the ones in other communities. He looked forward to them and dreaded them. He resented Linda for the distraction she represented. In Nyaru, he was aware of too much anticipation and not enough concentration, half his mind forever elsewhere.

HE CAN REMEMBER the feeling now, but he does not experience it. He reaches into his imagination for favourite erotic stimuli, but they produce no reaction now, either mental or physical. He hopes his lack of arousal is a result of the medication he is on and not a permanent result of his injuries.

33

IT DID TAKE hold of him early on; he remembers that now. How, the following time he came, or maybe the time after that, he got Sandra to pull up outside the jilimi. Doris was in front of the house, sitting in the middle of a huge canvas, applying dots with a stick. A younger woman was working on a smaller canvas opposite her. They were both singing. There were other women there as well, sitting together on the verandah of the house, and a group of children playing around the side.

'Can I have a quick word with her?' Elliot asked. Sandra turned off the engine. They got out and waited for Doris to acknowledge their presence. There were two big women in the back of the troopy, both diabetic, both on their way to the clinic for overdue blood tests. They craned their heads around so they could see out of the open passenger door. It must have been late afternoon, after school hours anyway, because all the children were home. There was a little mob of girls sitting in the shell of a car beside the end wall of the house, and a smaller boy kicking a deflated football around in the dust.

'Is that Stan?' Elliot asked Sandra. 'Is his foot better?'

Doris still hadn't looked up. The back door of the car opened and the two women peered out. One of them said, 'She painting.'

Elliot said, 'We can see that.'

'She showing that jukurrpa to Audrey. Leave her, eh,' said the other woman.

'I want to see how her chest is,' Elliot said. 'And I want to look at Stan's foot.'

'All better,' said the first woman, who had been complaining of a need to piss since she got into the car.

'It's fine,' Sandra said. 'I saw it during the week.' She made a hand gesture to one of the children in the car but got no response.

Elliot said, 'Where is their mother?'

'Gone for bush tucker, might be,' said the woman with the full bladder. Abruptly, she pushed the back door wide, lumbered down the fold-out steps and began making hand signals. As though her eyes were permanently attuned to that form of communication, Doris looked up from her work. For a moment, she appeared confused, like someone just waking up. Gradually she focussed, saw the troopy, responded with hand signals of her own then started talking breathlessly, waving the hand with the painting stick in it, sending flecks of dark colour flying. Their passenger clambered back into the car and pulled in the steps.

'She gone back to her husband,' she said. 'Took the baby.'

'No good that fella, eh,' said the other passenger, and muttered something in language which made them both fall about laughing.

Elliot felt a flush of irritation. He blamed it on the pitch of the women's voices, but he was dimly aware of a deeper disturbance that he was reluctant to examine. He called across to Stan, who looked up from the ball, saw who it was and legged it around the side of the house. There was no sign of a limp. Elliot would have liked a closer look, but he didn't fancy his chances.

Doris was watching. She said. 'All better now.' When Elliot showed no sign of moving, she made a casual hand gesture, an unmistakeable dismissal, then wiped her stick on a rag, shuffled a few centimetres forward on the canvas, and began to paint again. Elliot, more slighted by the rejection than he wanted to admit, got back into the car. Sandra started the engine.

'They're fine,' she said. Elliot nodded.

He said, 'Can Linda do that? Just leave her kids here and go back to her husband?'

'Ah, she won't stay there long,' Sandra said. 'She comes and goes a lot. She wants to stay here but she has obligations. Sometimes he comes and gets her, and she has to go. She always comes back, though. And the kids are fine. The jilimi is like a big family for them, you know? And Doris makes sure they get to school.'

'Does she make a lot of money out of her art?' he said.

Sandra shrugged. 'She might do. They fetch thousands, some of the bigger ones. But you know how it is out here. Money gets spread around and no one ever has anything much to show for it.'

34

ELLIOT DREAMS that he has finally learned to purr. It is such a divine experience that he wants to keep doing it forever. It is the philosopher's stone of audible sound, superior to Om. It delivers the purrer directly into nirvana. Elliot wants to tell the whole world, but as he wakes up, he discovers some link in his brain has broken down; the purr program won't load. He wakes full of confusion and it is some time before he remembers where he is, and he is devastated to discover it has been a dream.

35

LUKE NEVER CAME to Elliot's clinic for treatment, and their chance meetings were few and far between. They met a second time outside the store one day, and another time they bumped into each other at the airport in Alice Springs; Elliot on his way to sort out some business in Melbourne, Luke heading out to a meeting in Darwin. Both of them were looking unusually smart. They had time for a beer in the airport bar, and Luke told Elliot about his years working at the gold mine, driving earth-moving equipment. He said he hated it, every minute of it; his wages were like blood money for injuring the land. When he was younger, a lot of his people had jobs, but it was harder to get them now. Every kind of job was looking for some kind of qualification. It was a new thing that so many were unemployed and living off handouts. There used to be jobs in the community for yapa, but the intervention closed down the Community Development Programmes and now kardiya were sent in to do all the work.

As far as he can remember, he didn't ask what kind of meeting Luke was heading for in Darwin that day. Perhaps he remembered the appearance of that petition and was afraid that he would get an answer he didn't know what to do with. Instead, he had moved the conversation on to safer ground.

'So did you ever make that trip out to your country?'

Luke looked worried. 'No. My family on my back to go and look after that place. You want to go?'

'Yes, I want to go. You promised to take me. Remember?'

'Yeah. We'll go, then. When you want to go?'

'When is a good time?'

'Now is a good time, when I come back from Darwin. But I don't have my car.'

'Where is your car?'

'My son-in-law got him. Took a big mob out to his country, it's way down in Pitjantjara country. But might be he'll bring it back soon. Definitely he will. We can make a plan.'

Elliot's flight was called for boarding and he stood up. 'Let's make a plan, then,' he said.

'Yeah. When you come back. We make a plan. We go soon, eh?'

36

ELLIOT WAITED, hopefully at first, then with less optimism. A few times he tried Luke's mobile number, and he looked for him when he was in Nyaru, but he didn't succeed in making contact. He was disappointed. Visiting that vast, red country was why he had come here, and it had always been his intention to get a vehicle that would take him into it. But he had made a rash decision when he first arrived in Alice and bought an unsuitable car. It had been a bargain, and he had been hustled into buying it against his better judgement, by an American technician who had finished her stint working at the intelligence installation at Pine Gap. It was a good car, an all-wheel drive station-wagon that would handle the main dirt roads with no problem, but it was not designed to do the kind of driving that Elliot wanted to do. It would not take him along the four-wheel drive track beside the Finke river, or back along the Old Andado Road, and it wouldn't stand a chance on the French Line, the track he most wanted to take, across the Simpson desert. For that kind of driving it was widely accepted that there was only one suitable vehicle, the one so widely used in the area that its brand-name had become part of the desert people's vocabulary.

There was nothing to stop him getting one, apart from the fact that he found it increasingly hard to get round to things. The job took up no more of his time than he had expected, but it did take up more of his energy. The clinic days were long and often frustrating, and living and working in the heat was far more exhausting than just passing through it. Every winter, when it was cool, he managed to pick up a virus, which was a thing that hadn't happened to him since he was a child, and each time he got sick it seemed to take him longer to shake it off. He felt perpetually under par, always just lagging behind himself a bit. Jyoti had often complained that he lacked initiative and that if she didn't get on his case he would never do anything. He had always disagreed, of course, but he had to admit it at times. If he didn't get a push from some external force, he was capable of drifting for years along the path of least resistance, avoiding major decisions until they actually blocked his path.

37

HE DREAMS about an old man who runs and hides behind a house. He follows the old man, all his medical paraphernalia hanging from his shoulders, clinking in his pockets. The old man is sitting beside a stream, eating witchetty grubs with a spoon. Elliot takes one and is about to eat it when it jumps from his hand into the water. It swells up and turns into a big white brain.

38

THE SEPARATION between the yapa and kardiya populations was evident in all the desert communities. The interaction between service providers and users stopped at the end of each working day when the teachers and social workers returned to their government houses and closed their doors. The differences in philosophy, particularly where money and possessions were concerned, were too far apart for comfortable accommodations to be made. Exceptions existed, but they were few and far between.

But as time went on and Elliot got to know the community and how things worked, he relaxed into the unhurried pace of life there and became more tolerant of the differences in culture. He came to know most of his regulars on first-name terms and often knew the people Sandra was talking about when she phoned him for advice or prescriptions. She soon entrusted him to make the home visits by himself, even when the clinic car got changed for a brand new one that converted to an ambulance.

Nyaru consisted of four main streets built on an irregular noughts and crosses grid, all becoming dirt roads where they met the edge of town. Some of these were well-travelled yapa roads, short-cuts to other communities. Others were less defined, meandering around in the bush on their way to local ceremony sites or hunting grounds. New roads had been added in town, some official, like the one for the kardiya houses, some unofficial, like the one which ran between the north edge of town and the small collection of humpies beyond it, where the community overflow set themselves up to wait for more housing to be built. But even with these extensions, it was a tiny place, and it was practically impossible to drive around town without passing the jilimi at least once.

Linda and her children were there sometimes; less than half the time, probably. Sandra inferred that Linda and her husband had a stormy relationship, but Elliot never asked for more details, unwilling to expose the extent of his interest. In retrospect, he sees it must have been obvious, and he appreciates the restraint of all those women, in that they never challenged him or teased him about it. He supposed it was because he never acted on his infatuation; had no expectation that it could lead to anything. Or maybe acknowledging a thing like that would have made it more dangerous. In any event, they must have known. Linda did, anyway. He is sure that what she did was an attempt to exploit his feelings for her.

WHAT SHE DID. What did she do? Something is stirring uncomfortably close to consciousness. He sees Doris; her hands and her tee-shirt are spotted and streaked with acrylic paint. She looks like an early stage of one of her own paintings. A huge one lies unfinished on the ground between her and the verandah. A thin, brindled dog lies across one corner, scratching itself. Nearby another dog, a black one, is sprawled in the shade of the house. It has nearly as much paint on it as Doris does.

Elliot can see the painting clearly, as though he is floating above it. The background is a deep red, covered with bold black lines and circles, which are gradually being infilled with dotting of salmon pink, peach, mustard and white. As he watches it, his discomfort increases, until suddenly it erupts into a massive disturbance within him and, for the first time, he reaches overload, finds himself yelling for the hospital staff in half-formed words that he himself cannot understand. They administer some kind of chemical cosh and he goes under.

For a long time, maybe a couple of days, he can't concentrate well enough to explore any more memories. There is ongoing activity around his bed. People come and go, asking him to do this and that. He does as he is told, or he tries to. Physically he is beginning to gain a little control, and he is happy to avoid any more shocks to his system. But eventually, the level of the drug in his bloodstream is reduced. His mind and his memory begin to return. Doris is there, waiting for him, in her beanie and heavy winter jumper. And Linda, in a jumper as well, her face turned away.

HE DREAMS that he has a tail. It's a fine tail, admired by all. But he realises he has made a terrible mistake in not hiding it, and everyone is laughing because all the bones are falling out of it, one by one, little vertebrae like beads clattering on the floor, and his tail is limp and useless; empty like a snake skin. When he wakes, he connects the dream to his lost libido, and for the first time, he laughs out loud.

39

He tries to resurrect his passion, but there is no lust or longing in him now. He tries to understand what it is about Linda that aroused his desire, and it feels to him as though he is slipping into a familiar and well-used chain of thought, as though he has tried to analyse those feelings many, many times before. He had loved Jyoti and, on the whole, had wanted to stay in the relationship with her, but he had never felt the same urgency of desire about her or anyone else. He thinks that what attracted him to Linda might have been her grace, that elegant economy of movement that she shared with most desert people. That was part of it, perhaps, but it wasn't all. There was something within her; something he was forever trying to connect with and forever failing. She had a quality he lacked, and that he wanted. She had a certainty about who she was and what she wanted out of life. She carried it within her like an unfaltering flame, no matter what she was going through.

She came to his clinic one day with a swollen wrist. It was clearly fractured, with a laceration and extensive bruising, already several days old by the time he saw it. She told him she had trapped it in a car door, and that the swelling on her jaw had been caused the same way. The wind had blown the door while she was leaning into the car. She acted it out for him, and he saw that it could happen; stray winds often blew up in that area. He asked her where it happened and why she hadn't told Sandra. She didn't answer.

He said, 'You'll have to go to Alice. It needs to be x-rayed and properly set.'

Later on, he asked Sandra what she knew. She said, 'She didn't come to me about it because she's afraid I will tell the police who did it.'

They were sitting together in the clinic, going over the day's notes. Elliot said, 'It could have been an accident, I suppose.'

Sandra shook her head. 'That man of hers is bad news. He lives in town, in Hoppy's Camp. He only comes out here when he wants to fetch Linda and the kids or to humbug Doris. Then he pisses it all against the wall. Doesn't contribute a penny towards his kids.'

Elliot said, 'Are you saying we should report it?'

Sandra said, 'I don't know. There's a bit of a story behind it.' Elliot waited, and she went on, 'She took his car. He got this souped-up saloon thing, had it shipped up from Adelaide, you know? Ridiculous thing. Boy racer car. And Linda...' Sandra burst out laughing, and it was a minute or two before she could bring herself under control. 'She filled it with jerry cans and drove it all the way out here along that road. Knocked a bit of the shine off it along the way.'

'Even so,' said Elliot.

'He had to come out on the bush bus to get it back, that's all I know.' Sandra shrugged. 'Nothing we can do if she chooses not to report it. She's not a minor.'

Elliot was no stranger to injuries caused by domestic violence, nor to the excuses women made to protect their men. But the idea that Linda was in an abusive relationship or that she wouldn't come clean to him about it was, for some reason, difficult for him to accept. He took her into Alice on the plane when it returned that afternoon. Technically, flights were reserved for emergencies, but there were always grey areas when there was available space. Seven hours of corrugations and washouts on a dirt road was a form of torture to someone with a serious injury or a developing illness.

'Did someone else do this to you?' he asked her. She had brought Audrey, who she called her sister, to help out with the baby. The other children stayed in Nyaru with Doris. Linda's wrist was so thin and fragile it seemed to Elliot as though a tap with anything heavier than a pencil would break it. She was reluctant to say any more about it, but he insisted, and she sketched the trajectory of the door in the air; how it had clipped her jaw before slamming on her arm. She was distant, uncomfortable in the sterile interior of the plane, inclined to turn her back and concentrate on the baby. Audrey was more willing to talk to him, but he did nothing to encourage her.

He said to Linda, 'You must tell me if anyone hurts you. I'll stop them. I won't let them do it.'

He could hear how ridiculous he sounded and was aware that her brief glance and nod were given to humour him, and that there was a grin and a giggle behind it that she was struggling to keep hidden. It was one of those moments when he realised how little insight he had, or ever would have, into the lives other people led.

40

AND OF COURSE, it was numbskull behaviour like that which set him up as a target. He is getting closer to remembering; the events that followed are hovering around the peripheries of his consciousness now. Target is the wrong word. It implies a plan, a mercenary streak that he is sure neither Doris nor Linda possesses. But he set himself up, nonetheless. He was asking for trouble.

41

TWO OR THREE times a year he stayed overnight in Nyaru, sometimes because of unusually large numbers of patients, sometimes for more specialised reasons, such as a vaccination drive or a screening programme, occasionally because bad weather put the airstrip out of use. But when he stayed there, he generally had dinner with Sandra or kept to himself, taking advantage of having no internet to catch up on some reading or get an early night. He was aware that some kardiya who lived and worked in remote communities had much closer relationships to the residents, but he wasn't sure whether he wanted that. He came to understand that, as long as he didn't accept a skin name, he would never get close to anyone, but if he did accept one, the resulting trust and intimacy would inevitably be accompanied by obligations and assumptions which could make his practice as a doctor very awkward. He knew that other people managed to make it work. Sandra was clearly loved and trusted, and Drew had yapa friends who came to his house in Alice. But the nearest thing Elliot had to a yapa friend was Luke, and it was clear that Luke didn't see things the same way.

No phone call came and, as time went on, Elliot began to suspect that his offer of a trip was a fob-off. He told Sandra about it, and she said that no, it wasn't a fob-off; Luke needed to go back to his country.

He hadn't been back for too long and was always talking about it, but he was often too busy with other business to find the time. Elliot was never entirely sure what Luke's other business was, but it involved a lot of meetings: Land Council meetings, royalties' meetings, land lease meetings, many of them in other parts of the Territory, and sometimes even further afield.

42

SANDRA'S MOTHER comes to visit several times. She's a serious woman, thin and grey and energetic, outspoken and amusingly cynical. She brings books with her, and quite often Elliot wakes to find her sitting in the visitor's chair, reading. She tells him Sandra's health is beginning to break down and she is resigning from Nyaru. When she comes back next time it will be for good. Not soon enough, as far as her mother is concerned.

'Just wearing herself to the bone,' she says. 'And what has she got to show for it? Sacrificed her own family life to the people out there. I never understood why she does it.'

43

ONE DAY, Doris and Linda came to see him at the end of the day's clinic. When was it? Not that long ago, he thinks, though dates are difficult, and the effect that powerful memories carry often make them feel more recent. It was one of the occasions when he was scheduled to stay overnight in the community. In the morning he was running a special clinic to check on all the children's ears ahead of an upcoming visit by a specialist.

Neither Doris nor Linda was on his list for the day and he was surprised, delighted in fact, to see them. But there was something about them that alerted him to the fact that they had an unusual motive for being there. There was no paint on Doris' latest tee-shirt. Linda was wearing jeans and a smart pink hoodie, which made her appear younger, and more worldly. There were no children with them, and they both looked fit and well.

Doris said, 'We not sick. We want to ask you something.'

Elliot pushed back his seat and came around to the front of his desk. He leant on it and it slid away from him, so he sat on it.

He said, 'Of course. Is it health-related?'

He glanced at Linda, but she looked away. He sensed that fierce determination in her, that ember burning brighter than ever.

Doris considered his question for a moment, then said, 'Yuwayi. It's health related.'

Linda said, 'Big time.'

Elliot nodded. 'Go ahead. Fire away.'

The two women exchanged glances, came to some silent agreement. Doris said, 'Yeah. We looking for...some way to get money, you know?'

Elliot's interest recoiled, shrivelled into a hard, defensive knot in his gut. Doris read his reaction. 'Nah, not humbug, Doctor. This a different thing.'

'We need money for our place,' said Linda. 'We want to make it... proper culture centre, you know? Where can we get money for that?'

Doris said, 'We need a fence. Stop those kardiya in the new houses looking in. And we need a toyota so we can go out on country. For ceremony.'

Elliot nodded. 'But it's not really my department,' he said. 'Health and culture are different things.'

There was that pause again. Elliot watched Linda and Linda watched Doris, waiting for her to speak. 'No,' she said, at last. 'Not here. Our young people getting lost. You seen it. Drink and drugs, suicide, all that bad stuff. Young people got nothing to live for if they don't know their culture.'

Doris' words were measured, and her slow, quiet delivery gave them authority. When Linda spoke, her voice was full of that passion that Elliot had always guessed was there and had waited all this time to see. 'We need the old people to teach us the law. If we don't get it from them, it's gone, you know? When they finish, law finish too.'

She held Elliot's gaze for only a fraction of a second, but it was long enough to send a jolt of hot energy through his blood. Then she turned to Doris and said something quietly in language.

Doris said, 'So how can we get money, you think?'

Elliot did his best to gather his wits. 'I see where you're coming from,' he said. 'I can see why you would make that connection. But it's definitely not something the health department would get involved in.

You would need to make an application for funding. Get a direct grant. I'm sure there is money for cultural things.'

Again, the two women conferred, quietly. Then Linda said, 'We don't want government money. If we get funding, we need an administrator and we don't want that. This for us, our people, we want to do it our way, you know? No reports, no audits, no putting on dancing for whitefellas.'

Doris said, 'Can you help us, Doctor?'

Linda, unleashed now, continued. She spoke more rapidly than Doris, but with a similar quiet authority. 'Is there money in England for us? She our queen too, isn't she?' Elliot drew breath to answer, but Linda went on, 'Or crowdfunding. We heard about that. Can we get money from crowdfunding?'

Elliot said, 'I don't know. I don't know anything about crowd-funding.'

'Can you find out for us?' Linda said. 'We can't look. We don't have internet here.'

Elliot shrugged. 'Ok. I'll have a look when I'm back in town. But I doubt...'

Linda made to stand up, but Doris made a subtle gesture with a long, thin hand and she relaxed back into her seat.

Doris said, 'Have you been out on country, Doctor?'

Elliot said, 'Well...Not much. Not recently anyway.'

Doris said, 'You can come with us. You can get two tails in the store. Maybe some potatoes.'

'Soft drink,' Linda added

Elliot said, 'Well, I'm not sure,' but he found that he was. Even out of the blue like this, even if there was an ulterior motive, he was ready for a trip out on country. Especially one that involved Linda.

44

ELLIOT DREAMS of the dog fence, the farmlands of the southeast rich and green and, on the other side, the arid red heart of the country. Dingoes are prowling along it and he is afraid that they will break through the flimsy-looking structure. Then he realises that they are not dingoes, but German Shepherds, snarling attack dogs, and that they are on the farmers' side of the fence, not the desert side.

But he doesn't seem to be on either side. He is perched on the top wire, not a wire but a terrifyingly high ledge, on a narrow path that is about to peter out entirely.

45

HE WAITED OUTSIDE THE STORE, the frozen kangaroo tails sticking out of one bag, another bag filled with foil and potatoes and an assortment of bottles. He wasn't sure why he let himself be talked into buying soft drinks, which, in his book, were as harmful out on the communities as cigarettes. He felt soiled by the act, a hypocrite at least; at worst a kind of pusher.

He waited and waited. He had wanted to take the clinic troopy and do the driving himself, but Sandra wouldn't allow it. The car was meant for emergencies and had to be available. He was dependent, therefore, on whatever kind of arrangement Doris and Linda could work out, and it was clearly taking them some time. He looked at his watch again, self-conscious about hanging around for so long, and about what was in his shopping bags. He was afraid that they had forgotten or just decided to do something else instead.

A blue saloon car with a cracked windscreen pulled up. The side windows were all either open or missing. A young lad was driving, and an old man was in the passenger seat. Neither of them got out of the car. Neither of them paid him any attention. He recognised the younger man from a visit to the clinic, but he didn't remember his name. It wasn't until a second car, driven by Linda, pulled up beside them that

Elliot realised they belonged to his party. Doris was in the passenger seat of the second car. The back seat was heaving with exuberant children, Audrey in among them, but barely visible. There wasn't a seat belt in sight.

When the women had been into the store and done their own shopping, they piled all the bags, Elliot's as well, into the boot of their car. Elliot, following instructions from Doris, got into the back of the men's car. The seat wasn't bolted in and it rocked around on unsteady supports. He leaned forward and held on to the front seats.

'I'm Elliot,' he said.

The old man introduced himself by his skin name, Jakamarra. His eyes were pale with cataracts and there was only a single tooth visible when he spoke. He ignored Elliot's offer of a handshake and turned back to the road. The younger man said nothing, as though he were a taxi driver and not involved with the enterprise in any personal way at all.

The women led the way, heading out along the main road. The corrugations rattled the car so hard that Elliot was amazed it stayed in one piece. After a few kilometres, they turned to the south along a narrow little track that showed red among the yellow grasses. It was less predictable than the main road, much smoother in most places, but interspersed with hazards at random intervals. They went much more slowly, so it wasn't as hard on the bones. Termites had built towers in places, hard as concrete bollards, and previous travellers on the road had forged little detours around them. Grass swished under the belly of the car, and sometimes harder things which Elliot could feel grating beneath his feet. Occasionally, there would be a clunk, as some part of the chassis hit a stone or the hard edge of a wheel-rut. Despite their moderate speed, the drive set Elliot's nerves on edge.

They passed stretches of country that had been recently burned, and others where burning in the previous year had encouraged new green growth. Every couple of hundred metres or so, Jakamarra pointed something out to Elliot, but between the noise of the car and the lack of clarity in the old man's speech, he picked up on hardly any of it. When they had been on the road for about twenty minutes, the first car

stopped, and all four doors flew open. Everyone got out. Linda and
Audrey and the children spread out across a stretch of clear, green
country. Doris stayed where she was, and Elliot went over and leaned
against her side of the car.

'They are looking for bush tucker,' she said. 'Little sweet ones.' She
pointed at something, but Elliot couldn't see it. The children were busy
around little bushes, which looked dry and withered. Linda came back
to them with a small handful of yellow and brown berries, which she
shared among Doris and the men. Elliot was dubious but instantly
converted by the first sweet taste.

They stopped a few more times along the way, for firewood, which
they piled on to the roofs of the cars, and for other kinds of wild food.
Elliot doesn't remember the names of those things now: neither the
sweet berries nor the bigger, sharper ones they stopped for further on,
nor the tiny beans they picked from trees near where they made their
campfire. He knew them all once, their Warlpiri names as well as their
English ones. He worked hard to remember, but there is nothing left
now. He doesn't remember the names of the places they passed, either.
Not even the special men's place he visited with Jakamarra and their
silent driver.

Thirty minutes or so out of town, the cars went separate ways.
Elliot had already lost track of how many little junctions they had
encountered and which way they had turned each time. The side road
the men's car took was very like the others until they got near the end,
where it pretty much disappeared in a chaos of deep ruts and washouts,
and the three of them got out to walk the rest of the way to the small
field of jumbled boulders which made up the site.

Elliot was amazed that Jakamarra could still see the things he was
pointing out and explaining to him. A lot of it he couldn't catch, and it
seemed rude to continually ask the old man to repeat himself. Sometimes he turned to their young companion for clarification, but he
appeared to be in a world of his own, disconnected to what was going
on around him. So Elliot stayed quiet; absorbed what he could, allowed
the rest to flow over him. There was a story involving two men, an
emu and a tree that still stood on the site. There were some faint ochre

paintings beneath a leaning slab, which were the things women and children weren't allowed to see, although Elliot never learned the meaning of them or the reason they were taboo.

The thing he remembers most about being there is Jakamarra's singing, which seemed to emerge from him spontaneously, without self-consciousness, without the need for Elliot or anyone else to acknowledge it. Sometimes he paused it, to point something out, or offer another impenetrable explanation, then he would continue, his voice rising and falling as he traversed the site, immersed in a relationship with place that Elliot knew he would never begin to understand. It evoked power in the landscape, somehow, and gave Elliot the holy shiver. It was the closest he had come to the numinous experiences of that first Australian trip and reminded him of why he had come back; confirmed him in his decision.

They didn't stay long in that place, but by the time they caught up with the women and children, the fire they had made had already burned down to embers, and the kangaroo tails and potatoes were buried beneath them, cooking. They were in another rocky place, and the older children were climbing and jumping. There were extras with them, friends or cousins. The toddler was sprawled across Linda's lap, fast asleep. The baby was at her breast. Elliot averted his eyes.

Doris said, 'You like that place? Men's place?' Elliot agreed that he did, and she went on, 'There are women's places too. Places men can't go. We can't show you that.'

Elliot nodded. He remembered that there was a reason he had been brought there, but even that could not spoil it for him. The light became richer as the sun dropped towards the horizon. Audrey, always cheerful, stirred bean pods at the edge of the fire, gave him a handful of hot little beans, another one of berries. He realised how tired he was, and lay on his hip, leaning on his elbow, and pulled the brim of his hat down over his eyes. The sounds around him made no demands on him: the children's happy chatter, the women's conversation, all in language that he couldn't understand. He was alone among strangers, and yet he felt completely secure. The sounds became blurred and echoey, and Elliot dozed away the time until the food was ready to eat.

. . .

DORIS AND JAKAMARRA swapped seats for the return journey. Again Linda's car went ahead and was soon lost in the gathering darkness. The blue car had only one weak headlight, and their young driver craned over the steering wheel to see the road ahead. Elliot said to Doris, 'Why doesn't he speak?'

'He just shy one, little bit,' she said. 'My grandson, this one.'

'Linda's husband?'

The young man laughed then, for the first time, and shook his head.

Doris said, 'Grandson different way.' And Elliot knew enough about the complexities of yapa relationships to let it go at that.

It took far less time to get home than it had to get out there, without the stops and the detours. Insects flitted across their headlights, but they saw no wildlife apart from an owl, which skimmed the high edge of their headlight beam and vanished into the night. Elliot watched the stars until the streetlights of the community came into view.

They pulled up outside the jilimi. There were people there: a group of women sitting around the dull embers of their fire. The driver got out and began to untie the ropes holding the firewood on top of the car.

Elliot said, 'Thanks for taking me, Doris. It's beautiful country.'

Doris made no move to get out. She said, 'Yuwayi.' Hanging between the two of them was the unacknowledged purpose of the trip.

Elliot said, 'I was thinking. One thing you could do is some kind of cultural tour, you know? A few communities are running them now. I've seen them advertised around town.'

Two of the younger women from the jilimi came over and began to carry the firewood across the yard. It made Elliot aware that he couldn't see Linda, or her car. He went on, 'You get tourists to pay for a trip out on country. Give them bush tucker. Like what we just did. Maybe you could get a loan for some better cars.'

Doris said, 'No, we don't want to sell ourselves to kardiya. That's why we can't go for government money. Any place get government money, they have to get a kardiya to write reports and apply for money, all that stuff. That women's centre there, I'm on the committee. Four times a year we have to make a report. Audit, they call it. Every penny we spend, every little thing we do. That woman who is running the place there, half her time is writing, writing, always on that computer.'

Elliot could empathise. A lot of his time between bush trips was spent on paperwork of various kinds. 'Maybe it's what you need to do, though, if you want to get money.'

The wood was all unloaded. Some children had appeared and were throwing lumps of it around in the darkness. Doris shouted something at them, and they raced off across the yard. When she turned back to Elliot she said, 'We want to run this place yapa way, just for us. We want to keep out culture going proper way.'

Elliot said, 'Can't you just buy a car, Doris? Don't you make a lot of money from your paintings?'

'I got cars before, ' she said and indicated the remains of a couple of them that lay beside the house. 'When the art centre was open, that was a good time. They used to help. Keep some of that money. Save it up for me. But now, when I get money for painting, we are not like white-fellas, that money is for everyone. And some of those young people, they can get cheeky, you know? Her husband, worst one.'

'Linda's husband?' he said.

Doris didn't answer. Linda's car pulled up beside theirs, driven by someone else. Doris said, 'We don't need much.' She waved one hand in a gracious semi-circle. 'Little bit of fence around the back and that side. Make it safe, for women dancing, you know? And one toyota.'

Elliot was watching Linda, who got out of the passenger side and, assisted by Audrey, began pulling sleepy children out of the back. He said to Doris, ' I thought you didn't mind people seeing your culture. I thought you liked sharing it with whitefellas.'

'Some parts we don't mind,' Doris said. 'But that little dance we do for people, over there in town sometimes, special times, that one not our culture, not proper one. Same with those paintings. They are just one little bit, one story. That's like you read one page out of the Bible and think that is your whole law.'

She fell silent, perhaps aware that Elliot was only half listening, was still watching Linda who had now stepped into the circle of women and whose face was being lit by flames in the revived fire. Beside them, the other car reversed and drove away. Their own driver got out and went round to help Doris get out. He kept his back turned to the yard.

Elliot was suddenly aware that he was letting Doris down. He got out as well.

'I'll look into it, Doris,' he said. 'I'll find out about this crowdfunding. See if it's something that could work for you.'

'Yuwayi,' she said. It took another few moments for her to fully straighten up. 'Can you give him twenty dollars? For petrol.'

There was a commotion as an over-excited child flung a stray piece of wood onto the fire, sending up a shower of sparks and glowing embers. Elliot watched Linda step back, checking over her little ones, running hands over their hair. When he looked back, Doris was walking away and the car engine was already running, ready to return him to the clinic.

46

ELLIOT DREAMS of a cloth shopping bag with a smiling pink ice cream on the side. He wants to see what's inside it, but he can't. It belongs to a man who is holding on to it tightly. Elliot edges around it, trying to get a different angle on it. The man sees him, opens the bag. It is the entrance to a massive cave or wormhole which tunnels and twists into the rock. There are strange symbols on the walls. It goes on for miles. Elliot knows he will never find the end of it or understand the symbols. He wakes in a cold sweat.

47

THE CONSULTANT PHYSIO comes to see Elliot every morning. Now that he is no longer attached to a drip, he can exercise in bed. She has been teaching him to bend and flex his fingers and toes, his wrists and ankles, his elbows and knees. He has done everything she asks, but when she is gone, he forgets to continue. He is all past and no future. What he did back then is something he has no wish to return to. He no longer wants to see people suffering from diseases he cannot treat. Some of the symptoms he can ease, but the underlying problems, the reasons people don't look after themselves, those are things he can't cure. But if he doesn't go back there, what is there for him to do? He has a feeling that he has missed a move somewhere, made a wrong decision at some crucial juncture in his life. He is not where he ought to be. He knows that what he is looking at is despair, and he knows how dangerous that can be, but he can't, or won't, articulate it. To articulate it would be to make it solid, and even harder to evade.

HE DREAMS OF A WHIRLWIND: a huge red toxic storm of rage and despair blowing through the desert. He is running behind it, trying to repair the damage it is causing, but he is already too late. People have been infected, hollowed out. They are staggering around, committing violence, searching for their souls.

THE PHYSIO and some of the nursing staff are going to get him up. There is a big, comfy chair with all kinds of levers and knobs. They swing his legs to the side of the bed, support him to stand for a minute and it feels good to be standing, even though he can't tell whether he is actually supporting any of his own weight or not. Then they turn him around and gently lower him on to the chair. He practices his smile and says, 'Thank you.'

The physio brings up another chair and sits with him for a while, passing the time of day until he gets used to being upright, then showing him some more exercises he can do in the chair. He is pleased to see that he can lift his legs and make jerky circles with his ankles. He can lift his broken arm above his head, though he can't straighten it yet. His right arm won't go higher than his shoulder. The physio tells him to keep practicing all those movements. He will get better and better every day. The more he does the exercises, the faster he will improve. She exacts a promise from him, to do them several times an hour. But after she has gone he forgets. He shrinks from his colourless future and slides back into his luminous, vermillion past.

48

HE DID his bit of research, as he had promised, and was surprised by what he found. Crowdfunding was huge, and there were sites which didn't require the fundraisers to be registered charities or, indeed, to be officially recognised in any way. It didn't look difficult to start a campaign. The challenge, as far as he could see, would be to get it seen by the right kind of people. Elliot had a Facebook page, but it was only to keep him connected with his brother and his nephew, and he really had no idea how it worked. And since they had no telecommunications in Nyaru, it wasn't going to be possible for anyone to run it from there. All the same, it was worth investigating. Linda might know other people in town who could help.

49

THE NEXT DAY he is helped out of bed and into the chair for the second time. The physio asks him whether he has been doing his exercises, and he lies. She tells him they will be taking him to the gym within the next few days, and giving him a more serious work-out, but he can't tell whether or not she is joking. She runs through the routine with him again and adds some finer details. She leaves a pen and some small blocks on a side table for him to pick up and put down. She gets him handling his own cup and drinking from it with a straw.

'No worries, Elliot. Not a bother. Keep on working away and she'll be right.'

50

It was the end of a normal enough day in the clinic, and he had made a couple of house calls. On the way back to the clinic, he drove past the jilimi to pass on what he had learned about the crowdfunding idea. Doris and Audrey were painting. He could see Linda over near the house, moving things around, creating a lot of noise. There were ten or twelve children there, and when they spotted Elliot, they danced over, singing out to him. He knew nearly all of them by name, from visits to his clinic.

'Tell Doris to come,' he told them. 'And Linda.'

They raced off in a laughing stream, and Elliot watched them go. Nyaru, for all its faults, was a lot better off than many of the Aboriginal communities, particularly some of the ones nearer town. It wasn't free of suicide or violence, which, according to the most recent figures, had increased since the intervention, but it did have less of both than the other places where Elliot worked. And, despite the ramping up of compulsory reporting, he had seldom needed to express concern about Nyaru's children. He wondered what it was about life out here that turned so many of those happy, healthy kids into self-destructive teenagers and unstable adults.

One child stayed behind with him. Elliot slid down on to his haunches, back against the wheel arch, and little Rose, who had been a toddler when he first met her and had now just started school, sat down beside him, leaning against his knees. The flies were bad that day. He brushed them from Rose's eyes, and from his own. Doris had stopped painting and was looking over. Linda had finished her banging in the house and was standing on the verandah. The air was still and hot.

Doris stood up slowly and began to walk over, her stiffness easing as she came. Audrey followed, and Linda caught up with them as they reached the waist-high fence rail.

Elliot stood up. 'How are you?'

Doris nodded. Audrey beamed and said, 'Good, good,' but Linda did not acknowledge him. Her attention was elsewhere. A child Elliot didn't recognise, a boy of about ten, came pedalling up on a bicycle. He stopped at the roadside and spoke to Doris in language. What he said first seemed to please her, but what he went on to say changed her mood entirely. She looked disappointed, then angry, and she began to complain to Linda, berating her as far as Elliot could see. For a long time, Linda said nothing, but finally, when Doris ran out of steam, she spoke, and what she said clearly took the wind out of Doris' sails. For a moment she stared silently at her granddaughter and then both women turned their heads and looked at him.

51

ON HIS THIRD day in the chair, Elliot gets a visit from the police. The sight of them in uniform fills him with anxiety, because he is sure they are going to ask him how he got his injuries, and he hasn't got there yet. Sandra's mother has given him an explanation, but he can't connect with it at all. It sounds like something that has happened to someone else. In terms of any proper memories, that part of his life is still a complete blank.

But as it turns out, the police have come about a different matter. They have come with the news that his place in Alice Springs has been broken into and pretty much trashed. The police there have gone through what was left, clothes mainly, and papers; his passport is safe. They want to know whether there is anything of value that might have been taken, and the landlady wants to know whether he is going to take care of it and come back or whether she should fix it up herself and get someone else in. It isn't good to leave places empty. Elliot makes his first clear decision since regaining consciousness. He is not going back to Alice.

He can't actually remember where he lived, let alone whether there was anything of value in there, and initially his most pressing worry is his cat, which might not have been fed since he left. But after the police leave he remembers more; he can visualise his little unit out the back of his landlady's house, and he remembers that he had a laptop, and a stereo with good speakers that he used for listening to the radio, but no cat. His landlady was fine with him having a dog, but she wouldn't allow a cat unless it was indoors all the time, and Elliot couldn't justify doing that. He is relieved, but also strangely disturbed by the thought of cats, and he senses that ominous movement beneath the surface of consciousness; more surprises still to come.

He can't write yet, and he still can't speak clearly, but he gets one of the nurses to make a note of those things for him so he won't forget, and later he asks her to add a portable TV that he remembers buying, and still later a Gibson guitar, although that turns out to be a dream fragment and not a real thing at all. There is something else as well, though, he is sure of it. He can't see it yet, but something of great significance is waiting in the wings and about to make an appearance.

52

LINDA WENT BACK across the yard and into a storeroom at the end of the verandah. She emerged with a long roll of canvasses, their painted faces inwards, their grey linen backs to the outside. The roll was as tall as she was and clearly heavy. Elliot sent Rose back to the other children and reached over the fence-line to help.

'Take it,' Linda said. 'You sell them for Doris.'

'What?'

'Paintings. Doris made them. Worth a lot of money, eh?'

'Yes, but—'

Linda was in the grip of some urgency. 'Put them in the car,' she said. 'Take them to Alice. Buy us a toyota.'

Elliot was struggling to resist but failing. Linda was steadily herding him towards the troopy, all the time looking out along the road. The boy, the little messenger, was looking in that direction as well, fiddling with the brake levers on his bike, and somehow Elliot had a moment to notice that they weren't connected to anything. There were no cables. The chain was encrusted with red sand.

'So we can take the old women out on country,' Linda said. 'And the children. Teach them culture.'

When Elliot still made no sign of having understood, she reached for the back door of the troopy and tried to take the roll of paintings back from him. He was surprised by her strength.

'Put them in.'

He didn't so much help as cease to resist. She pushed the roll through the back door, and along the centre of the car, between the lengthwise rows of seats, and Audrey slammed the door on them.

Linda said, 'Don't bring money. Bring us a toyota. One like this one.'

Elliot found his voice. 'I can't do this. I don't know anything about art. I wouldn't know—'

But she wasn't listening to him. She had returned to the jilimi and was nervously tidying the edges of the fireplace, tossing cinders and half-burned sticks towards the centre, pulling scorched tins and twisted pieces of cutlery out to the sides. Doris glanced towards the road and gestured to him to leave. She said, 'They don't follow our law, those people. The law is gone.'

Elliot said, 'Is someone humbugging you, Doris? Is there something I can help you with? Do you want me to make a complaint?'

She looked at him as if he had two heads, then turned her attention to the road again. He could hear it now, the sound of a diesel engine. Unaccountably, he was filled with the same urgency as the women were. He climbed into the car.

Doris said, 'Money no good. Too much humbug. Bring us a toyota. She can drive it.'

Elliot put the car in gear and drove away. He didn't pass the other vehicle, which had taken the only other possible route across town.

And when, soon afterwards, he loaded the paintings on to the plane, no one took any notice. Art had been collected by every kind of visitor to Aboriginal communities since it first started being produced. There was nothing remarkable about a doctor picking up a few paintings and taking them home.

53

THE VISION of the paintings returns to him in the middle of the night, and he lies wide-eyed, going over it all, again and again, each time with more of the story falling into place. Eventually, in a state of extreme agitation, he calls for the night staff and demands that he be put through to the Alice Springs police immediately. He knows now who has broken into his place and why. They have stolen something worth thousands of dollars, and he has to get it back, not for himself, but for some Aboriginal woman who lives on the edge of the Tanami Desert and wants to get out on her country. 'It was Nickerson,' he keeps saying. 'Buggy Nickerson. I'm ng-going to get him.'

The nurse calls for back-up, and two of them quietly and calmly try to talk Elliot down. They explain that it is the middle of the night and that no one in the Alice Springs police department will want to talk to him at this time. He tries to explain that it is an emergency, that 'Nickerson' might be gone in the morning, back to his house in Rose Bay, that he has to be arrested before he leaves town, and that only Elliot can explain how to find the lock-up where he keeps the stolen goods. In the end, reluctantly, the nurses give him a sedative and he is pressed back into sleep.

But his determination isn't gone by morning. He is put through to the police in Alice, but his speech is so slurred and incoherent that they think he is a drunk, and hang up. To humour him, and to dampen down his dangerous rage, the hospital arranges for the Adelaide police to come back and take a full statement from him, which they might then hand on to the Alice department. They send a different officer this time, a young lad, barely more than a cadet, but patient as a mule and fully prepared to take Elliot seriously. He writes everything down, reads it back for confirmation, and goes away. But if the report is ever handed on or Dougie Nicholson investigated, Elliot never finds out.

PART II

1

IT SHOCKED ELLIOT, when he looked back through his email account, to see that it was well over three years since he had last been in contact with Miles. He wondered whether that was normal; whether friendships just lapsed after a certain length of time, but he knew there was something more to it. There was a reason why thinking about Miles had become uncomfortable.

It had happened over time, the distance growing between them. They had stayed in touch with each other when they were back in England following their Australian trip. Miles made several more visits to Australia. Sometimes he let Elliot know beforehand and sometimes he didn't. In a small way, he had become a bit of a dealer at home. Aboriginal art was on the up and up, he said. He had space in a friend's gallery in London, and he was forever in the process of setting up a website, though if there was an end result, Elliot never saw it. He continued trying to persuade Elliot to buy paintings as an investment. 'Better returns than the stock market,' he said. 'Come with me next time and get a piece of the action.'

But even if he had wanted to, Elliot wasn't in a position to take that kind of time off again. Once he had made the decision to emigrate, though, he assumed things would be different. Instead, they had begun to get weird.

One of the first news items Elliot remembered seeing on Australian TV when he moved to Melbourne in late 1999 was a report of an auction in Sotheby's the previous day, where record prices had been fetched for Aboriginal art. He was unpacking at the time, taking books out of boxes and shelving them. It was the mention of Papunya that caught his attention and he stopped what he was doing to watch. The report showed several examples of early boards; very similar to the ones Miles had bought in Alice. All of them had sold for breath-taking prices, several hundred per cent higher than what Miles had paid. None of the artists' names was familiar, but it had been a long time ago and Elliot wasn't sure whether he would recognise them even if he heard them. On impulse, he phoned Miles. It was late at night there, but Miles was still up, and there were noises in the background: voices, and clinking and clattering. Elliot waited while Miles moved to a quieter part of the house.

'Am I disturbing something?'

'It's over. Just clearing up.'

'Party?'

Miles giggled. He sounded distant and strung-out. 'Are you OK, Elliot? Is it something in particular?'

'Not really. Just saw the results of an Aboriginal art auction and thought of you.'

'Oh, yeah. It's really picking up. Those boards did well for Uncle Roly. Told you they would, didn't I? He sold two of them earlier this year. And a few of the other things I bought for him in Alice that time.'

'Good for him,' Elliot said, hoping he didn't sound as sour as he felt.

'I've done well too. You should have bought something that time, Elliot. When are you going to learn to recognise good advice when you hear it?'

'Are you still in that business, Miles? Still dealing in art?'

'Oh, that would be a bit of a stretch,' Miles said, and then paused as someone came barging into the room, laughing at something, then fell silent and left again. Elliot couldn't tell by the laughter whether the someone was female or male.

'I should let you go,' he said.

'No, no. No problem. Are you in Australia?'

'Yes, in Melbourne.'

'How is it?'

'I don't know, really. I'm still jet-lagged.'

'You'll get over that,' Miles said. 'I wouldn't really call myself a dealer, you know, but I still come over now and then and pick up a few pieces. I'll look you up next time I come.'

'That would be brilliant. Give me a bit of notice and I'll get some time off. I'm dying to go to Alice again. Dying to go driveabout.'

Miles laughed. 'It was a good trip, wasn't it?'

'Yes. It was.' Elliot was suddenly ready for reminiscences, and he wanted to catch up on what Miles was doing, but Miles was finished with the call. He said he had to go and help with the washing-up. 'I'll ring you back,' he said, but he didn't take Elliot's number, and even when Elliot sent it to him by email, along with a careful outline of the best times to get him, he didn't call.

HE ONLY EVER HAD ONE more conversation with Miles when he phoned, completely out of the blue, to invite Elliot to his wedding. He said he had scaled down the Aboriginal art and gone to work in the city, for another uncle that Elliot had never met. Now he was about to get hitched to a solicitor who worked in the same company. Elliot was disappointed. It sounded to him like a boring outcome to a promising life. He told Miles he would come to the wedding, but he never really intended to go.

Where had it taken place? The Bahamas? The Seychelles? The party was to be held on a yacht, anyway, or a fleet of yachts. It wasn't that Elliot couldn't afford to go, but that he couldn't stomach the extravagance. He had recurring nightmares, still ongoing, about turning up at some function that had Miles at its centre and realising that he was wearing completely inappropriate clothes. Polyester suits, or hospital scrubs, or workman's overalls. Once he woke in a sweat, following a dream in which he was wearing no pants at all. And he thought that maybe the friendship was finally over by then, with the realisation that he couldn't dress for Miles' wedding, even if he wanted to go.

But, all those years later, he emailed him about the paintings anyway, to get his advice, or any kind of useful leads he might have. Then he phoned Drew and asked his opinion of Doris' work.

'Are you going to buy one?'

'No. Just wondering what they might be worth, that's all.'

'The value of a painting generally depends on how big it is, how good it is, and who is selling it.'

'So, how long is a piece of string, is that what you're saying?'

'Yeah, maybe. I have a couple of her early ones, but I have no idea what they would be worth now. You could probably do a web search; see what's on offer. That would be a good place to start, anyway. But don't believe everything you see online. There are a few main players who can name their price, but a lot of gallery prices are just wishful thinking.'

Elliot came clean, explained why he needed to know. Drew's tone changed dramatically, his characteristic warmth receding.

He said, 'Don't get involved, mate. Give them back.'

'You serious?'

'Absolutely. There's a lot of money in this business and a lot of people sniffing around after it. Shark-infested waters, mate. Stay out of them.'

'I'm not setting up in business, Drew. I'm just—'

'Yeah, I know. I know. But don't. There's a whole hierarchy of players and you're not even on the bottom rung. Why would anybody buy paintings off you? Take my advice, will you? Don't get involved.'

Elliot, with a poor attempt to disguise his disappointment, said, 'Well, it's a bit late now. I am involved.'

Drew said, 'Good luck to you then. But I can't help. I know how to buy paintings, not how to sell them. I wouldn't know where to start.'

2

WHILE HE WAITED for a reply from Miles, Elliot found out what he could about Doris on the web. Most of the links that came up led to paintings for sale in galleries that had online outlets, and for sites which offered to tell you what price auction sales had realised, but only if you paid a subscription fee. Very few of the galleries gave prices for their stock, but one or two did, and Elliot was surprised. The artworks he was looking at were for sale at between four and twenty thousand dollars.

He began to see the paintings as a liability. The security in his house did not match their value, and he was constantly aware of the risk of losing them or having them stolen. It made him more restless than usual and he checked his email continually, impatient for a reply from Miles that didn't come. By the time his first free weekday arrived, he was in a state of anxiety, checking his email so regularly that he came to realise he had put all his eggs in one basket; at the back of his mind was the idea that Miles would solve the problem instantly by making an offer for the lot and wiring funds straight over. It wasn't going to happen, and no other solution was presenting itself. He didn't know where to begin.

But in fact, when he stopped deluding himself and sat down to think about, the place to begin was obvious. At ten in the morning, he parked the car under the trees in Leichhardt Terrace and walked through to Todd Mall, where Aboriginal artworks filled windows and leaked out on to the street. He felt awkward and conspicuous with the big roll of paintings. He had bound it in three places with surgical tape to keep it stable, and he started out with it across his shoulder. But there was something too workmanlike about that. It was disrespectful somehow, and there was a chance that the paintings might bend in the middle if they were carried too far like that. So he was carrying them vertically in his arms, hugging them to his chest, which took both hands, leaving him vulnerable to a couple of flies that had ventured in from the bush and were trying to climb into his eyes.

He came close to losing his nerve. He felt he had been badgered into something he wanted no part of. If the figures he had seen online were anything to go by, Doris was capable of making several times the money he did, and he wasn't sure how he felt about making a fool of himself because she was too feckless to manage it properly.

At the end of the street, he turned and walked back, looking a bit more closely into the galleries he passed. One of them had a couple of attractive watercolour landscapes, vivid with the local reds and oranges, and he could imagine having something like that on his wall if he ever moved back to Melbourne or England. Another had some paintings from Arnhem Land, made up of figures, human and animal, intricately shaded in distinctive cross-hatching. He could live with something like that as well, if he had to. It was the just the dots, the endless dazzling displays of multicoloured dots that he couldn't understand.

He was nearing the end of the street where he had started, and he paused to look around. He couldn't have been as conspicuous as he felt, because no one was paying any attention to him. All these places had to source their artworks somewhere. How hard could it be to sell them a few? There were four galleries within view, and he picked the nearest, took a deep breath and pushed open the door. A bell rang, but there was no sign of life in the deep, air-conditioned hall of the interior. Every wall was covered with paintings, from tiny ones the size of a book to huge ones of several square metres. They were nearly all dots and leaf designs. Counters running beneath the paintings held displays of greetings cards, photographs, fridge magnets and bags. Towards the rear of the long building, he could see swathes of unframed canvases, hanging from high rails. He was on his way to have a look at these when a young woman appeared in a doorway in the wall. Behind her, Elliot caught a glimpse of an office with a computer and filing cabinets.

'G'day,' she said and then, seeing the roll of paintings in his arms, 'is Maria expecting you? I'll take you through.'

She led him to the back of the showroom where she opened another door with a keypad code. Behind it was more open space, dim and dusty like a warehouse. It took his eyes a moment or two to adjust. More racks of hanging canvases ran along the walls and canvas rolls like the one he was carrying were bundled and stacked in the corners. On the floor were several knee-high piles of small paintings, and a woman of around Elliot's age was in the process of sorting through them. She looked at him, taking her time to appraise him, identical blue and green leaf-design canvases in each hand. Her face was familiar to him, but he didn't think they had been introduced. She was clearly having a similar problem.

'You'll have to help me out,' she said, dropping the paintings onto a central heap and dusting her hands on her skirt. 'Have we met?'

'I don't think so,' Elliot said. 'I'm sure I've seen you around town, though. Elliot Fielding. I'm with CAHS, working the remote clinics.'

Revealing he was a doctor seldom failed to break the ice or open the right kind of doors for Elliot. It worked here. The woman smiled and held out a hand for him to shake. 'Maria Perris,' she said. 'I thought I'd seen you around.' She turned her eyes to his paintings. 'Special delivery?'

Elliot said, 'Not exactly. I've got some paintings I want to sell.'

Maria Perris tried to hide her disappointment. 'Did you buy them here?'

'No, no,' he said. 'They are Doris…' he hesitated, suddenly lost for her name. He knew her skin name. 'Nampijinpa,' he said, and then remembered her husband's old station name that she used for her paintings. 'Banks,' he said. 'Doris Banks. I'm selling them for her.'

Maria Perris said, 'Why?' Her expression had hardened considerably. 'Why isn't she selling them through one of the galleries? Or through Dougie Nicholson? He's her usual dealer.'

Elliot was on the back foot. He had no good answer to that, not without going into the business of the car, which suddenly felt to him like a personal matter and no one else's business. He said, 'She asked me to.'

'Did she?' There was no attempt to conceal it now, the cold hostility in Perris' tone. 'On what basis?'

'I'm sorry?'

'On a commission basis, is it? Or did you give her money upfront?'

'Nothing like that,' he said. 'I'm not doing this for money. It's just a favour.'

She turned back to the paintings she was going through and picked one up, but she didn't look at it. 'Well, whatever your reasons are, it's not a good idea. The Territory is swarming with people ripping off the artists and trying to make a quick buck. You can't just walk in off the street and expect to sell paintings.'

Elliot flushed. 'Did you not hear me? The artist is a friend of mine. She asked me to do this for her.'

Behind him he was aware of the assistant, twittering an apology. 'I thought he was...'

Maria Perris, the painting still in her hand, said, 'Well, if you want my advice, you'll stay out of it. Give them back to her. Let someone with credibility sell them for her.'

'Credibility?'

'If you knew the first thing about Aboriginal art, you wouldn't have brought those paintings to me. I deal pretty much exclusively with painters from Utopia. I don't sell any art by painters west of Alice.' He was silenced by this, and her manner softened a little. 'Take them back to her. Sometimes these people get impatient when their stuff doesn't move fast enough, but it's no good for them as artists to sell for a quick buck. They don't realise it, they're not good with money and they don't understand how the system works. It's better for Doris to be patient and sell her work through the proper channels if she cares about her reputation. She's a good painter.'

While Elliot was trying to absorb what she was saying, he felt the assistant's hand on his arm. 'I'll show you out,' she said.

Back in the white ferocity of the desert sun, Elliot found the nearest street bench and sat on it. He took a swig from his water bottle and waited for the sting of humiliation to wear off so he could begin to think straight again. He had learned a lot in a very short time, and he was having difficulty processing it. He deeply resented the assumptions Perris had made about his motives but there was something else bothering him as well. Who was she to decide what Doris should or shouldn't do? Doris was, he couldn't remember how old, but surely getting on for eighty. He didn't know whether she cared about her 'reputation' or not, but she was entitled to make her own decisions about what she did with her paintings. He wished he had said it to Perrin back there in the gallery. He was tempted to go back in, but the moment had passed. Instead, his annoyance helped to firm up his resolve. There were plenty more fish in the sea.

He set out along Todd Mall again, taking his time, looking more carefully into each of the galleries, accompanied, irritatingly, by the bush flies. He looked for the names of the artists on the paintings in the windows and tried to get an idea of the style of artwork sold by each gallery. He recognised the name of another artist from Nyaru on one of them and thought he could see work in a style similar to Doris' in several others. Some of the galleries were clearly aimed at casual passing trade; they carried books and boomerangs and cuddly marsupials, and their paintings were mainly small ones. Others appeared to be more seriously aimed at collectors, with nothing on display except artworks. He picked one of these at random and went in.

This place was much, much smaller than Maria Perris' gallery. There was barely room to turn round in it. The woman at the counter looked up and gave him a breezy welcome, then returned her attention to her computer. Elliot took some time to look around. Despite his lack of expertise, he was able to see that there was a variety of styles of art on display: cross-hatched turtles and tall, gangly figures from the Top End, dot paintings and watercolour landscapes from the desert and a few precisely executed abstract paintings that looked very modern. All were strung up on the walls haphazardly, wherever they would fit. Along the centre of the room was a long, narrow table, laden with small canvases at one end and watercolours at the other. More small framed works leaned against the walls at the level of his feet, eight deep in places. There was no shortage of paintings in town; that was beyond doubt.

The woman at the counter took a phone call, so Elliot made a second circuit, this time paying closer attention to the prices, which ranged from a couple of hundred dollars to several thousand. There was nothing in five figures though, and nothing bigger than a metre square. He wasn't sure what was in his roll, but he could tell by the length of it that at least one of the paintings was a lot bigger than that. He was coming round to the possibility that he had picked the wrong kind of place again when the woman finished her call and turned to him.

'Did you get something nice?'

'Hm?'

'You got some nice paintings?'

Elliot said, 'Oh, yes. They're very nice. Doris Banks.'

The woman said, 'Oh wow. One of my favourite artists.'

'Really?'

'Yeah, really. She's a great painter. Good investment you have there.'

'Oh, I didn't buy them,' Elliot said. 'I'm selling them. For Doris, that is. She asked me to sell them.' The woman appraised him shrewdly and he explained the situation to her. Everything except the bit about the car. 'So I thought you might be interested. No problem if it's not your thing. Maybe they're a bit big for this place anyway.'

'That's not an issue,' she said. 'We have partner galleries in Sydney and Melbourne: no problem selling big paintings. It's just we generally do our own deals directly with the artists, see? We don't deal with middlemen.'

'Oh, I'm not a middleman,' Elliot said. 'I'm not looking for commission, just doing it as a favour.' He held out a hand. 'Elliot Fielding.'

Behind him the door opened, and he turned to see a pair of backpackers, fully laden, edging their way in. The owner greeted them in the same cheerful way as she had greeted Elliot, then turned back to him and shook his hand. 'Sally Cameron. I'll take a look at the paintings. I'm always interested in seeing Doris' work. We don't get many of hers through here.'

Elliot rested one end of the roll on the floor, but it was clear that there was no room to open up the paintings while the backpackers were in there.

'Where you from?' Sally Cameron asked them.

'From Israel and Holland,' the woman said.

'Oh right,' said Sally. 'Israel and Holland. And are you enjoying Australia?'

'Yes, we like it. But it's a bit too hot for me. He doesn't mind it.'

'Let me know if there's anything I can help you with.'

There wasn't though, and they took their time; browsed their awkward way around the cramped space, along every wall, always on the point of bumping off the central table or putting an unsteady foot through one of the canvases at ground level. It looked to Elliot as though they were appreciating the air conditioning more than the artwork.

'You could do with a bigger shop,' he said.

'Gallery,' Sally said. 'And we're looking into it. We had a place a few streets away but hardly anyone goes beyond Todd Mall. Have to have a presence here.'

They waited again, and eventually, the tourists left, hefting their rucksacks wearily out into the sun. Sally locked the door behind them. Elliot unwound the surgical tape. There was nowhere near enough space to lay the paintings out flat in the gallery, so Elliot unrolled them one at a time and held them up by the corners for Sally to inspect. There were six of them, ranging in size from around ninety by a hundred and twenty centimetres to a hundred and fifty by a hundred and eighty.

Doris used desert colours; reds and oranges, yellows and browns, and pastel shades of the same range. When he saw her work laid out in front of her house in Nyaru it looked synthetic, too bright and fresh against the dust. But here, under the artificial light and contrasted against the wider range of colours on display, the paintings looked drab, almost dingy. The dot-work was fairly tidy in most places, but paint had spread beyond the primed edges on to the grey linen surround, and several of the paintings had smudges in prominent places. As he held them up, one after another, Elliot looked down the length of them from above. He couldn't get a proper sense of them from that viewpoint, but he could see flaws in nearly all of them, and he was struck by the uncomfortable possibility that these paintings might be substandard; a kind of reject pile, not good enough for the gallery owners or her regular dealer, whatever his name was. Were she and Linda playing him for a mug, trying to get him to sell a pile of rubbish for her?

But Sally Cameron didn't dismiss the paintings. 'How much is she asking for them?' she said. 'Did she give you a price?'

They were looking at the last of them, not the biggest but the most intricate, with dozens and dozens of little walled-off sections, almost like fields on an aerial photograph.

'I suppose you should make me an offer,' Elliot said. 'What would you give Doris if you were dealing with her directly?'

Sally took a calculator out of her desk drawer and did some sums. 'Look, I can't make you a definite offer until I talk to my dad. He has the keys to the safe, if you know what I mean. But we would be talking somewhere in the region of fifteen thousand.'

Elliot began to roll up the paintings. It wasn't as much as he had hoped; nowhere close to their real value, but at least it was a start. It meant that it was possible for him to sell the paintings and that gave him confidence.

'I thought they were worth a bit more,' he said.

'Like, how much? What were you thinking?'

'I've seen some of the bigger ones going for twenty grand online.'

'Twenty K each?' she said. 'Ah no, mate. You're on the wrong planet there.'

'I don't think so,' Elliot said. 'I can show you the websites if you like.'

Sally shook her head dismissively. 'Asking it maybe. But are they getting it? Seriously, mate, you can't expect to get anything like that kind of price for them. And don't forget we have to allow for our mark-up. You're only getting the artist's rate, there.'

The paintings were on the floor where Elliot had dropped them. Cameron nudged a couple of them towards him with her foot as if she was in a sudden rush to get rid of him. There was something sacrilegious about the gesture, and Elliot bent to pick them up. They were all separate now, in soft, unstable rolls which he tried to gather into his arms. He knew there had to be a way to get them back into one roll, but he was too flustered to work it out.

Cameron said, 'Are you a collector yourself?'

Elliot said, 'No,' and buttoned his lip just in time; before he went on to confess both his ignorance and his scepticism.

'Well, if you were, you might understand how it works.'

'Educate me, then,' he said.

She passed him another of the paintings. 'There's a collector's market for the super-rich. It's all managed by certain people who got their foot in the door early on and think they own the market. Some of them have big, flashy galleries in Sydney and Melbourne and some of them deal via their networks directly, but all of them charge sky-high prices. Think they own the artists as well, some of them. Take out exclusive contacts with them, or think they do.'

She watched him for a moment, as he struggled to unroll one canvas while simultaneously rolling another. 'Here. Hold them like this.' She put the corners of the biggest paintings in his hands and added the others one at a time, letting gravity unroll them.

'So they convince the big auction houses that they are the only ones to deal with. Only paintings supplied by them have proper provenance.' She parenthesised the last two words with her forefingers. 'But it's just a kind of control; they want to clean up. They maintain they're the only ones who look after the artists properly, but the artists don't seem to agree.' She swept an arm around her, indicating the overcrowded space. 'We have artists lining up to sell us paintings. We have a place out on the edge of town where they can come and paint in peace and quiet with no one humbugging them.' She pointed to one particularly messy smear on the last of the paintings as she fed the edges into his fingers, and she laughed. 'No dogs. No babies.'

They rolled up the paintings and Sally produced masking tape to replace the surgical tape, which was now under their feet, sticking in squashed lumps to their shoes. 'We want to sell paintings to people who want to hang them on their walls and live with them, not lock them up in a bank vault or stash them under the bed for their super.' She hesitated, as if she had caught herself in an error. 'I mean, not that there's anything wrong with buying paintings as an investment. They're a good investment. But we make work by good artists affordable to pretty much everyone, you know? And everyone's happy with that except for the control freaks. The establishment. We're treading on their territory, see? They try to discredit us. Call us carpetbaggers, accuse us of running sweatshops in town, you know? Accuse *us* of exploiting the artists.'

Elliot, who could put exquisite bands of strapping on damaged human limbs, was struggling with the masking tape, which was reluctant to stick to the dusty linen. Sally took it from him and wrapped it round and round, so it stuck to itself and stayed stuck. 'I never see their faces in the hospital, though,' she went on. 'I never see them looking after these old people when they are sick and dying. I've never seen any of them take someone in for their dialysis. That's where my dad is now, by the way. He has taken Daly Jack into the centre there.' Elliot said nothing, and she went on, 'Daly Jack? Daly Tjangala?' She indicated a group of paintings on the furthest wall, just unidentifiable splodges of colour as far as Elliot could see. 'Very collectable,' she said. 'His father was one of the founders of the art movement and he was mega. This fella will end up the same way, you'll see.'

Elliot was keen to get back on the street. He hefted the paintings and said, 'Well,' but Sally was still talking.

'So that's where Dad is. He'll pick up Jack after he's finished, and we'll take him to our place for a feed. He might paint if he feels like it. And if he paints he goes home with a pocketful of cash. He doesn't have to hang around for months or years waiting for a gallery or art centre to sell something.'

Elliot edged towards the door. Sally nodded at his paintings. 'Did Doris give you a price? Some idea of what she's expecting to get?'

'She wants a toyota,' Elliot confessed.

'No surprise,' Sally said. 'We come across that all the time. You'll get a car for fifteen K. You'll get a troopy for that, out on the Stuart Highway.'

Elliot said, 'I want a good one. One that will last.'

'You can't control that,' Sally said. 'You can give her a car, but you can't decide who she lends it to or who just takes it when they feel like it. Cars are common property out in those places and common property always ends up in the hands of the bludgers and the bullies.'

All these lectures about the failings of Aboriginal people were making Elliot uncomfortable. He turned away from Cameron and had his hand on the doorknob when she said, 'Hold on a minute, Elliot.' He waited while she went into a stock cupboard behind the counter and returned with a length of white water-pipe, about 20cms in diameter. She slid the canvases into it and pushed on the plastic end cap.

'They're lovely paintings,' she said. 'Keep them safe, whatever you do. If you don't get a better offer, come back to us. I'll talk to Dad and see what he says.'

She gave him a business card and he left.

3

ELLIOT KNEW he ought to be optimistic now, but something was dragging at his mood. What Cameron had said about people taking cars had
reminded him of the last time he saw Luke, maybe six months ago. He
was sitting outside the store in Nyaru, looking older, rougher than
usual, carrying a few days' stubble with quite a lot of grey in it and
drinking from a bottle of something green and viscous, which might
have been undiluted cordial. He returned Elliot's greeting politely but
not enthusiastically, and Elliot was disappointed. He bought fresh cups
of tea for them both and, since there was nothing much in the way of
alternative, apple pie with tepid, glutinous custard.

'Still waiting, Luke,' he said.

'For what?'

'Our trip. To your country.'

Luke broke sugar sachets into his tea.

'Not sometime soon,' he said.

'Are you OK Luke? Are you sick? Is there anything I can do?'

'Not sick,' Luke said. A young man passing behind him on his way
out of the store leant down and put a handful of cigarettes beside his
teacup. Luke nodded in acknowledgement and handed one to Elliot. He
hadn't smoked in years, but he took it, waited while Luke found

someone who had a light, then smoked it, just for the sake of compan-
ionship. It made him light-headed and nauseous.

Luke said, 'Some buggers stole my toyota.' It clearly pained him to
say it. 'Right outside the hotel up there in Hall's Creek, they took him. I
was there for a meeting. Young fellas. Smashed him up good. Burn
him up and run off.'

Elliot said, 'Oh, Luke, I'm sorry to hear that.'

Luke shrugged. 'Might be I get another one. Not sometime soon.'

'Well, what if I got one?' Elliot said. 'I might get a toyota too.'

'You?' Luke said.

'Why not? I want to go out driving, seeing places. Maybe I'll get a
car and then we can go.'

Luke grinned. 'Yeah,' he said. 'We can do that. You get the toyota, I
can show you the country. Here. Take my phone number.'

'I have it, Luke.' Elliot was disappointed that Luke didn't remember.
'And you have mine. Haven't you?'

Luke scrolled through his contacts list. Elliot said, 'Look under
'doctor'. I think you might have put it under 'doctor.'

HE HAD DONE nothing about it. He was still driving the station wagon,
still being swept along by the momentum of his life, which sometimes
left time for small detours but seldom left energy for them.

4

FIFTEEN THOUSAND DOLLARS wasn't enough, but it was a start, and Elliot was encouraged by it. His next stop was just a few doors along, a big gallery, all open space with a counter in the middle of the floor of one section and a bench and chairs in another. The walls here weren't crowded like the other galleries, and the artworks on them were numbered, as in an exhibition. There were no racks, and instead, piles of artwork on grey linen lay on the floor, arranged by size. At one of these piles, a middle-aged couple were browsing. The man supported himself on a stick and the woman, who was on the heavy side, was clearly finding it uncomfortable to bend down, but they were intent on their search and their eyes were bright with anticipation.

In the other section of the gallery, a big family was occupying the available seating. All of them, even the children, looked anxious and gloomy. Two men, one elderly and one middle-aged, were standing at the counter. Their conversation with the assistant was clearly inter-rupted by Elliot's appearance. He nodded briefly and set out to examine the paintings on the walls while they finished their business.

To his untrained eye, the paintings in here looked very like the ones he was carrying. They made use of a similar range of colours, reds and yellows and browns, very little in the way of blues and greens, and it was nearly all dot-work. No watercolours, no Arnhem Land hatching. Some of them even had smears and smudges.

'What about this one?' The woman of the couple held up a canvas to show the man.

At the counter, the conversation continued: the voices very soft, but audible all the same in the quiet space. 'She told us this morning. She said we could pick it up for her.'

The other members of the family, even the children, were watching discreetly.

'I don't think so, but I'll have a look,' the assistant said, turning to the computer and typing.

'Truth,' the old man said, stretching his arms out wide. 'Big one.'

Elliot began another dawdling circuit of the walls.

'Well, I like it,' said the woman at the pile, but her partner clearly didn't.

The assistant shook his head. He looked about nineteen to Elliot, but he was probably thirty. 'I don't have any record of it here. Have you got any record of it, David? Any paper?'

One of the women stood up and spoke to the men in language. The old man tried to quietly hustle her away, but she was not to be closed down. 'She give him the paper from Clive. He been leave it at home, stupid bugger.'

The assistant said, 'I'll have a look out the back.' Elliot was tempted to give the family fifty dollars himself, partly just bugger-off money, partly because the children looked so anxious. They were beginning to drift around, restlessly. The foragers had moved on to another pile and the woman groaned as she bent to look through them, lifting the corners one at a time to see what was underneath. The assistant returned, empty-handed.

'Phone Clive,' the older man said, a slight hint of aggression entering into his voice. 'He'll tell you.'

'I can't get him, David. He's out of coverage.' He turned his attention to Elliot. 'Anything I can help you with there?'

Elliot straightened up and retrieved his roll. As he approached the counter, the others moved away from it, regrouped around the few chairs, the adults speaking softly in language, the older kids standing so the men could sit.

Elliot said, ' I have some paintings to sell. Doris Banks. She asked me to sell them for her.'

The assistant's manner changed abruptly. His tone was cold and flat as he spoke. 'I think you're in the wrong place. This isn't a private gallery. It's a cooperative.'

Elliot said, 'Oh, I didn't realise.' As the assistant went on, he was suddenly aware of every eye in the place upon him. 'Doris isn't a member, and even if she was, we wouldn't be accepting her work through an agent.'

Elliot said, 'I'm not an agent. I'm just doing this as a favour.'

Now the assistant's tone was loaded with derision. It seemed to Elliot that he was using his superior height as an added provocation. 'You'd be amazed how often we hear that around Alice Springs. All the people trying to help out the poor artists by dealing in their paintings.'

His tone was now so full of acid that Elliot had the impression he was on the receiving end of a week's worth of frustrations.

'Look,' he began, with all the authority he could gather. 'That's a step too far, mate. You can't just insult me like that.' He wanted to tell everyone that he was a doctor, but he dried up, suddenly aware that it was irrelevant.

'I'm not a dealer,' he finished, lamely, but there seemed to be no one interested now. The assistant was typing. The collectors were turning to the next pile. The older members of the family were still in discussion and the smallest children, released from tension, were beginning to run and jump. Burning with rage and humiliation, Elliot made for the door.

5

HE RETURNED to his car and sat in it for a few minutes, gazing out over the riverbed. Despite the bit of shade it was standing in, it was still too hot for comfort, and he started the engine and ran the air-con. Predictably, although somehow he never did quite predict it, his nose began to bleed. He wound his seat back as far as it would go and lay back, pinching his nose with a handful of tissues, forced into a stillness that his mind would not reflect, no matter how hard he tried to calm it. He replayed the scene in the gallery again and again, until finally, the energy began to go out of it, just around the same time as his nose stopped bleeding. He looked at the tissues. There wasn't too much of a blood loss, but he felt washed-out all the same. He found an unopened bottle of water under the passenger seat. It was warm and chemical, but he drank some of it anyway and used the rest to clean up his face and fingers.

What was he doing? Why had he allowed himself to become a hustler on someone else's account? He would never try to sell something of his own in that way. It was all the more ridiculous because he had so much money that he knew what to do with it. Two of the four trips home he had made had been for funerals: his father's a year or so after he emigrated, his mother's just two years ago. They had both been only children and had each inherited houses from their own parents, and the whole lot was divided between Elliot and his brother Matty. Even after death duties had been paid, Elliot had nearly enough money to retire on.

A man laden with shopping bags passed in front of the car. Beyond him, the riverbed was empty and still. Elliot had once seen a video of the water on its way into town, the little vanguard stream nosing its way down the sandy creek, the weight of the river gathering behind it, as yet unseen. He had seen the Todd flowing a number of times, but never that first trickle: never its arrival. It was one of the few things he still wanted from the place.

He lived close to the centre, on the old East side. The most direct way into the business district of town was straight across the riverbed, but he was there a long, long time before he came to use that route. Like most people in town, he drove everywhere. It was quicker and cooler, and there was often the excuse of getting the shopping home. But most people in town didn't spend a large part of each working day advising other people about the benefits of exercise. The time inevitably came when he ran out of excuses and started walking in.

To begin with, he went along the walkway at the Wills Terrace crossing, even though it required a slight detour. But as time went on he began to feel ridiculous, sticking to the paved road when he could go directly across the riverbed on foot. Still he hesitated. He told himself he might get sand on his shoes or run into a snake. The truth, when he brought himself to admit it, was that the riverbed was where Aboriginal people gathered to yarn and play cards and drink. He was less afraid of encountering hostility than of being caught going into a place where he didn't belong. The Todd was like a band of wild country reaching in, dividing the town from itself, out of bounds to whitefellas.

Eventually the day came when he took the plunge and found that the riverbed was not the dark and haunted place he had feared. There were footpaths and cycle-tyre marks across the soft sand, and the tracks of a four-wheel drive running along the centre. Ancient trees stood on sand islands out there, and beneath many of them were the white ash remains of small fires, and empty tins, plastic wine bottles, broken glass, an occasional upturned shopping trolley. But these things, this detritus of urban hinterlands, were familiar to him from every town he had lived and worked in. In a strange way, they legitimised his presence there, and after that first time, he never went around the long way again, despite the sand that did, in fact, collect in his shoes. He came to love the crossing, amazed at the amount of space that could exist in such a short distance. He became familiar with the individual trees on his route, those ancient river gums with their bloodhound skins, their blackened, fractured limbs, their determination, despite everything, to continually send out new shoots.

The sting of his recent embarrassment had begun to wear off, and he found he had just enough energy to try one more gallery that day. But as he opened the door to get out, he saw he had managed to smear blood from his nose across the leg of his white chinos.

He closed the door again, wondering why he was putting himself through all this. He could buy a good four-wheel drive with no pain at all, so why not do that? That would be perfectly acceptable to Doris and Linda, he was sure of that. It was one of the things he liked about yapa; their lack of embarrassment around money. They could give it and receive it as easily as water, and forget about it just as quickly. He couldn't though. It wasn't in him. He wouldn't mind spending the money, but not without getting something in return. He didn't want the paintings and he didn't understand the importance of culture and ceremony well enough to cough up that kind of contribution to it.

So was it Linda? In his dreams, his secret, forbidden dreams, Linda and her children lived with him in a big, weatherboard house in an inner-city suburb of Melbourne, far from dust and flies and chronic infections. Linda was happy, free from domestic violence and obligation. Everybody was happy in fact, but there was no more. That was as far as his imagination could run before being pulled up by reality. Even if Linda had not been married, he knew that she would never leave her country. She was unusually committed for someone so young, to keeping her culture strong. He thought she must draw on it for that passion he saw in her. There was nothing in his country's culture that inspired in him anything remotely comparable.

There was no fantasy version of a future in which Elliot accompanied her in her life, on her community, in her own country. He knew there were whitefellas who had taken that route, but it was too hard a task for his underused and underdeveloped imagination.

In the cold light of this understanding, everything became clear. He should go home and put his feet up, then return the paintings to Doris next time he was in Nyaru. He should never have agreed to take them in the first place.

6

WHEN HE GOT HOME, there was a note from Drew pinned to his front door.

We are invited to a party by Leslie James, who is the gallery owner I mostly deal with. She says you should talk to Dougie Anderson about the Doris paintings, and he will be there. Tomo at 8ish. I will pick you up.

7

WHEN HE SAW the white pipe, Drew said,

'Mate...'

Elliot put the paintings in the back and got into the car.

'What?'

Drew just shook his head, tight-lipped, and drove in silence until they crossed the river at Stott Terrace. Then he said,

'Mate, you do understand about provenance, don't you?'

Elliot said, 'Yeah. I think so. About where the paintings come from and stuff.'

'Stuff,' said Drew. 'Yeah, the stuff bit is probably quite important, though. You know?'Elliot said nothing. They crossed the Stuart Highway, then Milner road, and soon afterwards, just outside the Araluen precinct, Drew pulled in at the kerb and put on the handbrake. He said,

'You don't get it, do you? It's like, all the artwork around here, all the stuff in there,' he gestured towards the Araluen complex, 'who decides what it's worth?'

Elliot decided not to play. Drew waited a while, then went on, 'Those bloody experts we're going to meet, that's who. They're the ones who will decide the value your paintings, and they have given themselves the license to bestow legitimacy on some works of art and not others. Provenance, if you like. A piece of paper. A Certificate of Authenticity. That's what makes the same paintings worth three figures in your bit of plastic pipe, and five figures a piece in someone else's bit of plastic pipe. That's the stuff, Elliot. That's provenance.' He looked out of the window at the passing traffic for a while, then said, 'Jesus. It gives me heartburn to think of all the money I've given them over the years.'

'Why do you do it then?'

'Oh, I don't know, mate. I used to think I was investing, but most of the paintings I bought aren't worth half what I paid for them. Most of them I couldn't sell anyway. I couldn't live without them.'

He looked into the rear-view mirror and pulled back out into the road. 'I only buy from art centres now. That was my new year's resolution, but don't tell anyone that tonight. Leslie still thinks I'm one of her best customers.'

Elliot said, 'Anyway, I got an offer of a lot more than a few hundred.'

'True? Who from?'

'Sally Cameron.'

'You're not serious. You haven't been talking to the Camerons?'

'Why not? What's wrong with the Camerons?'

'Bloody sweat shop central, the Camerons. Everyone in town hates them.' He slowed the car for a right turn. 'You better not tell anyone that tonight, either.'

8

THE JAMES' house was down a broad side street, on a huge corner block filled with trees and shrubs, all of it surrounded by a high cyclone-wire fence. Drew parked on the roadside and led Elliot in through the open gates. A large brindled dog leapt up from beneath a tree and barked wildly. It quietened at a word from Leslie, but approached them all the same, in a manner not entirely friendly, and took a complete olfactory scan before returning to its tree. Bats cruised the edges of the light dome, feasting on moths.

There were five people already there besides Leslie James: three men that Elliot didn't recognise and two women that he did. One was Maria Perris from the first gallery he had visited that morning. He couldn't put a name on the other one, but she was a familiar face around town.

Leslie gave Drew an air kiss and left him to his own devices. She took Elliot by the arm and drew him into the circle, which made him feel as if he was being exhibited and had him wondering what Drew had told her about him.

'Elliot what?' she said to him.

'Fielding.'

'He's just started working with the RFDS.'

'Actually' he began but Leslie continued to talk over him.

'Julia Scholz,' she said. 'Manager at Eusebia art centre.' Elliot nodded and shook her hand. 'It's probably the best of the art centres,' Leslie went on. 'The one the others try to emulate.'

Elliot nodded again, appreciatively he hoped, and Leslie continued around the gathering. 'Maria Perris.'

'We've met,' said Maria and Elliot together.

'Dougie Nicholson, the Sydney Swagman. Pioneer of Aboriginal art. First boot on the ground in a lot of the outlying communities. Currently advises and supplies the obscenely wealthy all over the world.'

He must have been in his late sixties to have become involved so early, but he didn't look it. He was tall, rangy, leathery, one of those Australian outback men that made Elliot feel inadequate. He was wearing a singlet, all the men there were. Long sleeves and trousers made Elliot feel taller and more substantial. But here, on this sweltering evening, he felt overdressed.

'Adam Dukes,' Leslie went on. 'Also owns a very successful gallery in Sydney. Understands the internet and social media and stuff.'

Dukes looked pretty rugged and dusty as well, not like someone who spent his life in front of a computer in a city gallery. 'Pleased to meet you,' Elliot mumbled.

'And last and very definitely least, this is my other half, Ollie.'

Ollie was standing behind a glowing barbecue. He was fleshier than the other two men and shorter, nearly as short as Elliot. He wore an apron and held a blackened implement in each hand. He waved them both at Elliot.

'Ollie,' Elliot said.

'Elliot has taken an interest in desert art,' Leslie said. 'I thought no one would mind if I invited him along.'

'How long has he got?' Ollie said, and the others laughed.

Elliot looked around for Drew, but he was over at the esky beside the barbeque, rooting around among the cans.

Leslie said, 'I've been trying to explain to him how to tell the sheep from the goats.'

'Sheep from the wolves, more like,' said Scholz.

'Wolves from the sharks I'd say,' said Ollie, spearing slabs of meat on the grill.

'Now now, Ollie,' Leslie said. 'Don't listen to him, Elliot. He says he doesn't know anything about art but don't believe him.'

'I don't know anything about art,' Ollie said. 'Believe me. I'm a windmill man. Ask me about windmills.'

'Ignore him,' Leslie said. 'Dougie is the one I was telling you about. The one you should talk to about Doris.'

'Doris?' said Dougie.

'He's the man with the nose for the up-and-coming. Or maybe he's the man with the influence to create overnight sensations.'

'Not the only one, Leslie.'

'True enough,' she said. 'But most of them don't keep it secret until the price goes beyond us mere mortals.'

'I always share my hunches,' Nicholson said. 'You mob don't listen, that's all.' He turned to Elliot. 'So, which Doris are you interested in?'

But Leslie James literally pulled Elliot away, stuck a paper plate and a napkin in his hand, and pointed him at Ollie, who said, 'Take your pick.'

Even though he had eaten something before he came, the smell of the meat made Elliot hungry. 'The burgers look good,' he said.

'Point the finger,' Ollie said and Elliot, a little self-consciously, picked the darkest one. Ollie flipped it up and slapped it onto the plate. Elliot thanked him and reached for bread.

'Don't believe a word any of these bastards tell you,' Ollie said, loud enough so he was sure everyone could hear him. 'They're all bloody sharks and charlatans, ripping off the poor Aboriginal people.'

'Don't listen to him Elliot,' Leslie said. 'Come and—'

'Put your money into windmills,' Ollie went on. 'Moulded polycarbonate and cast aluminium. That's aluminum if you're paying in American dollars. All-steel gearing mechanisms. Absolutely beautiful and minimal maintenance. What could be more artistic than that?'

'He's a doctor, mate,' Dougie Nicholson said. 'What does he want with a windmill?'

'I'm offering him an investment,' Ollie said. 'Isn't that what you galahs are doing?'

Elliot said, 'I'm...' and 'But...' and 'Actually...' but no one was listening to him.

'He isn't here to buy art,' Leslie said.

'That's what he thinks,' Ollie said. 'That's what they all think. Be careful, young fella. This mob are professionals.'

'Do you work in the clinics out there?' Julia Scholz asked him, with a sweep of her arm which took in half the world beyond the lighted yard.

'I do,' Elliot said. 'I'm on a rota.' He named his three regular communities. 'Sometimes I do fill-ins or emergency runs. I've seen most places at this stage.'

'Must be a bit of a shock to the system, seeing what they're up against out there.'

Elliot saw his opportunity to shake off the impression that he was a newcomer. 'Actually,' he began, but the people here all seemed to behave like steamrollers.

'Do you get any joy out of it?'

The phrasing of the question stunned him into silence. Joy?

'Let him eat his burger, poor bloke,' Leslie said, and somehow managed to turn everyone's attention away from him and towards a new focus, so while he retreated to a bench beside the dog's tree, the others, except for Ollie, turned their chairs into a circle, almost a huddle, and spoke at a volume level just below the reach of his hearing. Drew returned, handed him a dripping beer, and sloped over to get within earshot of the conversation. The dog sat up and gazed intently at Elliot as he ate. He wondered whether it had been a good idea to come. But the burger was good, at least, and just as he was finishing it, Ollie appeared beside him with a second one, cooked exactly as the first one, just short of being burned.

'Kept this one 'specially for you,' he said, sitting down beside Elliot.

'Appreciate it,' Elliot said. 'This is a bit of a treat for me. I don't really cook.' Ollie's mouth was full, so Elliot went on, 'I'm not new here, you know. I don't know where Leslie got that impression.'

'How long you been here then?'

'Three years now.'

'That's new,' said Ollie, but Elliot thought he was joking. He liked Ollie. He had one of those elastic faces that exaggerated expressions. People with that kind of face had to be clowns, in Elliot's experience, because if their faces weren't animated they looked suicidal.

'I'm definitely new to this art stuff,' he said. 'I don't know which way is up.'

'Really? But it's always up for the whitefellas, did you not know that? Up and up.' Ollie dropped a crust into the snapping jaws of the dog. 'Acquisition. What we're good at.'

'Well, I'm not trying to acquire anything. Actually, I'm trying to sell something. It's a bit complicated.'

'It's a bit complicated all right,' Ollie said. 'It's a bloody maze and a minefield. As soon as you think you understand it, someone pulls the rug out from under your feet. I stopped trying, to be honest with you. I let Leslie get on with it. Just help her spend the money.'

'And is there a lot of money in it?'

'Are you joking?' Ollie put his plate under the bench and the dog fell on it: appeared to be eating everything, including the napkin and the plastic fork. 'She wasn't kidding when she said old Dougie there has the ear of the obscenely wealthy. He has a bigger network than Telstra, you know? Been selling art for nearly forty years. He's the go-to man for the global billionaires.'

Elliot glanced across, but all the heads in the circle were still down, the murmuring voices still not carrying. The dog regurgitated shards of plastic at his feet.

'We're not in the same league,' Ollie went on. 'We just try and keep our heads down and not get carried away.'

'Carried away?'

'Oh, there are crazes. Every now and then some new talent is discovered, some poor old man or woman living a quiet life in some remote corner of Australia, and someone comes along and puts a paintbrush in their hand and they're an overnight sensation. Gold mines, each and every one, for the buggers who call the shots. They don't give a shit what effect it has on that old person's life. Maybe it's a good effect sometimes, or maybe it's good for a while. They get a lot of money and get to decide who they'll buy a car for. All that community politics shit. You've seen all that, I suppose, where you work.'

Elliot tried to work out whether or not he had, and Ollie went on,

'Then the big buyers run out, they've all had their fill, and the dealers lose interest, and where does that leave the artist? They're used to getting money, and their families and communities have all these expectations now, so they are under pressure to keep turning out paintings, and under pressure to sell them. So that's when the carpetbaggers move in. Like vultures. The artists start letting their paintings go for less and less. The dealers and the collectors hate it, because the value of their investments is being pulled down too. So then some of the dealers try and get exclusive with the artists, sign contracts to be their sole agent, that kind of carry-on. Works OK for some of them. Doesn't work at all for others.'

'I can see why you stick to the windmills,' Elliot said.

Ollie said, 'Um, yeah. I know. I shouldn't really be talking like this to you. Sounds all negative, doesn't it? Didn't mean to. Should be saying Aboriginal art is a great thing for everyone, artist and collector and dealer alike. Brings money into these impoverished communities. Keeps a few whitefellas afloat as well. What is there not to like about it?'

Elliot wondered whether he had seen any of the benefits art might have provided. He thought there was a lot of truth in what Luke had once said to him.

'YOU ONLY SEE THE BAD STUFF.'

They had been outside the library in Alice. Elliot was picking up DVDs and he met Luke with some of the lads from the Nyaru school footy team, who were in town for a weekend tournament. They were watching a video about the Yuendumu team and were being pretty well supervised by the library staff, so Luke left them and came out to have a smoke and a yarn.

'Great to see the kids enjoying themselves,' Elliot said.

'Our little kids are always happy, Elliot,' Luke said. 'They have a great time. Not like when I was a kid. We got music lessons out there for them. Studio where they can make recordings, all that. We even got half a footy team. You don't see the good stuff. You only see the bad stuff. The sick kids and the diabetes and all that.'

Elliot couldn't deny it.

'You don't see the people living on the outstations. Not so often you don't see them. Only if they sick and coming in for the clinic. Sometimes it don't work for them to live out there. Sometimes it's good. Some small communities, way out. You don't even see those people, Elliot. You only see the bad stuff.'

Elliot said, 'Don't you want to live that kind of life, Luke? Out there on your country?'

Luke said, 'My country too far, Elliot. Long way west, my place. Nyaru is my wife's country, all around there. Mother's country one side, father's country different way. All around Nyaru. She a proper owner for that place.'

Elliot tried to remember whether he had ever met Luke's wife or any of his kids. He realised he might have, without knowing.

'She teaching in the school. Teacher assistant. When we are old people, might be we go then.'

Elliot nodded. He thought he knew who she was, now. Luke smoked. Then he went on, 'I don't have the law for my country, Elliot. Only a little bit. How can I live on my country when I don't have the law?'

'YOU SHOULD TALK TO JULIA,' Ollie was saying. 'That woman is a force of nature. She runs the most amazing art centre, runs it like a proper business and makes it work. She has the respect of pretty much everyone on both sides of the fence.'

Elliot nodded. 'So if I was a buyer, and if I was concerned about the welfare of the artists, that's where I should buy my art from?'

'Ah look,' Ollie said. 'I always do this. I can't keep my mouth shut. If you were a buyer and you were concerned about the welfare of the artist, you'd be pretty safe to buy off any of the people here.'

Elliot nodded. He said. 'Pretty safe.'

Ollie nodded too, then said, 'Probably.'

'Probably,' said Elliot.

'Yep,' said Ollie.

SOON AFTERWARDS, the huddle broke up and Julia Scholz joined him on his bench with her plate. She told him that being so close to Alice Springs had advantages and disadvantages for the community where she worked. It was easier for the people to access healthcare and other services; they had some chance of getting jobs and a bit more choice about where to spend their money and use their basics cards. It was good for the staff there, too: easier for them to get away for a day or two. On the downside, there were worse problems with substance abuse, and the community was an easy target for grog runners and carpetbaggers and other kinds of predators.

Elliot's beer was getting warm. He tanked it down like a dose of medicine. 'What's the difference between a dealer and a carpetbagger?' he said.

'Well,' Scholz said, 'All carpetbaggers are dealers, but not all dealers are carpetbaggers. Does that make sense?'

She had a slight accent, European he thought, overlaid strongly with Australian vowels and idioms. German?

He said, 'No.'

Scholz said, 'OK. Well, everyone here is a dealer but they are all reputable, you know? Trustworthy. They care about the artists and their careers. It's in everyone's interests really, for the artists' work to find its true value. That can't happen if people come in from outside and drag down the value of the work. Sell it too cheap, buy it even cheaper.'

'Why isn't it up to the artist to decide? Why is it up to you people?'

'When you say, 'you people', which people do you mean?' Her voice betrayed her irritation with the question. 'You realise art centres are owned by their communities? They get funding from the state, but they are all run by a community board of management. When you hear some people, you'd think the art centre was imposed by government but it's the other way round. I'm employed to manage the centre. I don't make the rules, just try to implement them. So I'm not making anyone's decisions for them.'

She picked up her sandwich, examined the leading edge of it and put it down again. The dog crept closer to her knees. She went on, 'There's a general consensus in my community that all work should go through the art centre. It worked pretty well up until the crash in 2008, then everything got shaky, the big money dried up and some of the artists, mainly the better ones, unfortunately, they started selling to anyone and everyone who would give them a couple of hundred dollars. The whole art movement looked as if it was going down the drain.' She ducked as a huge beetle came blundering in, bumping and bouncing off the string of solar lamps hanging from the trees. When it crash-landed near her feet, stuck on its back, she stepped on it and ground it into the dust.

'Things are picking up a bit now and we're trying to bring people back into the fold, but if someone comes along with cash it's hard for people to turn it down. Some of the dreamings are simple and people can paint them quickly. Or they paint quick ones, real shabby versions of their better work. They get paid shit so they produce shit. Everybody gets what they deserve, you say. Except that the average Jill Soap out there can't tell the difference. So if she can get a Millie Nungarrayi for five hundred dollars instead of five thousand, why wouldn't she do that?'

Ollie came round carrying a plate of unidentifiable slabs of meat in one hand and a bottle of wine in the other. 'Anyone?' he said.

They both declined and he moved on. The dog seemed to consider him a better prospect than Scholz and followed. She went on, 'Thing is, even the good dealers are a problem for us. The work that gets sold through the art centre benefits everyone. Fifty per cent goes to the artist and the other fifty gets ploughed back into the centre and the community. Our place supports two or three other projects in the community. But if the likes of Deadly Dougie comes along and lures our best artists away, that's maybe good for them but it's not good for us. It's sales we don't get to make and money we don't get to spend.'

'Did I hear my name mentioned?' Nicholson strolled over, plate in hand.

Ollie came back and handed Elliot a cold beer. 'Still talking about windmills?' he said. 'Is there nothing else with you people?'

Nicholson pulled a chair up and Scholz said to him, 'Just complaining about you poaching our artists.'

'I could say the same thing about you,' Nicholson said. 'I was buying art from people in your place before you were even born. There wouldn't be any art centres, there mightn't be any art at all if it wasn't for people like me.'

Elliot had the impression that he was listening in on a well-rehearsed argument.

'People who make huge profits out of it you mean?' Scholz said.

'I make a living out of it. So do you.'

'Can't deny that,' Scholz said.

'No. Or that the artists get impatient waiting for you to move their work.'

'We move their work.' An edge had crept into her tone. 'We move it to galleries all over the world. I don't see why you can't deal through us like the others do.'

'We've been over this,' Dougie said.

'Have we? Everyone else seems to be happy with the art that we produce.'

Dougie turned to Elliot. 'We don't always see eye to eye on the aesthetics. The art centres try to steer the artists to produce certain styles of work—'

'We don't steer anybody!' Scholz said, and now her tone was unmistakably bitter. 'We don't manipulate anyone. We just like to give the artists opportunity to develop.'

'Same thing,' Dougie said. He was quite calm, not responding to Scholz's anger.

'Are you saying you don't instruct them just as much?' Scholz said. 'Are you saying you don't tell them what kind of paintings you want?'

'I just want them to do what they always did. Stay true to their culture.'

'We are trying to help them to develop as artists. You want to fossilise them.'

Dougie shrugged. 'All I want is authenticity. And anyway, a lot of these people are my friends, you know? Why should you try and stop me making my own arrangements the way I always did?'

'Which means setting your own prices.'

'Are we back to this again?'

Scholz said nothing, and Nicholson went on, 'Have you heard anyone complaining about what I pay? I was one of the first people to propose the code, you know? And one of the first to sign it. I'm not responsible for what people do with their money when they get it. I don't see that as my problem.'

Scholz muttered something that Elliot couldn't catch. It might have been in a different language. Nicholson took a deep breath and turned to Elliot, throwing his gaze skywards. He said, 'Ollie's banoffee anyone? I recommend it, Elliot.'

He offloaded his scraps to the dog and went towards the back of the house, where powerful lights lit up a long verandah with an open door into the kitchen. Scholz said, 'I shouldn't let him get to me, but it drives me crazy.'

Elliot looked around the garden. Drew and Maria Perris were in a huddle with Leslie James. Ollie was on his way over again, waving the bottle of wine. He looked more unsteady on his feet with each circuit of the party he made. He said, 'Tempt you, young fella?' Elliot shook his head. 'Tea or coffee then? You can help yourself in the kitchen,'

'That would be good.' He stood up and turned to Scholz. 'Want one?'

'I'm good, thanks,' she said.

9

NICHOLSON WAS IN THERE, leaning against a marble-topped island, eating something the colour and consistency of infant poo, with whipped cream on top. He waved his spoon at Elliot, clearly still hot under the collar.

'People go on about cultural obligations as if they're a bad thing,' he said, 'as if whitefellas can organise things better with their interventions and their managers and their artistic supervision. But those laws have kept these people alive and healthy for thousands and thousands of generations, you know? Why is it such a bad thing to share what you have instead of hoarding it for yourself?'

Elliot said, 'I suppose...' He wasn't sure which bit of the earlier conversation had given rise to this, or whether it was entirely spontaneous.

'It's true that it can be open to exploitation,' Nicholson went on. 'Show me a system that isn't. Look at the corruption all around us. Look at our pollies, for god's sake. No one is denying there's a lot of humbug goes on, but it's not the whole story. Most of the time people look after each other. Spread the good luck around, you know?'

Elliot shrugged noncommittally and helped himself to some of the banoffee trifle. Nicholson watched him, then said, 'Anyway, I hear you were wanting to talk about Doris. Which Doris would that be?'

'Doris Banks,' Elliot said. 'From Nyaru.'

'Oh,' Nicholson nodded his head softly, in a kind of reverence. 'She's amazing, isn't she? I really believe she's one of the greats. She'll go meteoric soon, you'll see. No two paintings alike. Every one a story, a journey.'

Elliot nodded, unwilling to reveal his ignorance.

'That's the thing, see? I hope you didn't get the wrong impression there with Julia. We're mates, you know. She's brilliant at what she does; the best there is. But you can't go leaning on these artists to start experimenting and pressurising them to change the way they work, just because certain colours and styles are in vogue with the tourists. People spit nails about family members helping artists with their paint-ing, but you don't hear people complaining about the art centres touching up the sloppy bits. Where's the *Four Corners* exposé about that, eh?'

'Do they do that?' said Elliot.

'Ah, who cares?' Nicholson said. 'It's mostly mass-produced stuff anyway. But these old artists, they are what they are, and they won't come again. The young painters, some of them are technically brilliant, you know, but they don't have the knowledge. They don't have the memory of that relationship with country, before first contact. And Doris has that in spades. She's one of the last people alive who has it.'

Elliot nodded again. 'I suppose that's true.'

'It is true, mate. No ifs and buts. She's a law woman and she's a great artist. Very rare, that. Never rushes herself, never devalues herself. I just love her work. You got good taste there, Doctor.'

Elliot suddenly realised that what he was hearing was a sales pitch, and he found himself on the back foot. He said, 'Oh, well...'

Nicholson put his bowl, empty now apart from yellow-brown smears, on the island and moved closer, too close, shoulder to shoulder in a matey way. Elliot would have to crane his neck now to meet Nicholson's eye. He looked away, his hackles rising.

'Truth is, I'm being a bit canny with the paintings I've got. Not in any rush to shift them, you know? I reckon they'll double in value over the next couple of years; even treble.'

Elliot said, 'Good, good. But actually, I'm not looking to buy one.'

'Oh?'

'I've got some to sell. Doris asked me to sell them for her.' Elliot still wasn't looking at Nicholson, but he felt him shrinking away, withdrawing his enthusiasm, if not his interest.

'How many paintings?' he said. 'What kind of size?'

'Six. Different sizes.'

'And when did she give them to you?'

'Just a few days ago,' Elliot said. 'A week or so. I was out there for a clinic.' Nicholson said nothing, and Elliot felt compelled to add, 'It wasn't my idea. I'm not looking for a cut.'

'So you're talking to me because?'

Elliot was surprised. 'Leslie said I should talk to you. She said you deal with Doris' work.'

'Oh, I deal with Doris all right,' Nicholson said. 'Did she tell you what she wants for them?'

'She wants a toyota. She wants it for a culture centre, to make trips out on country, teach law to the younger women.'

'Ah, the old toyota,' Nicholson said, stepping away from Elliot at last and turning on the electric kettle. 'Primary currency of the outback. They all want them, mate, but none of them can hold on to them. Some young bugger comes along and if she ever sees it again, it's upside down in a creek bed.' Elliot drew breath to protest, but Nicholson went on, 'We take them on trips sometimes, a few of them at a time, out to their country. Hundreds of kilometres, some of those trips, all of it off-road. Camp out there with them, let them reconnect, do their ceremonies and stuff, spend a few days painting. Great thing to do. Inspires them, reinvigorates them. Some really good work comes out of those trips. But Doris is a bit isolated out there in Nyaru. Not so many senior artists around there. Maybe it's time I organised something just for her.'

'Maybe,' Elliot said. 'But—'

'It's a great idea, actually,' Nicholson said. 'If she wants a trip out into the woopwoop we'll get it organised. Take some of her mates along too. Women's business, you know?'

'She wants a car, not a painting trip,' Elliot said.

'Well, we'll see,' Nicholson said. 'I'll talk to her about it next time I'm out there.'

Elliot waited for him to continue, and when he didn't he said, 'Are you interested in having a look at these paintings?'

'Very definitely,' Nicholson said. 'No question about that.'

'Great. They're in Drew's car. I'll just—'

'Ah no, mate,' Nicholson said. 'Not here. Not now. This is a social occasion. No business allowed. But I'm around town for another few days. Why don't you bring them out to my place?'

10

OLLIE WAS DRUNK. He poured red wine into Elliot's unfinished cup of tea. He said, 'Poor buggers. I feel sorry for some of them. Getting pulled and dragged every which way. Someone has this great gift and it ends up being a curse. Dealers leaning on them from one side and family humbugging them on the other. There are some old people round here that are just being used as cash cows by everyone. Break your bloody heart.'

He appeared to be in real pain, and Elliot backed away.

'Windmills,' Ollie called after him plaintively as he headed towards his car. 'No one gets damaged by windmills.'

11

THE NEXT MORNING Elliot's head wasn't good, and he was glad it was Sunday. He took some paracetamol and put on the kettle, then opened the door to the verandah, hoping the air outside might be cooler than the stuff inside. It was, but it wouldn't be for long. He found a clean tee-shirt and loose pyjama pants, put pretty much everything else he owned in the washing machine and turned it on.

The pipe containing the paintings lay against the skirting board in his living room, and as soon as he set eyes on it, he was filled with anxiety. It looked like nothing much, a grubby thing that had clearly seen a lot of use. It was covered in writing that had been crossed out or stickered over as the contents were changed and new names added. It wasn't an object likely to attract much attention, but if the paintings were really likely to double or treble in value over the next few years then they had a potential future value higher than his house in Melbourne. Quite a few people now knew that he had them, and while he didn't actively mistrust anyone in particular, he realised he knew next to nothing about any of them and couldn't take anything for granted.

He had little in the house worth stealing, and although he always locked up at night and when he went out, he was well aware that it wouldn't take much of an effort to break in. The place was built around an old demountable with extensions in two directions, perfect for someone like him but not designed for security. It rattled on windy nights. A good shove at any of the doors and windows would break their locks. It wasn't going to be a safe place to leave the paintings when he went off to do his clinic the following day.

He was half tempted to open them up and inspect them; get a proper look at them. In his imagination they were deteriorating rapidly, their smudges and paw-prints spreading to cover entire canvases. What if Nicholson didn't like them? What if he said they weren't genuine or were inferior to Doris' other work? And what if they actually were inferior? Nicholson could say whatever he liked, and Elliot would have no way of disputing it. He returned to the moment when Linda fetched the paintings from the house, found his mind beginning to circle on worn tracks, and was suddenly fed up with the whole business. He wanted to sign off on the deal with Nicholson and move on to the next step, the fun part, getting the car and delivering it to Nyaru. He ran the fantasy reel again, the moment of rolling up beside the jilimi house in a clean white troopy, such an obvious image of the knight in shining armour that it made him laugh out loud. But an idea began to form in his mind of how he might move things along. He looked at his watch, drained his coffee and went to get his phone.

The first two colleagues that he reached weren't keen to swap days. The third person he tried was Lena Holmes, and he didn't hold out much hope. She was the longest serving of his colleagues in Alice and if his previous experience was anything to go by, the least likely to agree to swapping days. But he was in luck.

'I won't change a day,' she said, 'but I'll do a day for you if you want. I'm finally taking that sabbatical and heading for Europe. I need all the cash I can get.'

Elliot said, 'Yes, absolutely. We can let them know in the office.'

'Deal, then,' she said. 'And as many days as you want between now and the end of next month. If I'm free I'll do them.'

They stayed on the line for a few minutes. Elliot gave her the details she would need, the time the plane usually left Alice, any particular issues she was likely to encounter in that community. He told her that a burst water pipe, left unmended for several weeks, had undermined the foundations of the clinic buildings and left them listing. They discussed the strong-willed ngangkari who often insisted on accompanying patients when they visited the doctor, and who Elliot seemed always to rub up the wrong way. It turned out that Lena had worked with him in the past and found him very helpful, so that led them into a discussion about the value of traditional medicine, and while all that was going on, in some other part of Elliot's mind that seemed to be working quite independently, pieces of a plan he wasn't even aware he was making were dropping neatly into place, one by one. So just as they were wrapping up their call, Elliot found himself saying, 'Hey, Lena?'

'Yes?'

'If you're really serious about doing more days, can you do the following Monday for me as well?'

12

HE WAS AWAKE EARLY the next morning, well before his alarm was set to go off, impatient as a child at Christmas. As soon as the town was open, he threw the paintings into the car and set off for the main Toyota dealer. They had a few suitable four-wheel drive cars for sale but only one that really interested him; an ex-government troop-carrier fitted out with long-distance fuel tanks, a roof-rack and a winch. It wasn't young but it was clean and had a relatively low mileage. There were a few months left on the rego and the dealer was giving a three month's guarantee on all parts. At slightly under thirty thousand dollars on the road it looked like a good deal to Elliot. He was dying to be behind the wheel of it and driving out towards the west on the red dirt roads.

'It won't be there for long, mate,' the salesman told him, and Elliot was inclined to believe him. He walked around it again, getting a good feeling. It was a car that was eager to get moving. He wanted it, and he couldn't tell whether he wanted it for Linda and Doris or for himself. Back in his own car, giving himself a talking to, trying to avoid making a rash decision, he decided it didn't matter. He had the money in the bank, and he could write a cheque for it right away. Dougie Nicholson was going to look at the paintings the following day and had told him, inadvertently perhaps, that their value was on the rise. It put him in a position to hold out for a really good price. He hoped it would be enough to buy that troopy twice over, but even if that was being over-optimistic it was a dead cert that it would easily cover the thirty grand. If Nicholson played hard to get, he was pretty sure he could push Sally Cameron and her dad up a bit, maybe get them and Nicholson bidding against each other. And if none of that worked out, there were still plenty of avenues he hadn't explored. Even in the very worst-case scenario, he couldn't go wrong, because he would just keep the lovely troopy and sell the station wagon, which was a thing he had been planning to do anyway. It was a win-win situation. A win-win car.

He took one more breath, one more moment for reflection. There were other dealers in town, and he hadn't even looked at Gumtree. He had the whole day and most of the next to look around and see if he could find a better deal. He knew he ought to do that. But the prospect of someone else coming along and buying that beautiful car was more than he could stand. Twenty minutes later, he was back at the dealership, signing the paperwork.

13

THE NEXT AFTERNOON, a few minutes before four o'clock, Elliot arrived at the address Nicholson had given him. It was clear that there was no one there. The place had been easy to find and was just as Nicholson had described it: a shipping container and a campervan behind the main house on a dusty block just off the Undoolya Road. The campervan, from the look of its flat tyres and welded-on awning, had not seen the roads for a very long time.

Elliot parked up beside it. He realised he hadn't taken Nicholson's phone number, swore at himself for the oversight. He knew it was barely four, but he checked the time again, and then again a couple of minutes later. Seeing the troopy and deciding to buy it had lit the blue touch paper in him, and he was in the grip of a restlessness as uncomfortable and uncontrollable as a virus. He had spent the last couple of hours being irritated by paperwork; just the run-of-the-mill clinic reports and expenses forms, but infinitely more arduous than usual, battling with a mind continually running ahead of itself. He was in no mood to hang around on Nicholson's whim.

There was, as always, a pile of reading in the back seat of the car; things he needed to keep abreast of; new guidelines and protocols, current research into the diseases he encountered most often and new approaches to treating them. He picked up a sheaf of the stuff, but he had no chance of concentrating. Instead, he thought about the drive he would be taking on Friday. He had been told it would take seven or eight hours by road and he was keen to do as much of it as possible in daylight. He was out at clinics for the next two days and he couldn't collect the troopy until Friday morning, so he had arranged with the dealership that he would collect it, checked over and filled up with diesel, the moment they opened. He had been planning the trip like a military campaign, writing lists and sourcing supplies. He had already done a supermarket run, bought a new billy and a flask, casks of water, nuts and energy bars, tea and milk powder; way more than was necessary, most of it just insurance against a breakdown. His swag, bought when he first arrived in Alice but hardly ever used, was hanging out in the sun to air and he had packed a bag with a first-aid kit and a few changes of clothes. He had dug out his old broad brimmed sunhat and a flynet, which he had twice removed from the pile and twice put back again. He wouldn't be seen dead wearing it in Nyaru, but he might need it if he stopped along the way.

He was parked in the shade of some wattle trees, but it was still too hot in the car, so he got out and wandered over to the house. There were plenty of signs that it was lived-in: there was barbecue gear at the back and a selection of stools and camp chairs, but no one answered when he knocked on the door. On the other side of the block was an abandoned vegetable patch, raised beds full of desiccated weeds with plastic hooping and the tattered remains of shade netting. He went back to the shipping container. There were no windows, but there were vents with fans on the sides and another pair like chimneys on the top. He could see the nearest ones turning, and the container hummed gently, like an old radio. It would take an explosives expert to get into it without keys. Elliot wondered what was in there that was so valuable.

Paintings. It had to be. He walked around behind the campervan, got a whiff of stale urine from a dunny or a pissing tree, recoiled as instinctively as an animal entering a rival's territory. He was retracing his steps when Nicholson drove in, the big wheels of his Landcruiser grinding the gravel. As it passed him on its way to park beside his own car, Elliot noticed the raised floor in the back, the swag rolled up at one end. Elliot had seen that kind of layout before, with storage drawers underneath for cooking and camping gear. It was what he wanted for his own vehicle when the time came to get it, and he resisted a swell of envy for Nicholson and the life he led.

He waited while Nicholson got out, groaning, rolling his shoulders and shaking out his ankles and knees. 'You're early,' he said.

Elliot said, 'No, I'm—' but Nicholson went on, 'How you going? Let's get a beer before we shrivel up.'

He reached back into the car and pulled out a bunch of keys that looked like a small munitions dump.

Elliot said, 'Yeah, why not.'

While Nicholson unlocked the camper and climbed inside, Elliot went over to his car and collected the paintings. When he got back there was a cold beer for him on the edge of a tin door which lay across two barrels, serving as a table. He reached for a folded camp chair and checked it for red-backs. Nicholson took a long swig of his beer and lit a cigarette. He nodded at the paintings and said, 'So tell me again how you came by these?'

Elliot opened his beer and told the story again, just the bare bones of it. Nicholson nodded and said, 'When was this, exactly?'

It was easy for Elliot to remember because his clinic routine was so regular. He said, 'A week ago. Thursday afternoon. Why?'

Nicholson reached across and took the end cap off the pipe. He pulled out the paintings, deftly stripped off the masking tape and unrolled them on to the gravelly dust of his yard. He examined them with an expert eye, quickly flipping through the pile. He said,

'I hope you didn't take me too seriously when I was having a go at Julia the other night. It's just a thing we have going. We wind each other up.'

Elliot shrugged. He hadn't given it another thought, serious or otherwise. Nicholson went on, 'The art centres are OK. They get people painting who might never have done it otherwise. There's a whole movement going on in the APY Lands just now, amazing painting going on there, all coming through their little art centres. It all depends on the managers, in the end. Some of them are too hands-on, that's my only complaint. Some of them give the artists too much direction.'

He looked through the paintings again, lifted the top three off the pile to reveal the one beneath them. It was done in umbers and rust, with strong waves in paler shades running in several directions across most of the canvas. In one place, so far off-centre that it was almost in the corner, was a small arrangement of concentric circles, horseshoes and ovals.

'Could be part of a dreamtime story going back thousands of generations, or it could be a women's ceremony they hold every year. Or both. That's the thing with Doris. She paints them all according to her mood. The paintings are timeless. I don't need to know what they are. It doesn't matter to me.'

He dropped the other canvasses back into place and leafed through them all again. 'Most buyers don't care either, but you get the odd one who wants the whole nine yards, you know? Artist bio, dreaming story, mystical and spiritual significance. I have to give them some guff.' He laughed. 'They don't want to know if it's Doris and her family cooking tail just outside town.'

Elliot was suddenly interested. 'Is it?' he said. 'Could it be?'

Nicholson shrugged. 'There's still more cultural significance in that than there is in a lot of the art being produced these days. There aren't many of them left, you know? The great old originals. A lot of people they call artists now just do the same painting, over and over and over again. A production line is a production line, whether it's in an art centre or a sweat shop. That's my opinion, anyway.'

He stood, rolled up the paintings with practiced ease, and slid them into their tube. Elliot said, 'But Doris liked the art centre. She told me. She said they helped her manage her money.'

'Some of them do that, it's true,' said Nicholson. 'It's not their job, though, strictly speaking. Not mine, either. I give my artists a fair price for their work. It's up to them what they do with it.'

'What, so you just rock up there with thousands of dollars in cash?'

Nicholson flared. 'You know what? That's between me and Doris, and it's none of your business. I've signed the Indigenous Art Code. My books are at your disposal if you want to make an application through the proper channels.'

Elliot said nothing. Nicholson reached for his keys.

'Let me show you how it works.'

Elliot followed him to the lock-up and waited while he opened mortice locks and padlocks and pulled open the heavy door. Nicholson turned on an overhead bulb powered, like the fans, by a single wire strung across from the house. The first thing Elliot noticed was a dozen or so lengths of water pipe standing on end in the corner beside the door. Like the one Sally Cameron had given him, they had writing on them in different coloured markers, much of it scrubbed out.

'Paintings I've been picking up on this trip,' Nicholson said. 'I'll take them all back to Sydney with me when I go.'

Elliot looked past him into the interior of the shed. It was like the stockroom of an artist supply store. One entire wall was lined with steel shelving and stacked with acrylic paint; boxes and bottles and tubs and buckets in every imaginable colour. Shelves along the short wall held bolts of grey linen, and the rest of the space was taken up by wooden frames and canvases in different states of preparation. Nicholson indicated these. 'We stretch them here and prepare them. They get primer first, then whatever colour the artist wants. Red or black most often, but some of them ask for other colours.' There were all sizes of canvas, square and rectangular, with sides ranging from fifty centimetres to two metres. 'Joannie from the house there, she does most of this. When they're dry we take them off the stretchers and hand them out to the artists. Stock them up with paint and leave them to it. Go back and collect them a couple of months later, or whenever I'm back in the area.'

Elliot was uneasy. His mind was beginning to engage, but too slowly. Nicholson had to spell it out. 'Those ones you have out there. They began life here, like this, see? Strictly speaking, those paintings are my property.'

Elliot reversed out of the shed and looked towards the pipe on Nicholson's makeshift table. His sunglasses were there beside it, and the light at this angle was cutting into his vision, another assault, disorientating him. He could find no reliable bearings in this new world he had stumbled into. Every time he thought he knew what was happening, the ground shifted again. Was he now going to hand the paintings over, shamefaced as a schoolchild caught in possession of someone else's property? He wondered, momentarily, whether he could stop the deal on the troopy.

'Sit down again, mate,' Nicholson said. 'Finish your beer.'

Elliot couldn't meet Nicholson's eye. He sat back down in the folding chair. Nicholson went on, 'I'm not accusing you of anything. It's a bit of a jungle out there and I wouldn't blame anyone for making mistakes. I hardly ever get the same number of canvases back as I hand out. A few losses are built into my estimates. I can't expect to have total control.' He disappeared into the campervan and reappeared with two more beers. 'But when you get someone like Doris and everyone can see she's on the up and up, suddenly there's collectors and carpet-baggers swarming all over her like cockroaches and I could be pouring my materials into a black hole. See where I'm coming from?'

Elliot said, 'I'm not a carpetbagger.'

'I know that, mate. But the thing is, I have an arrangement with Doris. With her and her family. She's a bit naughty handing over my paintings to you like that. We have an agreement that says she won't do that.'

'Maybe you don't pay her enough,' Elliot said. 'Maybe you should buy her a car and then she wouldn't have to ask me to.'

Nicholson threw up his hands in a gesture of futility. He said, 'Look, mate—' but this time Elliot talked across him.

'I've already bought the car.'

'You've what?'

'I've bought them a car. A good one. I'm going to drive it out there on Friday.'

Nicholson said, 'Bought it with what?'

'Not your business,' said Elliot. He stood up and reached for the paintings. 'And as far as I'm concerned, these paintings are my property. The artist gave them to me in return for a car and I intend to honour that. If you don't want to buy them off me, someone else will.'

Nicholson stayed where he was, sitting on the steps of the camper. 'You think so?'

'I'm certain of it.' Elliot was shaking with rage. 'You can't do that to people. You can't tell Doris who she can sell paintings to and who she can't.'

'There's nothing to stop you buying them, mate. But you can't sell them. They've got no provenance, see?'

'Oh, stuff your fucking provenance,' Elliot said, crossing the gravel yard towards his car. The hairs on the back of his neck stiffened with fear. Nicholson was a couple of decades older than he was, nearly an old man in effect, but he was rangy and strong, and Elliot had never been a fighter. But Nicholson didn't move. He watched as Elliot opened the hatchback and threw in the paintings.

'You're an idiot, mate,' he called. 'You have no idea what you're doing.'

Still fuelled by adrenalin, Elliot turned the car round, drove out past the house and off the block.

PART III

1

ELLIOT IS secure in those memories: he has built them up painstakingly, piece by piece. He remembers driving along the Undoolya road, shaking so hard that for a minute or two he wasn't sure whether he was fit to drive, and he remembers the panic subsiding when he got into town and the endocrine overload beginning to clear from his system. He has a lot of other memories as well, of what happened between then and his arrival in Adelaide General hospital, but he isn't sure which of them are reliable and which might have been invented to fill inconvenient gaps and which are things he thinks he remembers but in fact has been told or has dreamed. His doctors are not worried about any of this. It is all quite normal following a head injury. But Elliot is someone who likes certainty. He likes clarity. He likes control.

THERE WERE two days of clinics in between that meeting and his departure for Nyaru. He has no memory of them at all, but nor would he have been able to recall any particular day out of the previous three years of clinics unless something particularly memorable had happened, like the freak shooting accident that happened one day when he was in Saint Margaret, or the teenager he met in another community who had been going round with his foreskin stuck in a zip for four days.

'Do you get any joy out of it?' Who said that? Well he did, he saw now. He got joy out of getting sick people back on their feet again, of nipping a case of OM in the bud and saving a child's hearing, he got joy out of meeting lively old people who wanted to yarn and made him laugh. And there was satisfaction in finding that one person in a hundred who took his advice and changed their habits and got their drinking or their diabetes under control and became an inspiration to their community. But most of the time it wasn't like that. By the time of the meeting with Nicholson, Elliot was worn out with giving advice to people who wouldn't or couldn't follow it. For all the endless changes in regulation and protocol, he could see no significant improvements in people's lives, and he had no optimism that there was any change coming. He could see now that he was already close to burn-out back then. It might have been why he made decisions that, looking back on them now, seemed out of character.

2

_____

ON FRIDAY MORNING he packed up his car and drove to the dealership, where he transferred everything—the swag, the food, the water casks, his overnight bag—into the troopy. It started instantly, and the big diesel engine ticked over sweetly. Elliot pulled out of the dealer's fore-court, finally heading out of Alice Springs in the way he had dreamed of doing for so long.

He followed the Stuart Highway until he came to the turn-off for the old beef road that crossed the Tanami desert on its way to the Kimberley. There was a lot more bitumen than he remembered; he was still on it when he reached the limit of the town transmitter and the car radio faded and died, still on it an hour or more later when he reached the turn-off for Nyaru. After that, there would be no more bitumen, and he sailed into a big wide arid world with horizons so distant and flat that he might have been crossing an ocean. This was what he had come there for. There were no demands on him now; no bills, no emails, no texts or phone calls. He was unreachable, alone beneath the vast desert skies and he remembered, fetched from deep within himself, the reason behind his longing for the place.

Memories of the trip with Miles began to return. An early morning, a rock wallaby coming to drink at a waterhole, the clear song of a butcher bird, that still and sacred aura that such places held; the sense of a watching presence. Sometimes, if he went for a walk on his own in the early morning, he got the impression that something went along with him, something glimpsed out of the corner of an eye but never seen. Out there he could enter the stillness, the mood of the desert, the timescale of something that made human life seem insignificant. He was a transient presence in a tiny white capsule, dragging its little comet-trail of red dust.

Gradually he got his eye in; began to see patterns in the vegetation, ripples the wind left in the sand, tracks of creatures big and small on the banks pushed up by the graders. The first abandoned car, lying on its roof, stripped of every reusable part, was a reminder of the dangers of careless driving out here. There was roadkill as always, most of it dry and shrivelled; a bullock skeleton with paddy-melons growing up through it, several indistinguishable lumps of shrivelled skin. Some of it was still fresh enough, though, to entice the massive wedge-tailed eagles which played chicken with him as he approached, always heaving themselves up into the air just in time and flapping away to a nearby perch, hardly rising above mulga-level.

Was that a memory or an image from a dream? Was any of it memory? It felt like it. But if it wasn't, if it was just a construction based upon earlier experiences of the terrain, what did it matter? He made the drive; of that much he is certain. Close to the road, he saw crested dragons and frill-necks, a huge goanna, several slow and clumsy blue-tongues. Further from the road, he saw herds of camels and brumbies, all of them stopping and turning their heads to watch him pass. In the troopy he felt as though he belonged out here, in a way he had never felt in the station wagon. It wasn't just currency, that car, not just status. It made things possible, and Elliot felt liberated by it.

He remembers, too, a sudden insight; a thought that struck him so forcibly he slowed for a minute to contemplate it. Hadn't another life been offered to him? Nicholson's life? If he had listened to Miles, got interested in the world of art instead of rejecting it, couldn't he have ended up just where Nicholson was now? If he hadn't sneered at Roly's investments but had taken his advice instead, like Miles did, might they have become partners in the business? He envisioned a life driving around the heart of Australia, dealing with artists of all kinds, getting to know people like Doris in the positive light of their abilities and achievements, instead of endlessly trying to prevent the 'bad stuff', or fix people up when it was already too late. He could have been out there for weeks and months on end, sleeping in a swag, living on that country instead of forever flying over it. He would have made that buying trip with Miles that time instead of just catching him on his way out of the country. He would have showed him around, then stayed in the desert while Miles went back to do all the sales stuff in Europe and America. Instead of being the idiot drawn into something he didn't understand, he would by now be a renowned expert on Aboriginal art, up ahead of the wave, discovering new brilliance in forgotten corners of the outback. Briefly, he flirted with the idea of trying to do it now, of resurrecting his friendship with Miles, firing up his enthusiasm for Aboriginal art again, winding him up like a clockwork toy and aiming him at people with money. But he knew it was too late. As fast as the inspiration had appeared, it vanished, leaving him momentarily subdued. He was not Dougie Nicholson, and he never could have been.

After a couple more hours he took a left turn onto another unsealed road; one he had often looked down on from above, forging its way, ramrod straight, towards the mines and settlements in the far west of the Northern Territory. It was wide enough for two vehicles to pass, but badly in need of grading, and there were stretches that went on for miles where he could find no happy speed for the car, weaving across and around wheel ruts and deep drifts of bull dust. From time to time he passed a sign at the head of some faint little track leading into an outstation. Sometimes they could be seen from the road, mostly just a couple of tin houses and a rainwater tank. He saw no sign of life in any of them, but several times he saw smoke on the horizon. Whether it was from deliberate burning of country or wild bushfires he had no way of knowing.

3

ONE THING ELLIOT is sure of is that he arrived in Nyaru in the morning and not in the evening. It means he stayed a night on the road instead of completing the drive in a single day, as he had intended. There are plenty of reasons why this might have happened, but Elliot has practically no memory of that night at all, or of the decision to stop driving. He likes to believe that he just chose to stop; that once he got out into the open and away from phone coverage, a new mood entered into him and the sense of urgency left him. He could have just decided to spend a night on his own under the stars and looked for a likely spot, or it might have been the other way round: that he saw an enticing creek bed running away from the road and stopped to have a look, and then decided to stay. He has no memory of any particular place at all, but he does have a series of images associated with somewhere, it must have been there, of cars passing, sometimes in convoys, of headlights waxing and waning in the night. He isn't certain that the images aren't part of a dream, because they seem related to another one, in which he fell down a sinkhole and found himself in a second Australia that existed beneath the surface, an entire level of industrial processing which had to be hidden away where the tourists couldn't see it. There were bright lights, huge trucks coming and going. Above him the land was flat, two-dimensional, and underneath it, the bit that he could see was grey linen canvas. But it is also possible that those cars really did pass him in the night because he thinks they were accounted for by some of the extra vehicles he saw when he drove into Nyaru the next morning.

He passed the huge blue and white board that once informed visitors they were entering a Prescribed Area and weren't allowed to bring alcohol or pornography into the community. It is covered in graffiti and dents and bullet holes, but it is still there, even though the community has permission from the Licensing Commission to remove it. He drove under the archway that marked the official, if not the actual, edge of town, then turned right, heading towards the conspicuous grey roofs of the teacher's houses opposite the jilimi, feverish with excitement at the prospect of handing over the keys to Linda. For the first time, it occurred to him that she might not be there. What would he do if she wasn't staying with Doris? What were the odds?

He slowed down, suddenly aware that one of the houses had large numbers of cars parked around it and a big gathering of people in its yard. He knew what it meant, and he knew the family that lived there. He would like to have found out who had died and called in to express his condolences, but he was suddenly unsure what to do. When he was on duty, doing his rounds, he would have always been informed of any business going on in town that he needed to avoid. Sometimes the days of his clinics had been changed to accommodate sorry business or important ceremonies. If there was a protocol for situations like this, he was unable to remember it, because he had never been faced with it unexpectedly before. He pulled up and was still trying to decide what to do when two men stepped out into the street and approached the car.

Elliot's window was already open. The nearest man leaned into it. 'Town closed,' he said. 'Go back.'

Elliot said, 'What?'

The man repeated himself at higher volume. Elliot said, 'But I'm your doctor. I work here. This is probably one of my patients.'

The second man stepped forward and Elliot recognised him as one of his regulars. He said, 'No clinic today. Sorry business.'

He seemed to be apologetic and Elliot wished he were better at remembering names. But the first man was neither apologetic nor diplomatic. He stood in front of the car and said,

'Turn round. Bugger off home!'

Elliot turned to his patient. 'Look, I don't need to go this way. I can go round by the clinic. I just have to—'

He was cut short by the boom of the other man's hand slamming down on the bonnet of the car. To Elliot's left, three other men were approaching rapidly, and he understood there was no room for discussion. He lifted both hands, palms outwards, and said,

'OK, OK.'

As he reached for the gear lever, the passenger door opened and one of the three newcomers got in. Elliot experienced an instant of blind panic before he realised who it was.

'Luke,' he said. 'What the hell's going on?'

Luke said, 'Ochre business in town. Big law man, that one.' As Elliot got the car turned round, he pointed out the extra cars and people. 'Big mobs come in for ceremony. No kardiya here today.'

'Really?' said Elliot. 'What about Sandra? What about the teachers?'

'Different for them,' Luke said. 'They can stay at home.'

'Well, I can stay out of the way too. I won't intrude.'

'You got a permit, Elliot?'

'A permit? Why do I need a permit? I work here.'

'You not working now. No clinic on a Saturday. You need a permit same for any visitor.'

Elliot's blood began to boil. He was familiar with the permit system, put in place back in the seventies in an attempt to give people some control over their own affairs. Everyone who wanted to visit an Aboriginal community was supposed to have one, whatever the nature of their business. But that law had been rescinded at the time of the intervention, along with a number of other land rights.

'There is no permit system,' he said. 'The intervention took it away.'

'Fuck the intervention,' Luke said. 'Land council still asking for permits. Our business. We have a right to do that. You shouldn't even be on our roads without a permit.'

Elliot opened his mouth to swear, but Luke was tapping on the dash. 'Stop here, stop here.'

They were out past the town boundary. Elliot stopped, and Luke turned round and looked into the back. He said. 'Nice car. Want to make that trip? Visit my country?'

Elliot took a deep breath, disorientated by the turning and over-turning of events. He tried to think. If he really couldn't get into Nyaru for the next couple of days, maybe he should go with Luke. It was something they had been talking about for years, after all, and he had come to believe it would never happen. This could well be his one and only opportunity. But he wasn't ready. He wasn't psyched up for it. Spontaneity was not in his toolbox and he was full of automatic resistance. He said, 'Don't you need to be here for the sorry business?'

'I been spend time with that mob already. Not my family though. Not my ceremony business.'

Elliot looked at his options, which were few. Return to Alice. Park up in a creek somewhere and live off water and nuts for two or three days until the ceremony and its aftermath were over. He felt a surge of adrenalin race through him as he said, 'OK, Luke. Let's do it.'

4

IN ORDER for them to get back into town and fill up with fuel and provisions, Luke had to take over the wheel. Then they had to go around town collecting containers for water and jerrycans for diesel from three different houses, and to another one for bedding and a shovel, and finally to Luke's own house where he picked up a plastic bucket full of chipped pannikins, a .22 rifle and a big cotton shopping bag with a smiling pink ice cream cone printed on the side. Several times he pulled up to chat to people at the roadside, always in language, never anything Elliot could understand. It felt like hours later when they made it to the store. While Elliot filled up the car and six jerrycans with diesel, Luke took a trolley round the supermarket part. By the time Elliot joined him he had filled two huge boxes with bread and cheese slices, tins of meat and powdered milk, packets of flour and tea and matches, a length of blue rope. Beside the boxes in the trolley was an armful of frozen kangaroo tails and half a crate of tomatoes. Elliot added two extra casks of drinking water as insurance. He offered to pay half, but Luke dismissed him with a wave and paid for everything with his bank card. Some of the food didn't make it as far as the car because Luke handed out packets and tins to a couple of people who asked for them. Even so, it seemed to Elliot like an excessive amount of provisions for two people.

Luke climbed up on top of the car and Elliot handed up the jerry cans of diesel and water and a couple of the rolls of bedding. The rest stayed inside the car, with the food supplies and their personal things. Luke took his time, tying everything down securely, making the car rock on its springs as he moved around up there. This was not at all like the trip out to Doris' country. These preparations were taking on the characteristics of an expedition.

Elliot said, 'How long are we going to be gone?' While Luke considered this he went on, 'I have to be back at work next Wednesday.'

'No worries, eh,' Luke said. 'We can get you home for your work, no problem.' He dropped down from the roof and closed the back door of the car. Elliot assumed that was it, and now they would be on their way, but Luke went over to some old men who were sitting on the concrete base of one of the fuel pumps. He started talking to them, then sat down beside them. Elliot fumed silently. His head was beginning to ache, and he realised with a flash of insight that he was craving caffeine. He went back into the store, decided once he was in there to pick up some of the kinds of food he liked to eat. There wasn't much of it in that place, but he got a few tins of beans, a block of cheese, long-life milk, some Tim Tams and a few cartons of iced coffee. At the counter, he was held up by a group of middle-aged women who were negotiating with the manager about how to buy two drums of flour with their combined basics cards. It appeared to be extremely techni-cal, insurmountable perhaps, and Elliot thought he might never have escaped from there if one of the young staff members hadn't spotted him waiting and opened up another till.

He put his own box in the back of the car. Luke saw him and got up, accompanied by two of the other men. Elliot hoped to get the keys back, but Luke passed him and swung up into the driver's seat. The other two got in the back. Elliot, a little irritably, got back into the passenger seat and handed round the iced coffees. He said, 'Are they coming with us?'

Luke said. 'No. Not those fellas.'

SOMEONE ELSE WAS, though.

'Stupid young buggers,' Luke said. 'Too much trouble. Getting into bad ways.'

They had to go and find them first, but it wasn't too difficult. There was a derelict house a short way from town. Elliot could see no clue as to its original use but plenty of evidence of its present one. There were beer tins and spirits bottles, many of them broken, scattered around the focal point of a fire, just charred embers now, the whole scene reminding him of the aftermath of an explosion.

'You know what this place is?' Luke said.

Elliot had seen places like this before. There were plenty of them on the outskirts of Alice, outside the town boundaries, outside the areas that were still prescribed, even though the blue and white signs might be gone. He said, 'Looks like a drinking camp.'

Luke said, 'You know what they saying now? More domestic violence in our communities since the intervention. More suicides too. You hear that?'

Elliot nodded. He was not the fan of the intervention he had once been. People who wanted to drink were always going to find ways to do it. The troublemakers just got tanked up outside town and then went home to traumatise their families and communities. Or they moved into urban centres such as Alice Springs or Tennant Creek, where the prohibitions did not apply and made trouble there instead.

Luke said, 'If you want to make a man angry, take away more of his power. Just keep taking it, keep taking it.' He paused and Elliot said,

'I didn't take anything.'

He had forgotten that dark, political side of Luke that had been evident the day he first met him, at the table outside the store. He sat for a moment now; they all did, in silence. Then he said, 'You stay in the car, Doctor. We get those fellas.'

Elliot waited. The realisation was dawning on him that this was not going to be the trip he had envisaged. He wondered whether there was still time to pull out; whether he could find some excuse not to go. He looked at his phone, remembered there was no coverage out there. He couldn't even fake an emergency that required him to go back to Alice.

The old house had only a couple of tin wall panels left standing. The men disappeared behind them and for a while, all Elliot could hear was quiet voices. Then, abruptly, there was a high-pitched wail and a shouting match erupted, the boys' voices husky and loud, the men's low and soft, barely audible. It didn't last long, and then everyone emerged together, the boys surrounded, bundled into the back of the car, the door slammed behind them. Elliot turned to look. One was tall, lean and leggy, far too thin. He had self-harm scars down both long arms. The other boy had clean skin, no scars that Elliot could see, a nimbus of blonde curls around his head, his face turned away. Luke heaved himself in and started the engine. They drove off, leaving the other men to walk back to town.

The stink in the car was noxious. It had taken a while, but Elliot had grown accustomed to the smell of unwashed clothes, pretty much inevitable in desert communities. This was worse; teenage musk and sour drink heavily overlaid with tobacco. It nauseated him. On top of it all, one of the boys lit a cigarette and filled the car with smoke.

Elliot put his head out of the window. He tried to summon up the resolve to take back the keys and the control of his car and his life. He couldn't find it. Some other force was in charge now, and Elliot knew that what Luke had said was true. Losing control made men angry. It was his car, at least until he handed it over to Doris, and he wanted to drive it. What made Luke think he could just take over like this? But something prevented Elliot from speaking; some sense that a different set of laws applied out here, and that he had no choice but to abide by them, whatever his own sense of justice might demand. He said nothing, and the further they got from Nyaru, the harder it became to object.

Something very similar was happening with the boys. They spoke in language and in hand signs so Elliot couldn't follow much, but he heard mention of breakfast, and then Luke gave them permission to open the stores and hand around bread and biscuits, and soon afterwards he heard mention of cigarettes, and was pleased to realise they had finished their smokes and were not going to be allowed to go back to town for more. The blonde boy began to cry quietly. The other one began to rearrange the cans and boxes in the back, folded up the rows of seats, laid out one of the swags on the floor so they could resume their sleep.

The crying and complaining stopped. The vast country unfolded itself before them, mile by mile. They turned off the back road on to a broad mine road. Luke speeded up, and the car began to ride the corrugations. There was a sense of everyone settling in, resigning themselves to the long haul ahead.

Elliot said, 'I can drive if you like.'

It was meant to be a request for the wheel of his own car, but clearly Luke didn't interpret it that way. He didn't answer, and Elliot continued to fume in silence. A dust cloud appeared on the horizon ahead of them and a few minutes later a white truck with a big green corporate logo sped past. When they emerged from its hanging dust, Luke said, 'I used to work out there. Big mine, that one.' He gestured with his chin, but there was nothing ahead that Elliot could see apart from the straight orange road running into the heat mirage on the horizon. They crossed a deep creek bed with black and white depth poles marking the sides of the road. A big red kangaroo and her joey were standing in the shade of the river gums, maybe disturbed already by the mining truck. They jumped out and set off across the plain, so much more elegant in flight than they were at ease. Luke slowed the car, as though debating whether to go after them, then speeded up again. He said,

'I been working out there fifteen years. Before I was married.'

Elliot said, 'Is the mine on your country?'

'No. We go round him.'

Elliot resigned himself to being a passenger and began to slip into a familiar state of mesmerisation, watching the vegetation, becoming fascinated by the mulga trees. They had a beautiful shape, elegantly designed to collect the slightest bit of rainfall and funnel it down to their roots. Each bush stood in its own space, isolated from its neighbours as though they had been carefully planted with exactly the amount of ground they needed so that on occasions he was reminded of an orchard.

Luke said, 'They sleeping,' and it was a while before Elliot realised he was talking about the boys and not the trees.

'Why are they coming with us?' he asked.

'Senior men, we go out on country with young people like these,' Luke said. 'Might be two times in a year. Bush camp. We show them old ways, hunting, show them ceremony. Clean up their insides with bush tucker. Clean up their spirits, too. But these two never turn up, always around Alice Springs, making trouble.' He slowed to concentrate on a piece of road that was crisscrossed with washouts; tiny streambeds created by the last heavy rain. 'Tall fella there, he's my nephew. Other one too, same skin, brother for him, he met him in town at the footy, he's living there in Alice Springs, in Little Sisters. His dad works for the council, in the parks, you know? Works hard but he's drinking, too. His mother in Port Augusta, might be, feeding the pokies. Might be she finish. No one seen her.' He glanced back over his shoulder. 'Too much trouble, that little fella. Been stealing money, stealing cars, taking drugs. His father sent him out to Nyaru, try and keep him out of trouble, but that fella too much cheeky. He can find trouble anywhere.'

Elliot looked into the back. The blonde boy's eyes were open and he was staring into space, so still and unblinking that for a moment Elliot thought he was dead. But the car bumped over a washout and both boys stirred, readjusted their limbs, closed their eyes.

Luke said, 'Good that you came today with this toyota, Elliot. Might be those fellas don't make it till the next bush camp.'

THAT DAY and the next one are present in Elliot's memory, unaccountably so, given that the days on either side of them are completely lost. He has replayed them over and over, relived them, sometimes hoping to find an entry into the absent days, sometimes looking for evidence of Dougie Nicholson's influence in the events. He cannot find either of them.

THEY TURNED off the mine road on to another yapa track that criss-crossed a winding creek for several kilometres. Then they joined another graded road, crossed a cattle grid, saw Brahman cattle and a few horses, and in the distance a dust cloud thrown up by another moving vehicle, but it must have been going in the same direction because it never came any closer. They turned off again, left the cattle and their footprints behind and soon afterwards entered a landscape made up almost entirely of termite towers. Some of them were two or three metres high, others only a few centimetres, but there were thousands of them, millions, covering a vast area of ground.

Elliot said, 'Hmm. Ant farming, eh?' But the boys were asleep, and Luke made no response, far away in his own private world.

Eventually, they left the termite territory and came into a world of parallel dunes, red and orange, with broad plains of spinifex and low scrub in between. Luke stopped and engaged the wheel-hubs, put the car in four-wheel drive for the dunes. He took a run at them, slewing around where the sand was loose, coasting gently down the other sides. The steep, slaloming climbs woke the boys and, at the next bit of decent shade, Luke stopped the car so they could all have a break. He gathered firewood and put on a billy to boil. While they stood around waiting for it, Elliot introduced himself to the boys and, following a bit of pressure from Luke, they told him their names. Luke's nephew was called Tommy, which was short for a complicated family name too alien to Elliot's ear for him to remember. The blonde kid spoke so quietly that he had to say his name three times before Elliot caught it. 'Eric. Just Eric.' He seemed guileless; he had a tightness in his breath that Elliot associated with anxiety. He was the kind of vulnerable child that awakened his recalcitrant paternal instinct. It was difficult to believe that he could be the instigator of so much trouble, and Elliot wondered whether Luke had got it wrong.

The flies were terrible, and Elliot tried to stand in the smoke. His hat and flynet were in the car, but he couldn't bring himself to put them on in front of these boys. Instead, he tried, with very limited success, to imitate their version of the Australian wave, which was sparing and elegant. They drank tea and ate bread and tinned meat and jam. The boys' appetites seemed bottomless and Elliot wasn't surprised. They had the bloodless skin of addicts, and their bones stood out. He thought that Luke could have been right to suggest they might not last until the next bush camp. It was young people like these that ended up dying of overdoses or suicide or in police custody, or in prison. Service providers sprang up throughout the territory, throughout the world, in fact, to try and help disaffected adolescents like these. It was Elliot's understanding that they absorbed a lot of funding and had limited success.

As they packed up to leave again, Elliot adopted an American accent and said, 'Well Eric, Just Eric. Looks like we're all stuck in this bus till the end of the ride.' But if Eric understood what he said, he gave no sign of it. The boys, both of them, remained withdrawn and distant throughout the day, suffering through their enforced detox, clearly very unhappy to be there. It was a kind of kidnap, Elliot supposed, and he wouldn't have been happy about it either if it had happened to him when he was a teenager.

5

THE LITTLE TRACKS they were following became fainter the further they went until finally they faded out altogether and they were driving over unmarked ground. Luke was a master of dune crossing, choosing the shortest ascents and approaching with just enough momentum to get the car to the top. Occasionally they had to make more than one attempt, and once or twice Elliot and the boys had to get out and push, but in general, even when the terrain was difficult, Luke drove the car sweetly, keeping the revs low and regular, easing it over rocky areas, treating it with respect. There was no marker, no clear change in the environment, but in the early afternoon, Luke told Elliot they had left the Tanami desert behind.

'Out of Warlpiri country now,' he said.

Soon afterwards they crested a high dune and saw, to the North, the dazzle of a salt pan. Before long there were more, all straggly outliers to a huge salt lake.

'Another one south of here,' Luke said, and he gave the local names for them. Eric, leaning over from the back, said, 'Lake Hazlett this one. Other one Lake MacKay.'

Elliot nodded, remembering how they looked from the air, those huge salt lakes. Tommy gazed ahead dreamily. Luke began to sing the country, all he could remember, he said, of the little salt pans and the features in the land between them, and the jukurrpa which connected them all. Afterwards, he fell into a silence that Elliot was reluctant to interrupt. They had come upon a faint track, and they followed it for more than an hour as it wound unerringly between the salt pans until, finally, they left them behind. When Luke turned away from the track, Elliot thought he had made a mistake; pointed out where the faint ruts were heading. Luke said,

'That one going to Balgo. My father's country this side.' And then, remembering kardiya disability, 'West. We still heading west.'

ELLIOT DISCOVERED he had burned his left arm by leaning his elbow on the open window of the car. He thought he might even things up by driving and exposing the other arm, but he was reluctant to make a scene and, in any case, he wasn't sure how well-equipped he was for the kind of terrain they were passing through now. He had driven on dirt tracks but never completely off-road like this. He dug out his bottle of sunscreen, wished he had brought more, spread it on sparingly, just on the exposed arm. He suggested driving with the windows closed and the air conditioning on, but Luke said it would use too much fuel.

If Elliot had had his wits about him, he would have reached some obvious conclusions about their trip, based on Luke's concern about fuel. They had left Nyaru with the long-distance tank full: a hundred and eighty litres. On top of the car, there were the six jerry cans Luke had borrowed from friends and relations, each of them holding twenty litres. Even at the most conservative estimate, that should take them two thousand kilometres. It wasn't the kind of distance suggested by Luke's vague information about 'the other side of the mine.' But Elliot didn't do the sums, or if he did, he didn't remember having done them. He didn't remember having any worries about being back in time for work the following Wednesday.

AS THEY TRAVELLED DEEPER into it, Elliot got the impression that they had the Great Sandy Desert in its entirety all to themselves. They saw no one, no sign of human habitation at all, though there were plenty of animal tracks, which were the only things to draw signs of animation from the boys. They stopped once to dig out a little monitor lizard, which the boys brained on a rock and stuffed into the corner of the rear footwell. They stopped another couple of times for piss breaks and to collect a certain kind of heavy firewood in places where it was plentiful, but mostly they just drove.

'Is there a waterhole anywhere?' Elliot asked, once. He had a desire that was becoming overwhelming to get the boys and their clothes into a large quantity of clean water and spread them all out to dry in the sun.

Luke said, 'Where we're going. That jila.'

'And when do we get there?'

Luke shrugged. 'Might be tomorrow.'

They ran along the edges of dry claypans and circumnavigated the densest of the spinifex forts. As the day went on they left the dune country and were back to the more familiar broad plains of mulga and saltbush. Occasionally they passed through places where the country had been burned and was regenerating, and Luke pointed out various kinds of bush foods when he saw them, but they rarely stopped to investigate. From time to time their path was crossed by dry, meandering creeks. It was in one of these that they got bogged in deep sand.

'Fuck's sake,' Elliot said, getting out and slamming the door. 'Have you actually got any idea where you're going?'

Luke laughed. Elliot said, 'Seriously, do you?'

Luke said. 'Think I don't know my own country?'

'Is this your country then?'

'Not yet. Little bit more.'

'So how do you know where we are? How do you know which way to go?'

Luke was silent for a minute or two, eyeing up some nearby trees and examining the winch mechanism. When he had succeeded in getting the hook released he appraised Elliot for a moment or two, thinking. Then he pointed to his chest, 'I got a map, Doctor. In here.'

6

In the late afternoon, they left the plains behind and entered an area of low hills and rocky outcrops. There was very little sand here, and the sound of the wheels crunching over friable sandstone set Elliot's teeth on edge. They had two spare wheels on the roof-rack. After that, they would be travelling on the rims. In the back, the boys moved things around again. Eric tapped him gently on the shoulder and handed him some biscuits. They were his biscuits, the Tim Tams he had picked up in the store. He turned, saw his provisions box open on the seat, caught himself just in time. An eruption of possessive fury would be completely incomprehensible to the others; he knew that, but all the same, he had to work hard at keeping himself under control. First it was the car, now it was his food; what else were they going to take possession of before the trip was over?

Luke stopped the car and put on the handbrake. The gesture had an air of finality about it, but everyone sat for a minute or two, savouring the stillness and silence. They had stopped in a beautiful place, with a rock wall on one side and tall desert oaks on two others. For a moment, Elliot was overawed by it, by that sense of presence again, vast, ancient, at the same time indifferent and tolerant. He remembered why it was he had wanted to come on the trip, and all the petty anxieties and irritations slid away from him.

Luke tapped the dash and said, 'Good toyota, Doctor. You got a really good one.'

They got out. Luke mooched around beneath the trees, gathering firewood. The boys sloped off and were soon out of sight, but Luke didn't seem worried. Where could they go? Elliot pulled everything out of the car, draped the lizard over a rock, spread slabs of foam and blankets out in the sun to air. He couldn't see any signs of previous camps, but he was certain there had been plenty of them there. In quiet moments, when he paused in what he was doing, he experienced a strange sense of familiarity with the place, intimacy even, and the closeness of that presence again, the intangible essence of the land.

Glad to have something to do, he reorganised the supplies, repacked all the food into two boxes, handed over the empty one to Luke for lighting the fire. The boys reappeared, shuffling back through the trees, and Luke called to them, a little irritably. They came over to the car and began to gather up the swags. Tommy picked up Elliot's, the only custom-made one, a green canvas outer with a built-in mattress and fly-mesh. Elliot said,

'That's mine.'

Tommy turned to Eric, who nodded and continued over towards the rock wall, where he and Tommy began laying the beds out in a line. There seemed to be some disagreement about the positioning of them, and after a while, Elliot went over and reclaimed his from its position at one end of the line. 'I'll probably sleep over that side,' he said, indicating a nice flat place beyond the car, beneath the trees. But Tommy shook his head and tried to take the swag back.

Luke came over to join them. 'Men sleeping on the outside,' he said. 'Boys inside. Traditional way for our people.'

Elliot turned away to hide his irritation, found his attention taken by a tiny whirlwind, a willy-willy crossing the plain below, appearing and disappearing as it lost its cargo of red dust and then picked up another one. From nowhere a thought arose in his mind, that human life was like that; particles of matter picked up by an invisible engine, held together for as long as possible, then dropped back to the earth. The thought surprised him. He didn't believe in concepts of the soul, but what other explanation was there for the engine he envisaged? He looked at the others. They were watching it too, and he turned back, followed it until it disappeared completely and left the landscape still again, and silent. Luke and the boys entered into a long discussion, possibly an argument, since all their voices were raised well above the normal volume level. It ended with the swags being laid out in a new formation.

This time Elliot's was one of the inner ones. He knew why without being told. It was clear from the positioning of the swags that one of the boys, presumably Tommy, had been initiated, and as such he was considered to be a man. Elliot, on the other hand, was not. A patient had said it to him once,

'Kardiya don't know nothing. They got no law. They like children, never grow up.' She had laughed, and he had laughed with her, but he didn't find it quite so funny now.

He walked away from the camp, aware of how fast night could fall, aware too that one thing he had left off his list and forgotten to pack was a torch. He would like to have had one now, and for later, in case anything happened during the night.

Such as what, though? What was likely to happen during the night? Devil-devils?

The walk, the hour on his own in the rich light of dusk, was revelatory. He had arrived into Nyaru full of his own importance: a hero on a mission, a man with money and influence, but his status was entirely different now. He was the ignorant, runty little kid that nobody liked, but they had to let him play because he was the one who owned the ball. He was there because he had arrived at just the right time, in possession of a high clearance four-wheel drive.

But even that uncomfortable insight couldn't change the way he felt about the country. As soon as he was out of earshot of the camp, he was better, soothed by the evening sun, the soft glow of red sand and stone. He could, and would, put up with anything for interludes like this. On foot, wandering aimlessly, he saw thousands of details that were missed in a moving car. There was evidence of life everywhere, tracks of reptiles and insects, plant life hanging on to cracks in the rock, a solitary ghost gum high on the crag, almost bonsaied by the effort of staying alive.

By the time he got back, he was in a light, even high, frame of mind. There was a change in the mood among the others as well. Tommy had come out of his sulk and was joking loudly with Luke as they tended the fire. Eric was quieter, but he had a smile for Elliot as he returned, revealing a missing tooth. Luke had said both boys were fifteen, but Eric looked a lot younger. He was smaller, slighter, and the blonde in his hair was of the kind that generally darkened or grew out when kids reached puberty. If Elliot had encountered him at a clinic, he would have put his age at around twelve.

As night fell, everyone drew in closer to the fire. Elliot turned down a share of the lizard, much to Tommy's amusement, but he devoured half a kangaroo tail and helped the others finish another loaf and a half of the white bread that Luke had brought. The boys made short work of the last iced coffees.

The night wasn't all that cold, but Luke and Tommy took burning logs from the main fire and made little ones between the sleepers, each with a pile of sticks beside it so it could be kept burning throughout the night. The fires made Elliot uneasy because he had treated people for burns caused by rolling on to fires like them in the night, but Luke said only drunk people did that, and Elliot had to admit that he was probably right. He had seen fire scars on a lot of the older people, on their limbs and torsos, caused by rolling on live coals when they were little, but he rarely saw serious burns on children now, or on sober adults. And when he finally climbed into his swag, he was surprised by how comfortable and safe he felt in that line, and he didn't mind at all not being on the outside.

Luke told a story that made Eric laugh, but Tommy kept missing bits and asking for them to be repeated. It wasn't the first time Elliot noticed that he wasn't completely on the ball, and he wondered whether he had a learning disability of some kind. It might explain him hanging around with Eric, who appeared to be so much younger. When the story was over, Luke began it again, in English, for Elliot, but Elliot was gazing up at the stars and listening to the desert oaks, which were calling over like nursemaids, saying 'shhhhhhh, shhhhhhhhh', and Luke's voice became a gentle echo in his ears, and he fell asleep long before the story reached its punch line.

He woke to the sound of Eric whimpering in his sleep. He spoke gently to him and he quietened, but after a while, he started again. Sometimes Luke spoke to him as well, his voice deep and calm. Once Elliot woke for no reason that he could remember, and he looked over at Eric and saw his eyes were wide open, the blaze of the Milky Way reflected in them.

7

ELLIOT WOKE ONCE MORE in the night and for a moment he thought he had gone blind. He sat up, searching the sky for stars, found a patch at last, and then another. There was thick cloud up there, moving fast, but it was gone by the time Luke roused the camp at first light, and the sky was white, turning blue. He had already got the main fire going and the billy was on the boil. The boys coughed like miners and were slow to get up, but Elliot thought they looked better already.

The defrosted kangaroo tails would not last another day, so they cooked them and had them for breakfast. Afterwards, they drank more tea, sticky with sugar, while they packed up and loaded the car. As Elliot made to get into the passenger seat, he felt a hand on his arm, firm but gentle, and Tommy edged past him and got in first. He shunted over, so skinny he took up less than a third of the double seat and Elliot had plenty of room to get in. But it was different; like the positioning of the swags, it was a statement of a shift in the dynamic. It left Eric alone in the back where he began the day lying on the pile of foam and blankets, staring at the roof of the car.

'When will Eric get initiated?' Elliot asked.

Luke said, 'I don't know. Might be his father got some idea for him. Send him back to school, might be.'

'Does he want to be initiated? Do you, Eric?' Eric shrugged. Elliot went on, 'Can't you do it, Luke?'

Luke shook his head. 'Wrong skin for that, wrong family, wrong everything.'

They drove on into the west, the sweet chug of the engine lulling them all into a drowsy silence, but when they came to more dunes and began another series of crazy crossings, Elliot became uneasy.

'Is it much further, Luke?' he said. 'Are you sure we'll be home in time?'

'Don't worry, Elliot,' Luke said.

'But you have a meeting as well, don't you?' Elliot said.

Luke was silent for a few long moments, then he said, 'They never listen to us. Kardiya. All them meetings after the intervention. Tell us to talk, say what we think, say what our communities need. Then they take no notice. Do what they was always going to do, whatever they want, put in their shires and their business managers. Waste of time, those meetings. We stopped going.' He turned to Elliot, expecting a response that Elliot couldn't provide, then he went on, 'Now they got some new idea for consultation. More meetings. More talk. You think I should hurry back for that, Elliot?'

What Elliot wanted to say was that he didn't care either way about Luke's meeting, but that he had work to do, and had to be back, no two ways about it. But he couldn't think of a way of saying it that didn't sound confrontational. So he said nothing.

Eric sat up, made gritty sandwiches with cheese and tinned meat that they ate on the road. Tommy pointed to a long range of low, steep-sided hills and said, in English, 'Kangaroo wall.'

Elliot said, 'Eh?'

'Kangaroo wall. Old people build it. Keep all the kangaroos inside.'

In the back, Eric giggled, and Luke laughed as well, but Elliot sucked his tongue and turned to look out of the window. It was a wind-up and he braced himself for more of them, but they didn't come. In fact, it seemed as though the others were making more of an effort to include him, speaking in English as often as not. He appreciated it.

The dunes, deeply, darkly orange, seemed endless. There was more spinifex, sometimes very thick, and there were low stands of wiry shrubs, much tougher than they looked. On a couple of occasions, it became impossible for the car to pass through, and Luke had to reverse and find a way around. Occasionally he got out and surveyed the country, took new bearings according to signs invisible to Elliot, but mostly he just drove, singing to the car, the car singing back to him.

Shortly before midday they got their first puncture. Everyone had a theory about what caused it, and it seemed that they all had to be examined and discussed before anything was done. Elliot realised he had no idea where the jack was, or even whether the car had one, but the boys soon found it under the seats in the back, and there was a tin box in there too, with all kinds of other useful things: a wrench with some loose socket-heads, a plastic bag full of tent pegs, a folding camp-shovel which looked nearly new, a greasy tin of WD40, everything tangled up with frayed tow rope, bits of twine and electric wire. In the bottom was a thin sediment of small, loose things: screws and nuts and fuses.

Luke took the jack, Eric grabbed the wheel brace, Tommy pulled out the long jack handle from under the boxes. Elliot wanted to help, but whenever he thought of what needed to be done next, someone else had thought of it first. Tommy was up on the roof, throwing down branches to Luke, who was trying to build a stable platform on the sand to hold the jack. Inches from his head, Eric was bouncing on the wheel brace, pulling himself up with the help of the roof-rack and coming back down with all his weight. He had rolled up his sweatpants to keep them out of the way, and his calves were so long and so incredibly skinny that Elliot was terrified the continued impacts would break them. But Eric was enjoying himself, and he was succeeding, too. Only one of the nuts needed Luke's extra weight to shift.

Tommy heaved a spare wheel over the edge of the roof rack and Elliot found something useful to do at last. He stood it up and wheeled it around to the others. The first jack platform crumbled, and Luke went up on to the roof-rack to find better materials. Flies mobbed them. The heat was ferocious. Elliot rolled down his sleeves, got out his bottle of sunscreen and put a thin layer over his face and ears. Both boys were in singlets, and he offered it to them. It felt to him like a generous offer, since there was no way that small bottle would last them the trip. But Tommy shrugged and Eric shook his head.

'You people can get skin cancer as well, you know,' Elliot said. 'I've seen it plenty of times.'

But the boys just looked away, saving him the embarrassment of their ridicule.

Luke threw down some stronger bits of wood, and after a couple more failed attempts the construction held, and the wheels were changed over. They were not long on the road again when Luke stopped the car, and he and the boys engaged in a discussion in language about some tracks leading up the side of a dune. Then Tommy shoved Elliot out again, and for a moment he thought he was going to be included in the excitement, but they didn't want him. They took the wheel-brace and the long-handled shovel, and headed off up the dune at surprising speed.

'Perentie,' Luke said. 'Big one.' He sat in silence for a minute, then went on. 'They want to take my gun. I said no. Catch him old way. Dig him out and bash him.'

Elliot refilled his water bottle and noted that the second of the ten-litre water casks was feeling pretty light. There were two more left, and then they were down to whatever was in the can on top of the car. Elliot hadn't seen where Luke had got the water to fill it. It might be safe to drink and it might not, but he hoped they wouldn't have to test it. If anyone got an attack of diarrhoea out here they would die of dehydration.

Elliot sat in the tiny patch of shade created by his open door. He said, 'Is it much further, Luke?'

'Not far now. Little bit more.'

'It's just that I'm worried about water. There isn't much left.'

'Plenty water in that place,' Luke said. 'Jila. Always water there. Just maybe I have to clean it out, that waterhole.'

Elliot didn't like the sound of it. 'Are you sure, Luke? Because if you're wrong…'

For a moment, Luke said nothing. Flies were trying to crawl into his eyes and his mouth, but he didn't seem to be aware of them. At last, in a voice that shook with restrained anger, he said, 'You think I bring those two out here to let them die?'

'Ah, no…'

'I know my country, Doctor. Plenty water in that place.'

8

ELLIOT HAS no memory of telling Luke the story of the paintings and the car, or of making any mention of Doris or Linda. If Luke had any curiosity about why Elliot had come rocking up out of the dust on a Saturday morning in a clean new car, he never expressed it. It's possible that they had that conversation on one of the later days, the ones that are missing from his memory, but he considers it unlikely. He couldn't imagine any context in which he would have begun to explain the business with the paintings, and because of all the complexities in it —the fact that he hadn't sold them to buy the car; their dubious status with regard to Dougie Nicholson; his secret, impossible infatuation with Linda—it wouldn't have been something he was at all keen to talk about. So, to all intents and purposes, it was his car. Although, in view of what happened to it later, it made little or no difference.

9

UNABLE TO STAND the flies any longer, Elliot dug out his hat and its fly net, not caring what he looked like. There was about forty centimetres of shade on his side of the car and he sat in it, his back against the front wheel. Soon afterwards Luke joined him and sat against the back wheel. They waited. The flies swarmed over them. They were both asleep when the boys came back, carrying a sand goanna nearly two metres long; the biggest Elliot had ever seen, and maybe Luke too, from the strength of his initial reaction. The boys were pumped and breathless. Luke was quietly delighted.

ELLIOT HAD no idea of how far they travelled that day, but it was probably not as far as it seemed, because their progress was so slow. It was exhausting, going over that kind of terrain. The car tilted one way and then another and the passengers swayed with it, constantly adjusting their centres of balance. Elliot braced both feet against the dash, which helped a bit. It was worse in the back, but Eric still managed to make more sandwiches and hand them round. They had deep thumbprints, in which Elliot imagined he could see wheel-nut grease and lizard blood. He ate them anyway and fretted about the rapidly diminishing supplies.

There was a big bag of potatoes, still unopened, and that enormous lizard in the back, bleeding on to his bag the last time he looked, but they were nearly at the end of the bread and tinned meat, and he experienced a momentary fury with Luke for not managing things better, for letting the boys help themselves whenever they felt like it and mowing through the provisions so fast.

But between the bouts of anxiety, Elliot was lulled by the country and remembered that this was the drive he had been dreaming of. As they passed through it, the country changed, sometimes gradually, sometimes suddenly and surprisingly. They entered a place with more claypans, all empty and dry, but with greener vegetation around them as though there had been rain here recently. Luke stopped beside a sad little tree and scuffed around in the dust beneath it. There were seeds there, but they were all dried up and black, and Luke threw them aside, disappointed. In another place they stopped for bush onions, spending an hour digging up a double handful, which they saved in a pannikin for cooking later on, but mostly they drove, so slowly that Elliot developed the impression that their flies were following them like faithful pets, waiting to greet them ecstatically next time they got out.

In the mid-afternoon, back in dune country, Luke pulled up on a grassy crest and got out. He walked away from the car, stopping now and then and orientating himself, and then he took a cigarette lighter from his shirt pocket and set fire to the spinifex. Flames bloomed and raced along the dry stalks, crackling and hissing, sending up a huge cloud of thick, dark smoke. Luke waited, watching the horizon, until the flames died down. Then he got back into the car and drove on.

'Tell them we're coming,' Eric explained, leaning over the seat, picking grass stalks out of Elliot's hair.

'Are there people there?' Elliot said.

'Not people,' Eric said. 'Spirit of that jila. Taking care of it.'

Elliot turned towards Luke for clarification, but he was looking straight ahead, concentrating on the terrain, or on something else that Elliot could not divine. Twice more they stopped to light the spinifex, and the last time, Luke called out across the dunes. Elliot was mildly embarrassed, as he always was by any suggestion of the supernatural.

He glanced at the boys to see what they might be thinking, but their expressions were inscrutable. He still had no idea how Luke was navigating. If there was anything in the landscape that could act as a landmark, it was way too subtle for his uneducated eye.

Finally, in a broad hollow at the conjunction of two dunes, Luke stopped the car and turned off the engine. The place looked to Elliot like a hundred others they had traversed that day, but this, apparently, was it. Tommy was reaching across him to open the door, and he slid out before he began to climb over him. Luke got out and spoke to the boys in language. Something he said clearly displeased Tommy, who argued loudly with him for a while, then retreated into a sullen silence. Eric shinned up the ladder to the roof-rack. Luke said to Elliot, 'You mob stay here and make a fire.' He indicated the crest of the dune. 'Don't go up there. Don't come looking for me. You understand that?'

Elliot said, 'You don't want us looking behind that hill? What is it you don't want us to see?'

Luke gathered the things he needed, which included the shovel, the wheel brace, the bucket with a couple of empty milk tins in it and the bag with the smiley pink ice cream cone, from the top of which the blades of two boomerangs emerged. He said, 'I come back for you,' and disappeared over the shoulder of the dune.

Elliot turned to Tommy and shrugged, but Tommy was looking at the firewood Eric was throwing down, and clearly finding fault with it. He spoke in language, angrily, and Eric came down and Tommy went up. Eric picked up a few pieces of wood and began walking towards a sheltered spot below the lip of the declivity, and Elliot made to help, but again Tommy wasn't happy. He complained, in a voice heavy with disdain. He was looking at Eric as he spoke, but Elliot felt himself included and experienced a flush of anger. He said. 'Speak English.'

Tommy was slight but he was incredibly strong. He picked up a heavy branch and hurled it down. Elliot was much too far from the car to be in any danger, but the wood was unmistakably aimed in his direction. Tommy said, 'Over there. Fire is that side.'

Elliot met the furious gaze blazing down on him from above and, initiation or no initiation, decided not to play. He dropped the wood he was holding and went over to the back of the car. Luke's voice carried from the other side of the dune, calling out, and he turned in response, but Eric was shaking his head. Whoever Luke was calling, it wasn't any of them.

The reorganisation after the day's journey was Elliot's job, and one he enjoyed. It calmed him and, now that he was no longer involved in their fire-building, the boys seemed calmer, too, moving with their usual energy-saving grace, communicating almost entirely by hand signals. When the repacking was finished, he stood and watched the others for a while, but he was gasping for a cup of tea, anything with caffeine in it, so he got the water-can down from the roof, filled the billy and took it over to the fire. Under Tommy's stern supervision, Eric was scorching the skin of the goanna, lugging it this way and that, turning it over. The fire was long and narrow, quite different from the one on the previous night, and it was still burning too fiercely for Elliot to get close, but when Eric was finished with the goanna, he pushed a few small pieces to one side and deftly created a little bed of coals for the billy. It was like an indulgence given to a small child to keep him happy while the adults got on with the real business, but if Tommy disapproved he didn't show it. And when the billy boiled and the tea was made and poured and handed around with the last packet of glued-together Tim Tams, Tommy's mood lightened; he gave Elliot a rare smile and it felt as though they might be a team again.

When the tea was finished, the boys went back to work on the fire. The flames had died down and the wood was all glowing heart. The boys swept it to one side with some of the greener branches, then dug out a long pit with the billy and the little camp shovel. Eric dragged the lizard over and packed it in there, curling its tail around for a better fit, and then the hot sand and coals were pushed back over it. The mood in the camp was entirely different now; the boys larked around and laughed as they worked. Elliot left them to it and mooched across the hollow. After a while, Eric joined him.

'Very old place,' he said. His hands described the shape of the hollow in the dunes where they stood. There was grass growing up one side of the bowl and a small stand of acacias close to one edge. 'People coming here for thousands of years.' As they walked around, he began to point out the evidence. There were a few old flaking bones, some branches so ancient they were little more than papery tubes, a rusty fish tin, its winder key still attached. Near the trees was a flat stone with a declivity worn in the middle. Eric said, 'Women make it.' He picked up a smaller stone, a round one, and demonstrated grinding. 'Making damper,' he said.

LUKE CAME around the hill and called for Tommy, but Tommy didn't hear him. Eric had to alert him with hand signals, so he turned and saw Luke, and Luke spoke to him with more hand signals. He got up eagerly and ran across the sand. Elliot watched him go, annoyed and ashamed that it should have taken him this long to work out that Tommy was practically deaf. He saw it in nearly every clinic he took, the long-term damage caused by ear infections, and yet he hadn't spotted it in Tommy. He said to Eric, 'What's going on?'

Eric said, 'Cleaning out that jila. Only for initiated men.'

'Really? So we can't help?'

'Later we can go. When the water comes.'

Elliot waited a moment, then said, 'You think the water will come?'

Eric said, 'It's a jila. Means there is always water there.'

Elliot tried to make him out. He seemed to be a smart kid, and his English was better than either of the others, possibly because he grew up in Alice Springs and not out in the bush. Looking at his yellow-blonde mop, it was hard for Elliot to believe what Tommy had implied; that Eric was the one leading Tommy astray, not the other way round. But maybe Tommy's hearing impairment explained it.

As though he was aware of Elliot's attention, Eric turned and smiled, the lost tooth adding to his child-like charm. 'Bush onions,' he said. 'We forgot.'

'So we did,' said Elliot. 'You have to show me how to cook them.'

10

When Luke and Tommy came back at sunset, they didn't look like people returning from a successful enterprise. Both of them were bare-chested, carrying their shirts, both of them had sand up to their shoulders, so red in the setting sun that for a moment they looked like a pair of butchers. Luke put the bucket and the tools down beside the car. Elliot, always anxious about the whereabouts of the wheel brace, checked that it had come back, and saw that the shovel handle was broken near the neck. He couldn't imagine what they had been doing on the other side of the dune, and later, after they had eaten, Luke explained. He stoked up a bit of light from the fire and drew the jila in the sand. It lay at one end of a deep claypan, a hole in the rock that went a long way down to meet a permanent spring. The drawing reminded Elliot of the plughole in a bath. It reminded him too, with its lines and circles in the sand, of some of the artworks he had seen in town.

'Old days, people come here every year,' Luke said. 'They been living here that time. Keep that jila open, little bit digging him out every year. Sand in him now, all filled up. No one keep him open any more.'

Elliot didn't know what to think or feel. He was aware that there was an element of historic tragedy in what Luke was telling him, but his primary concern was whether or not they were going to find water. As well as that, he was worried about Luke's appearance. His skin was grey in the firelight and his hands were covered in weeping blisters. His movements had become stiff; he looked ten years older than he had when he set out over the dune that afternoon. It was unlikely that he got much exercise in the normal course of events, and trying to empty a bottomless hole full of sand was not a recommended way of easing into a new regime. If he took ill, they were all done for, water or no water.

He was saying, 'My people all up Kimberley way now. Not many of us left. Only a few of those old people speaking our language now. Sometimes we try and make a plan, you know? We got obligations to this place.'

'Didn't happen, eh?' said Elliot. 'I know how it is.'

'People all got too much problems,' said Luke. 'One brother working, another one in prison, too many of our old people got sick now. Too sick for that big journey, you know?'

Elliot nodded. He said, 'Well, I don't mind helping. Can't me and Eric be honorary men, just for the sake of getting down to the water?'

He wasn't sure whether Luke understood him. The look he was giving him suggested he didn't, and he realised it was his attitude and not his words that were incomprehensible. He thought about what Luke had said, realised he was describing the dying-out of his people, searched for a way of backtracking, but it was already too late. Luke was moving on. He said, 'We get there, no problem. Tomorrow we dig him out.'

Elliot finished his tea and scrubbed out his pannikin with a handful of ashes and sand. He said, 'Well, I'm sorry about your people, Luke. Sorry your plans haven't worked out, but at least we're here now. Can I suggest that we take more care with what's left of the water? Maybe ration it. Just in case.'

Luke said something in language and stood up. Elliot turned to Eric, aware as he did so that a new relationship was forming with the boy, partly based on their inferior status in the group, partly on his facility with language. 'What did he say?'

'He says we don't need ration. He says country will look after us.'

Later they made a windbreak from mulga branches, and when they were lined up in their swags beside it, Luke said, 'Those two Jangalas, they know where we are.'

'Is that the old guys?' Elliot said. 'The ones who came with us to find the boys?'

'Yuwayi. Those old fellas. They worry for us if we don't come back.'

'When?'

'Wednesday.'

'And what will they do, if we don't come back? How will they get us out?'

Luke shifted on his foam mattress. 'Might be Friday, I tell them. Might be Friday they look for us. If they remember.'

In the quiet of the night, Elliot could hear Tommy's light snores. He said, 'Maybe we should start back tomorrow, eh?'

But Luke didn't answer.

11

ELLIOT REMEMBERS THE DREAM. He was in the trenches, and he was trying to fill skin bags with water for the troops, but the bags had a one-way valve which only allowed water out, not back in again. He realised they were the foil bags from water-casks, and while he was wondering whether they had been invented yet, the artillery started up and he was being splashed with hot blood.

He gasped and opened his eyes. The boys were already on their feet and he joined them before he was fully awake. Another crash of thunder ripped through the sky, and then another. In the brilliant lightning-flash between them, Elliot saw the boys dragging their bundled bedding towards the car, Luke getting to his feet, his face distorted by pain.

Elliot said, 'Are you OK?' Balls of rain were exploding in his eyes.

'Get in the car,' Luke said, and Elliot grabbed his swag and ran. The boys had the back door held open for him and he flung himself in and pulled it closed just as Luke opened the driver's side and hauled himself in.

'Are you in pain? Elliot asked him.

'I'm really sore,' Luke said. 'Too much digging.'

The noise of the rain on the roof was deafening, and the next thunderclap hit the car like a physical impact. Elliot flinched and the boys whooped, but Luke was laughing.

'This your ration, Doctor,' he said. 'Mine coming next.'

For a few more minutes the storm assaulted them, then it passed over, moving slowly off across the country, grumbling and lashing out randomly like a cranky old drunk. The temperature, which had plummeted during the rain, began to rise again and with it came the stench of all the dirty, sweaty clothes and bedding, amplified by the damp. Elliot was aware that his own shirt was making a significant contribution. He wanted to get out, but there was nowhere to go. The ground outside was sodden and he could still hear water trickling down the car's gutters and dripping underneath it. There was no cover anywhere.

'What did the old people do?' he asked Luke.

'Might be in a cave,' he said. 'Good place, that. East from here, little bit. Next time, we go that way. Old paintings there still.'

Despite everything, Elliot found he was up for it. 'I'll come, definitely. Yes.'

Luke was quiet for a moment, then he laughed softly. 'Might be some time they get wet, too, those old people.'

For a while, they sat in the dark and listened to the drips and trickles slowing down, like fading music. Then the boys began to move things around, pulling down the folding seats and lying down along them, one on each side of the car. The stars were back, and there was just enough light for Elliot to see Tommy drag his overnight bag out from behind the front seat to use as a pillow. Peevishly he pulled it away and dropped it on the floor at his own end, near the door.

The space was cramped but Elliot managed to create a platform to lie on, with the boxes at one end and his rolled-up swag under his torso at the other. When he finally got half-way comfortable, he lay awake, listening to the car dripping and Luke snoring in the front, and Eric whimpering in his sleep, and then the sound of a new storm rolling over and the whole dramatic performance replaying itself again, and again, and again throughout the night. But he got some kind of sleep in patches here and there, and when he woke it was because the car was heating up and his nose had started to bleed.

He sat up and groped among the things in his bag for something he could sacrifice. He had one clean shirt in there and a singlet. He wriggled out of his smelly shirt and used that to mop himself up a bit, then leaned his head back against the door, closed his eyes and pinched his nose. He waited, swallowing the blood as it backed up into his throat, fending off nightmare imaginings of bleeding to death in the middle of nowhere. Gradually it slowed. He opened his eyes, found Eric watching him with wide eyes.

'Dose bleed,' he said, and Eric nodded and sat up. Tommy was still sleeping. Elliot tentatively removed the shirt from his face, holding his breath as he waited for the flow to start again, letting it out when it didn't. He was light-headed, though, and moved slowly and carefully, twisting around so he could open the back door and let himself out.

The world was wet and steaming. Luke had left barefoot prints in the sand. A few sets came and went from the car, and Elliot found his trainers among the rest of the shoes, all upside-down on the bonnet, left there to dry. The billy and pannikins were up there too, all of them half-filled with rainwater. He drank half the contents of one of the cups and used the rest to wash the sticky blood off his face and chest. The water was already warm, but it was sweet and fresh.

Elliot looked for more of Luke's prints and found them, heading towards the shoulder of the dune and the jila beyond. Behind him, he heard the boys coughing, then Tommy emerging from the car, speaking too loudly to Eric. He had opened one of Elliot's tins of bean and was eating them straight from the can with his fingers. When he saw that Luke had gone without him, he grew anxious, poured the rest of the beans into his mouth and took off after him.

Directly above them the sky was clear, but there were heavy clouds on three sides and Elliot was not optimistic about the rains being over. He had thought it might keep the flies away, but it didn't. If anything, they had multiplied. There were clouds of them over the firepit, where some of the bony remains of the lizard had been disinterred by pounding rain, and his bloody shirt, discarded beside the wheel of the troopy, was black and gruesomely animate. He waved them away as he got into his clean shirt and put sunscreen on his face and ears. He tried to resist the fly-net but he couldn't, and once, as he passed along the side of the car, he got a glimpse of himself in the wing mirror, looking like some weird alien insect-man in his wrap-around reflective sunnies and his green gossamer veil. It made him aware that, no matter how much he might want to, he didn't belong out there and never would.

He went over to the side of the hollow where the wattles grew and pissed there, with his back to the camp. The heavy rain had exposed other things; more old cans, an enamel pannikin with the bottom rusted out, all evidence of continuous visits to the place. Until when, though? How long was it since someone from Luke's family had made it out here? How many years of silt were in that waterhole?

From where he stood Elliot could see across the plain, the way they had come. It didn't look much different, but there were gleams of wet from a few of the claypans, and it occurred to Elliot that it might not be so easy to get home. Up here the rain had just compacted the sand: in some places, there was a wet crust that broke when it was walked on, the sand still dry underneath. But down there the water would not drain so fast. The claypans would turn into mud. There was every chance the car would get bogged. He looked over at the high part of the dune, behind which, somewhere, Luke and Tommy must have been digging now through heavy wet sand and mud. He hoped Luke had factored in the possibility of rain. He hoped he would get him back to Alice by Wednesday.

Was that possible? For several minutes he was unable to work out what day it was. Already, in such a short time, his unquestioned, cast-iron grasp on the calendar was slipping. He couldn't remember which day they had left Nyaru, nor how many nights they had spent on the road, and though he eventually worked out that it must be Monday, he found it almost impossible to believe. It was both too much and too little time for them to have been travelling. Too much, because it was already impossible for him to be back in Alice Springs by Wednesday, unless he got a lift in a helicopter. Too little because so much had happened out here, so many miles covered, impressions formed, assumptions turned on their heads.

He would have to phone them in CAHS and let them know. He had gone three steps towards the car before he remembered that there was no signal here. Time and again over the next few hours he went through the same mental process; the instinctive decision to phone, the realisation that he couldn't. There would be people expecting a clinic and it wouldn't happen. He would have a blemish on his record: a no-show without warning or explanation. Would they try and contact him? Would someone report him missing? No one from Alice knew he was here. As far as he was aware, none of his connections even knew he had gone to Nyaru, except maybe the man who sold him the car, but who would think of asking him? It was crazy. He had been completely irresponsible to come out here with Luke. What had he been thinking of?

Eric emerged from the car. He found the water on the bonnet and drank the contents of the billy, then picked up the empty beans tin and wiped the inside clean with his fingers for the last of the sauce. When he spotted Elliot over by the trees, he joined him there.

'No breakfast,' he said.

'No,' said Elliot. 'There might be some cheese left. Maybe we could get a fire going and make some damper?'

'Little bit wet, I think,' Eric said. 'More rain coming too. We can try it.'

There was more rain coming, and they sheltered in the car while it pummelled the ground all around, ran down the sloping sides of the declivity, making a soggy patch in the centre, near where the fire had been. Undoubtedly it would be putting more inches in the claypans Elliot had seen from the side of the hill.

He said, 'Fuck it. Will we be able to get home?'

Eric shook his head. 'Not today. Not tomorrow. After that, might be.'

'I need to be back for work. What about you? Do you have anything to get back for?'

Eric didn't answer that. Instead, he said, 'What skin are you?'

'I'm a whitefella. You know that. We don't have skins.'

'Lot of whitefellas have skin names. I think you are Japanangka, same like Luke. Father for me and Tommy.'

226

'I thought Luke was Tommy's uncle.'

'Same. Father's brother. Same skin.'

Elliot said, 'I don't think I need a skin name, Eric. I think it would make things complicated for me.'

Eric turned his face away, and any answer he gave was lost in a new crash of thunder.

Elliot said, 'You're a smart kid, Eric. Why don't you go back and finish school? You're not old enough to leave yet anyway.'

Eric didn't answer and, as though he was really looking at him for the first time, Elliot saw the dark roots in his hair and understood that he had been taken in by an illusion; that Eric's true blonde had grown out years ago, if he ever had it, and that his hair colour came out of a bottle. He was formulating a careful question, about why he would want to appear younger than he was in a society where most young men wanted to look mature, when all hell erupted in the atmosphere, and they raced once again for the car.

12

IT RAINED LONG AND HARD, bucketing down for an hour or more, making far too much din on the car's roof for any kind of conversation. Elliot expected the others to come back, but they didn't. When it finally ended and the sun returned, Elliot and Eric got out of the car and began trying to dry the firewood, stacking some of it in crooked wigwams to let the air get at it, the rest in the car away from any future downpours. The billy and the pannikins were nearly full again. They drank water and ate some cheese, then went back to the wattles, where Eric began to gather more firewood, lighter than the thick mulga sticks they had gathered along the way.

Elliot gazed out over the plains. There was water lying everywhere. The claypans were shining now.

Elliot shook his head. 'What are we going to do?'

As if in answer, a sound came to them from the other side of the dune: a rhythmic clacking that Elliot couldn't immediately identify.

'Boomerang,' Eric said, miming the action of two objects being knocked together.

Luke started to sing, his voice light, tenor, carrying clearly across the distance.

'He's singing that place.' Eric dropped his kindling, stretched his arms out beside him and bent his knees, then began to dance, making stiff jumps, stamping his feet.

'What does it mean? Have they cleared the jila?'

Eric shrugged. 'All the little kids learn dancing. But we don't know the law.'

He danced again, in the traditional way Elliot had seen many times at festival occasions in town. But as he went on, the dance began to change in subtle ways, becoming more fluid, more modern. Elliot stared, mesmerised, aware that he was watching an exceptional talent, but unsure why he knew that. There was unleashed power in Eric, the sense that he wasn't following the rhythm but creating it. And then, suddenly, with the ceremonial chanting going on unchanged, Eric stopped, looked out over the country and said,

'Maybe we have to stay here for a few days.'

Elliot said, 'A few days?'

'Yeah, might be,' said Eric. 'Or could be a week.'

Elliot lost it. He raved and swore and kicked over the carefully constructed piles they had made of the firewood.

Eric came running after him, his arms full of sticks. He said, 'Don't worry, Doctor. I can make a little fire. I can make you some tea.'

Elliot didn't answer him. He turned his back, was aware of Eric moving around, the smell of smoke, the hissing and spitting of damp wood, the clank of the billy. The sounds from the ceremony behind the dune came to an end, and soon afterwards Luke and Tommy appeared, trudging back across the wet sand. Elliot half expected them to be painted up but they were clean, their skin glistening in the sun. They were happy, and Elliot knew he should leave it, but he couldn't help himself. He launched his pent-up anger at Luke.

'Glad to see you're so pleased with yourself. Do you realise we can't drive out of here now? It's insane, Luke. What were you thinking of, bringing us out here into the middle of nowhere?'

Luke stared at him, stunned by the outburst, then turned his gaze away. From the corner of his eye, Elliot could see Eric making subtle hand signals for Tommy. The silence was ominous. It went on too long, and Elliot was aware of Luke's size and strength, and the intensity of the rage in him, bottled up over the years and the decades. Then Eric, with the practiced care of someone well-accustomed to defusing dangerous situations, walked over and bent down, began to draw in the sand. He drew circles within circles, he drew lines that radiated out and made connections to more circles, and more beyond those. He spoke to Luke in language, questioning him, and Luke began breathing again, responded, pointed, and Eric wiped out some of his drawings and replaced them, extended the map, eliciting the names of those ancient places. Luke stepped closer, leaving Elliot looking at his broad shoulders, lumpy with sorry scars. He pointed to the biggest set of circles in Eric's map and said, quietly, 'My father was born here. That old man jila been taking care of my people for all of our history, you know? Might be nowhere to you, Doctor, but this place is not nowhere to me.'

PART IV

1

THAT'S where Elliot's clear memories end. After that, he can only find fragments, and even then he is never entirely sure which are genuine and which are illusionary. No matter how hard he tries, he can't retrieve the lost days, nor can he work out how long they were stranded at the jila or how many days it took them to get back. He has a date for admission to Adelaide, but no date for when he left home. His phone is gone, and with it all his contacts in Alice. Even if it wasn't, he couldn't have phoned anyone. His voice is still not under his control.

2

─────────

Sandra's retirement in Adelaide lasts about three days. She tells Elliot she has been longing to have time on her hands, just to sit around and read, or wander into town for a coffee, but when she finally gets it, she can't stand it. She has underestimated her attachment to the community in Nyaru and is missing her friends there. She finds Adelaide one-dimensional. Time drags. So she takes a part-time job in the hospital, which works, she says, in the way nicotine patches work for smokers.

She fills in any of Elliot's gaps she can. Luke had been brought to Adelaide as well, also with a head injury, but nothing as bad as Elliot's. He had gone home after a few days. The boys had cuts and bruises that were treated in the A&E in Alice. Sandra says she hasn't seen either of them since and doesn't know where they are now. But Luke, when she last saw him, was making a good recovery, still getting headaches and dizzy spells but pretty much back to full capacity and getting on with business in the community. He hasn't told her much about the trip, but he said they eventually came out at Balgo, where they were able to fill up with diesel and get their punctures mended. They were heading for Alice, not Nyaru, because Elliot was keen to get back to work and Luke had things to do there as well, and they intended to make the trip inside a day. They had gone past Rabbit Flat and they were making good time. They were overtaking a road-train when they hit a wash-out and the car rolled.

Luke said it was a good place to have a serious accident. They were within spitting distance of the airstrip at the Granites mine. They couldn't have planned it better if they had tried.

THE OTHER BIT of information she passes on from Luke is that Elliot was behind the wheel when the car rolled. He is horrified by that, and by the fact that he can't remember it. He imagines the accident again and again, in a variety of ways. In one version the road is wet, the way ahead clearly visible. The washout is deep and narrow, and it is unmarked, so it's impossible to see it until it's too late to avoid it. In another, the road train is stationary, and he pulls out to pass it, unaware that it has stopped because of the road damage, which is wide and deep, like an earthquake crater, and they sail right into it. In a third version, the one he suspects is most likely, the road has already dried out, the road train is barrelling along it, sending up clouds of dust, obscuring visibility. He has flashed it and flashed it, but the driver either can't see him or doesn't care. Elliot waits, but he is impatient to get back to Alice. He becomes frustrated, and when the driver eventually does slow down he pulls out recklessly. As soon as he is level with the rear trailer he can see the road ahead, and the reason the road train has slowed. The washout is marked by its red flag, but it is already too late and he is travelling much too fast.

3

As well as a fractured skull, Elliot has a broken elbow and several broken ribs, one of which has punctured a lung and caused complications. By the time he is medically stable, he is ready to move on to the Brain Injury Rehabilitation Unit.

His first frustrating attempts to get the staff there to help him track down Dougie Nicholson end with him in an impotent rage and earn him a lengthy psychiatric assessment. After that, he is careful to keep his investigations to himself. It isn't easy, but then nothing is easy for him during that time. He feels as if he is driving a car where the controls don't work, and it is galling and sometimes terrifying. Over time his motor skills improve, but for months, maybe even years, there is a time lag between his brain sending out a message and his body obeying it, which gives him the impression that he is on both ends of a trans-global phone conversation with himself; tangled up in the delays, in a constant state of overlap.

His memory and thought processes recover more quickly, though, and he is beginning to get a fairly good grip on who he is and what had happened. He knows he is a doctor because in most of his memories of himself he is a doctor, but he doesn't remember much about the actual business of practicing medicine. Then one day, a few weeks after the accident, he has access to his medical knowledge again. It seems to him that it had always been there, but he has been looking for it in the wrong place. And along with it comes a landslide of associated memories of medical school, the exams, the registrar years in London, the day-to-day running of his practice in Melbourne. He begins to ask his doctors for details of his injuries and treatment, and he finds he can make sense of pretty much everything they say.

And around the same time, his memories of the recent past become clearer and more linear, although to begin with the idea that he was out in the desert with three Aboriginal people seems too far-fetched to contemplate. But it does come back to him, the memory of the trip, in dribs and drabs. He wonders—when he gets well enough to wonder, or to hold a single thought for more than three or four seconds at a time— how things would be if he had taken a skin name after all. Would his skin brothers and sisters come to visit him, bringing traditional medicines and bush tucker? Would they take him out onto the grass outside the hospital, drip stands and all, the way he had seen people do in Alice Springs? Would his wheelchair be surrounded by a huge extended family out there on the grass, the little kids in restless orbit around him, the teenagers eyeing up their peers in other family groups? If there were people whose skins made them fathers to him, would he get another crack at being someone's son?

He hopes Luke will come and see him, the boys too. He wants to hear their version of the accident, and the story of how long they were stranded on the dunes, and how they came to drive out. There is nothing coming back apart from isolated scenes, which he might be imagining. The round mouth of the jila lying beneath the surface of the water has been a recurring theme in his dreams, but one day he remembers actually seeing it; being invited to visit it, standing beside the pool that had risen in the surrounding claypan. He remembers looking a long way down the hole. Luke and Tommy had clearly done a lot of digging before the clay-pan filled and stopped them.

'Too much water now.'

He remembers a formal introduction to the place, like a baptism, in which Luke splashed water over his head and neck. He remembers being disappointed that it wasn't deep enough for swimming, but he did swim somewhere, and the boys did too, graceful as eels, while Luke read an Ian Rankin novel on the bank. He remembers orange rocks rising up out of the water, and the boys climbing out and diving back in. But the Ian Rankin book seems incongruous and he wonders whether he has superimposed it somehow. It might have been among the audiobooks, which he sometimes resents, sees as an onslaught of noise that interferes with his thinking.

None of these broken bits of memory is reliable. Some have the powerful emotional content of dreams. In one scene he is alone in the hollow in the dunes and he has been alone there all day. He walks to the highest point and looks around. The car is there, the keys are in it, but it is no use to him. The country is as alien and as hostile and as far away from home as the blood-red surface of Mars.

AND YET HE has a recurring memory or waking dream, in which he relives the sensation of a mild wind plucking at his shirt, tickling his back as tenderly as a lover, as though it knew him, or was trying to work out whether it knew him. Sometimes it calms him and sends him to sleep. Sometimes the enquiry becomes a demand; the breeze becomes a gale that tears at his clothes and his skin, trying to tell him something that he knows he will never be able to understand.

4

ELLIOT'S MOTOR skills and his speech are slow to improve, infuriatingly so since his mind has recovered much more quickly. He knows what he wants to do but can't do it, knows what he wants to say but can't say it. He is tormented by the idea that Linda and Doris didn't get their car and may not have received any kind of payment at all for the paintings. He is furious with Dougie Nicholson for taking the paintings from his house and he wants to know whether he paid Doris for them, but he can't find out. He is sure he could get hold of an address and phone number for Nicholson, but he knows he can't keep up one end of a conversation yet, let alone hold his own in an argument. He goes over and over and over the events leading up to the accident, determined to find evidence of Nicholson's hand in it somewhere, entirely unable to do so. The missing days, before and after the journey to the jila, are a source of irritation and anxiety. He tries all kinds of methods for getting into them—comes at them from different angles—but nothing works. They are lost. And deep, deep down, he knows that something of crucial significance is concealed within them.

5

HE DREAMS, or he remembers, everyone taking a turn with the Ian Rankin book, Tommy pretending he can read even though it's clear to everyone that he can't—he is turning the pages much too fast. He dreams, or he remembers, being left alone in the shade of the car while the others go hunting with the rifle. He wants to go with them, but he will fry in that heat. He makes shorter forays to collect firewood, which gives him a sense of purpose. On some of these occasions, he is observed, even flanked, by a solitary dingo. He imagines a friendship growing between them; he sees himself accompanied around Alice Springs by the coolest pet in town, but the dingo has other ideas. It never comes within fifty metres of him during the day, but at night, as though it is teasing him, it leaves paw prints across the camp, some of them just inches from his swag.

He sees the others coming home with witchetty grubs and bush potatoes and honey ants. He has an image of Luke trudging into camp with a huge red kangaroo over his shoulder, tied into a bundle with its own guts. And there's another image that recurs, a nightmare image: the boys coming into camp exhausted but happy, throwing down lizards, throwing down a dead cat and the cat's three dead kittens.

6

HE HAS to work hard at controlling his temper. The staff in the unit are skilled and patient, but some of them are still inclined to patronise him and sometimes all he needs is a bit more time to do or say something, and it sends him into a rage when they don't realise it. He gets some counselling for anger—it's a common complaint among head injury sufferers—and he memorises the techniques he is given and does his best to apply them.

As soon as he progresses to the use of the unit's computers he googles Dougie Nicholson. There isn't a whole lot there. He discovers that the name of Nicholson's company is Five Tree Gallery and that it has a website, which he succeeds in opening. He looks for an email address but there isn't one, just a contact form, and with the teachers and therapists hovering around he doesn't feel like attempting to fill it in. Besides, the effort of concentration required for something as simple as getting the cursor on to the right tab or box is exhausting, and Elliot knows that typing a message is still beyond him. In subsequent computer sessions, he finds other references to Nicholson, a few newspaper pieces about Aboriginal art, his name mentioned in connection with submissions to committees. It also comes up on the fourth or fifth page of a google search, in an article about an old art fraud case, and Elliot is disappointed when he discovers that Nicholson had no connection with the fraud but had been called as an expert witness. There is nothing that he can find anywhere to suggest the man is in any way suspect, but Elliot knows what he knows and will not be discouraged.

He thinks about Nicholson every hour of every day. He goes to sleep thinking about him, and he wakes up thinking about him. He knows it isn't healthy and he hides it from the staff in the rehab unit. He wedges a pencil between his uncooperative fingers and makes barely legible notes for the letter he plans to write as soon as he is master of his own destiny again. He lies awake, composing it, editing it, polishing it; he knows it off by heart and every day he adds or subtracts a line or two or comes up with a new, crushing put-down. Occasionally he laughs to himself, but he can see it concerns the staff and he learns to control that as well so that, in the end, he becomes a human crucible with the lid tightly sealed.

He was never fat, and now he has become a bag of bones. What muscle mass he arrived with has atrophied during his weeks of being bed-ridden. Initially, a few minutes exercise has him shaking like a jelly, but his obsession is a fuel-source and later, much later, he will come to see that it gave him a drive to recover that he was unlikely to have got from anywhere else. He paces the floors with his walking frame until his limbs judder with exhaustion. He attends all his occupational therapy sessions and spends hours practising the exercises that are set for him. He asks the doctors for literature and although the effort of focussing on print is initially intolerable, he concentrates, he improves, and eventually he reads everything they bring him about recovery from brain trauma. It all pays off, and he makes much faster progress than has been expected of him.

HE DREAMS about driving with Luke and the boys and arriving at a fence line. Luke pulls up, takes a pair of bolt cutters from the pink bag, leaves the engine ticking over, so sweetly, the sound as comforting and reliable as a heartbeat. On the other side of the fence, some distance away, two sleek Droughtmaster bullocks look on.

Elliot is instantly awake and alert. The image is a key, he is sure of it, to unlocking at least one lost day. But the short, isolated scene is all there is, and no matter how often he examines it, he cannot expand it, nor locate it in any kind of time frame.

7
———————

His brother Matty flies over, to help organise some of the trickier things. Elliot has decided he wants to go back to Melbourne, so the tenants need to be moved out of his house; everything done properly, by the rules. There is even more money in Elliot's account, now. The family house has been sold and the proceeds divided.

'It's good timing, really,' Matty says. 'You can retire in comfort if you don't get well enough to go back to work.'

'I w-will get w-well enough,' Elliot says. 'I w-will go back to w-work.'

Matty buys Elliot a laptop before he returns to London and, now that his computer time is no longer rationed, he finally succeeds in writing his letter to Nicholson. He is allowed to print it out in the office, with no one breathing down his neck, and he takes it back to his room with a great sense of achievement. It reads:

Dear Mr Nicholson,

I know you took the Doris Banks paintings from my studio in Alice

Springs, or had them taken on your behalf. The police have been informed of the matter. I will not press charges if you can give me proof that Doris has been paid for them.

YOURS SINCERELY,

Dr Elliot Fielding

HE IS DISAPPOINTED that it has turned out to be so short. In his huge, clumsy longhand it appeared meaty and substantial, but in type it looks puny. He goes back to the computer, tries making the font bigger to bulk it out, but it is still a short letter. Worse, seeing it in print makes him aware of how worthless it is. Anyone, especially anyone with Nicholson's experience and confidence, will see it for what it is: a hollow threat. He has no idea whether the police ever followed up on his report. And what could they have done if they did? What kind of proof did anyone have of money paid to artists out of the backs of cars?

Elliot deletes the letter from his computer and hides the print-out from the staff. He is embarrassed that someone might see how delusional his thinking has become. Later he tears it into tiny, unreadable pieces, an effort of coordination equivalent to any of the rehabilitation exercises he has so far been given.

THE EXPERIENCE IS ALMOST MORE than he can bear. It takes the wind out of his sails with drastic consequences, and for a few days, his progress comes to a complete standstill. His therapists notice his lowered mood and lack of motivation and try to find out what is wrong, but Elliot can't explain. Without Nicholson as a focus for blame, he becomes fixated on the mess he had made of it all, on his naivety, his recklessness, the image of that lovely car upside down beside the Tanami road, inevitably just a carcass now, like so many other rusting heaps along there, picked clean for its precious parts. Luke had driven the car over thousands of kilometres of trackless desert, but when Elliot got a turn behind the wheel, on a road as wide and straight as an airstrip, he had succeeded in wrecking things for everyone.

His obsession with Nicholson gradually returns, and his energy along with it. If he can't yet confront Nicholson directly, there might be other ways of discovering what had become of the paintings. The need to find out motivates him to go back to his computer and begin a new series of searches, this time under Doris' name. He finds new links this way, to some small, obscure galleries with moribund websites. Some have sold their Doris Banks paintings, some have them on offer but without prices, one or two have tiny art centre ones for a few hundred dollars. But one of the links he follows fires him up again. Five Trees Gallery.

When he visited the site before, he was focussed on finding out how to contact Nicholson. It hadn't occurred to him to look at the artwork for sale, but now the direct link has led him there he sees that Nicholson has eight Doris Banks paintings listed, with prices ranging from four to forty thousand dollars. One or two of them are from an earlier phase, with mostly pale colours and dots swimming in murky, mustard space. But most of them, about five, are recognisable to him, even with his lack of artistic appreciation. The same reds and oranges, the same dense dot-work and arrangements of lines, circles, angulate segments. He enlarges the images, searching for and finding the familiar paw prints and smudges.

He says, loud enough for a passing attendant to hear, 'You bastard. You fucking, l-lying bastard.'

8

ELLIOT DOESN'T KNOW who he is any more. He has a memory of a self that was fully formed and, in its own way, confident, but now he can't find it. He feels like a theatre of conflict, an accumulation of warring factions, a mass of frustrations with no central government. Anger is a huge issue. He is often afraid of being engulfed by it; though he doesn't mention this to the psychologist he is working with. His private name for her is spychologist, and he sees her as an examiner whose tests he needs to pass if he is ever to get out into the real world again.

But in his own meanwhiles—in the long strange silences that visit him throughout the day and night, when he is not quite awake and not quite asleep—he sees visions, of drinking camps represented by dots and lines; dots for discarded bottles and cans, radiating lines from a black centre: the drinkers all sleeping, temporarily released from that dreadful despair which turns so many men into brawlers and abusers, and drives so many children to alcohol and drugs. He sees them stirring, turning to him with huge, liquid pupils, and he gasps for air, and for something else, for the freedom from knowing that he once had, that he longs to have again.

9

WITHOUT LUKE'S NUMBER, he has no contact with Nyaru. Sandra's main point of contact there now seems to be with her replacement, whose occasional emails she forwards to Elliot. He is glad of the little reports, but none of them is of much interest to him. Someone he doesn't remember gets killed in a car accident. An old man he was particularly fond of dies of kidney disease. Two young women he knows have a fight that puts them both in hospital. All the bad stuff again, and no good stuff. No news of Luke or his youth projects, or of Tommy and Eric and how they are doing now, or of whether the plan to reopen the art centre ever got off the ground. No news of Linda or Doris.

10

_____

HE DREAMS that he stops to rest in the dry bed of the Todd, puts out his
hand to lean against an old river gum and feels, through its white skin,
the presence of its ancient heart. He knows that old tree is deeper than
it is high and that its roots stretch far down into a time that is governed
by a set of elementals he will never comprehend.

11

WHEN HE IS ready for discharge from the BIRU, Elliot has nowhere to go. His tenants in Melbourne are entitled to stay on for a few more weeks and the doctors agree that moving into an unfamiliar place on his own would be too challenging for him. So Sandra moves him into her place and gives him the bedroom in her little flat. Sometimes she stays there too, on the couch in the living-room, and sometimes she stays with some member of her family, to give him space and the incentive to do things for himself. He still walks very slowly and needs a stick for support, and it makes him feel vulnerable out on the streets, but the area is friendly, and people are helpful, and he grows in strength and confidence as the days go by. One night Sandra gets drunk and climbs into bed with him, and it seems to both of them the most natural thing in the world that they should share it after that. Elliot still has no sex drive, and they are both old enough to be practical about it. Neither of them expects anything romantic or permanent, but there are consequences. Over the weeks that follow, Elliot's libido begins to return, and Sandra, pragmatic and droll, gives him the help he needs to revive it.

'Gets the base chakras firing,' she says. 'Reboot the nervous system.' Elliot scoffs at her terminology, but he has to agree that it is powerful medicine. And when his house in Melbourne finally becomes vacant, and the decorators sent in by the property management company have finished, Elliot is as much disappointed as pleased, and in the end, Sandra has to book flights and help him pack and deliver him to his house in Thornbury. Theirs is never going to be a long-term relationship and they both know it, but she promises to come and visit and she does, a couple of times. It is not until then that Elliot learns she has a son, who moved to London with his father when he was still a child, and who she has never seen since.

He is shocked by the news and feels dreadful that he didn't know about it before now, that everything in their relationship had always been about him, and that he never asked her about her life.

'I can help,' he says. 'I can pay for an airfare if you want to go over. Or if he wants to come here.'

She shakes her head. 'It's not about money. I want him to come back, but there are issues with his father. He isn't well. Truth is I haven't been a good parent. I made promises to him that I didn't keep. It was Nyaru. I got too attached to the place and the people there. It became my whole life.'

Elliot says, 'Well, you can make up for it now, can't you? Now that you have resigned from there?'

Sandra sheds silent tears and he is embarrassed, helpless, because he doesn't know whether she is crying for her lost son, or for Nyaru.

12

THE MOVE IS an upheaval for him, full of confusion and disorientation, but when he finally gets his bearings, he finds he is glad to be back in Melbourne. He remembers the things he likes about it: the broad streets, the trams, the restaurants and footpath cafes serving really good food. He no longer needs to cook, though he does, from time to time, because it makes him feel virtuous.

IN ANOTHER DREAM, a recurring one, he is standing beside the troopy in the dunes and the sun is shining but the water is rising on all sides, higher and higher. He realises it is undermining the dune where he stands; it will level it and wash the sand away. He runs for the car, but it is already keeling over, the ground beneath it melting and bubbling.

PART V

1

It is fifteen months after the accident before Elliot goes back to work in the practice in Preston. He is still an outpatient with the head injuries unit in Caulfield, but he is down to visiting once a month, and soon after that his check-ups will be reduced further, to three times a year. To begin with, he insists on all his consultations with patients being held under observation, just in case, but he doesn't make diagnostic or prescribing mistakes, and his partner and colleagues are soon happy to leave him to it. The accident and its aftermath have turned Elliot into a much better doctor: more empathetic, a lot more patient. He is more attentive, and he finds he can now imagine how people are affected by their health problems. His manner is quite different. Patients who knew him from before prefer him now. He gives them more time. Sometimes just talking to him makes them feel better.

But he is exhausted by the effort of concentration required, and for the first year, he works only four days a week and only in the morning surgery. If he manages to go shopping on the same day, or to cook a proper meal, or read a few chapters of a book, he considers it an achievement. Mostly he sits in front of the TV. Sometimes he dozes. Sometimes he dreams, or remembers. He continues to be obsessed by Dougie Nicholson.

He understands that there is a large part of him that doesn't want the fixation to go away and that, perversely, he takes refuge in it. At night time, when he is waiting for sleep, it is where his drifting mind finds focus and, in the morning, it is one of the first things he checks in with, after his vision, which is all good now, and his extremities with their remaining numb spots; these are the measurements of his existence. Can he still see and feel? Does he still hate Dougie Nicholson?

Sometimes, knowing it is an indulgence, he imagines sticky ends for him. Deaths by fire, by drowning, by hanging, by every kind of accident: Dougie Nicholson has died them all. Many times he has been murdered, and that is what most bothers Elliot, because it is always him who is doing the murdering, and he fears he will lose the distinction between the real and the imagined, and one day find himself covered in Dougie Nicholson's blood.

He doesn't dream about him, though. He dreams about Doris and Linda, and about flights above the red landscape, and he hears the butcher bird so clearly some nights that he can't believe, when he wakes up, that it isn't outside his window.

The first time he heard it he and Miles were camped among the trees on a station north of Oodnadatta. He thought it was Miles whistling as he moved around the camp, making tea perhaps. When he opened his eyes he realised that Miles was still fast asleep, and the sound was coming from above him. As he watched, the bird moved from one tree to another, circling the camp, creating divine music for the dawn. It is a sound imbued with the same quality as the light, peculiar to that place; it has an extra dimension in it for which he has no adequate language. In Melbourne mornings, as he struggles with his diminished capabilities, he both longs for that unnameable presence and dreads the prospect of the effort that would be needed to reach it. He takes refuge in visions of revenge.

2

HE DREAMS that the red desert country has a rhythm. While he watches, Eric dances across its surface, animated by the beat in the ground as a jumping bean is animated by heat.

3

SANDRA PAYS a visit and he asks her if she'd like to move in, but he knows what her answer will be. She says she is too involved with work and family in Adelaide, and he doesn't doubt it's true. If it wasn't, he would have to face the uncomfortable reality: he isn't any kind of a catch, and probably never will be. He is damaged and may never get completely repaired. He doesn't have a life again yet, so how can he offer to share it?

There is that, at least, to be said for the years he spent in central Australia. They were interesting. They were different. They have left him with some colourful memories.

He misses the old cat that used to live with him in that Melbourne house, and he considers getting another one, but it will involve a lot of hassle with litter trays and curfews. He knows why Australians are ambivalent about cats; knows about the damage they cause to indigenous wildlife and their proclivity for turning feral and breeding in large numbers. He understands it better now than he did when he lived in Melbourne before and was a little lax about following the guidelines. He thinks he might be able to put up with the hassle, but there is something else that holds him back. He tries to repress the memory, but it is too vivid. The mother cat's mouth is open, teeth bared, pink fluid dripping. Her little kittens, already emptied of their innards, slap down on to the sand beside the fireplace, one, two, three.

4

ONE AFTERNOON, when he is watching TV, the ABC runs a documentary about Aboriginal art. Elliot has a couple of archive boxes open on the table. He is trying to find some documents the practice accountant has asked for, but he keeps an eye on the programme in case Nicholson's name comes up. It doesn't, but suddenly he finds he is looking at Doris. There are some wonderful shots of her sitting in the middle of a canvas, singing her country as she paints. He is completely hooked in there, but the clip is too short, the action moves on somewhere else and he is left open-mouthed, staring at the papers in his hands as though they are part of someone else's life. He is bereft, longing for something that he can't even identify. Is it Doris herself? Linda? Nyaru? Just that place, that red sand? The longing is profound and painful.

In the frozen backwaters of Elliot's life, something begins to thaw.

5

He looks up Five Trees Gallery and dials the number. His call is taken by an assistant there, who tells him Nicholson isn't in that day, but readily passes on his mobile number. He dials, and on the third ring, Nicholson answers.

Elliot is so surprised he has to remember to speak. He hasn't prepared himself; hasn't even run over what he intends to say. 'Dougie. It's Elliot Fielding. Do you remember me?' He is aware that his voice has changed a lot. Even close friends sometimes have difficulty recognising it on the phone.

'Can't say I do,' Nicholson says. 'Remind me.'

'The party at...' He can't remember the name of the woman who had invited him. 'The Doris Banks paintings. A couple of years ago.'

Nicholson says, 'Oh yes. I have you now. The doctor. You were in a roll-over weren't you?'

'Yeah, that's right.'

'They said you were looking for paintings up in Balgo.'

'Looking for paintings?'

'Weren't you?'

'No.'

'There you go,' Nicholson says. 'Way my mind works. Can't think of any other reason for a whitefella to be in Balgo.'

Elliot is momentarily stumped. Nicholson waits a moment, then goes on, 'So what became of those Doris Banks ones, anyway?'

'I think you know that,' Elliot says. 'You lifted them from my house.'

'I what?'

'Don't come the innocent.'

'Mate, are you drunk?'

Elliot begins to shake. It is reckless to be making this call. He can't handle it. He says, 'I am not drunk. I saw those paintings on your website.'

'Not those ones, you didn't. I never saw them again, and I have to tell you, I resent the accusation.'

'W-w-well someone…'

'Not me.'

'Who, then?'

'Nicked from your house in Alice?'

'Yes. While I was in hospital.'

'Jeez. Could have been anyone. Kids most likely. Probably just dumped them in a creek somewhere.'

Elliot says, 'But I saw them on your w-w-website.'

'You didn't, mate.'

'They l-l-look the same.'

'But they're not. Did you take photos of the ones you got from Doris?'

'No.'

'Well, shame about that. Worth thinking about next time you go out bush buying paintings.'

Elliot loses it. He yells at the phone. 'I did not go out bush buying paintings!'

Nicholson says, 'Steady, steady on.'

'I just w-want to know if Doris got her money. If she got her car.' Elliot's coordination is going south. His hand is shaking, and the phone is wavering about in front of his face.

'Take it easy, Elliot. Are you back in Alice?'

'No, no. Melbourne.'

'Let's meet up someday I'm in town and have a chat about it. I got your number here. I'll give you a shout.'

Elliot says. 'I just w-w-w,' but he is jammed. He hears Nicholson heave a sigh at the other end of the line before he hangs up.

He collapses back on the couch. The documentary is still running, the sound turned down, the final scenes meaningless without the voice-over. Todd Mall with its rows of galleries, a woman sitting on the grassy mound there, a few paintings spread around her, fade-out to the clichéd helicopter shot running along the Macdonnell Ranges, then sweeping away across the speckled red of the surrounding plains. Elliot is still shaking, unable to hold back tears of rage and frustration. Nicholson, the bastard, holds all the cards. He can do and say whatever he likes, and Elliot can prove nothing.

6

HE DREAMS that he is lying awake under the blaze of the desert stars, watching a hopping mouse explore his hat and flynet, just a few inches away from his nose.

7

OVER THE NEXT couple of days, Elliot continues to function, but only
just. He is inclined to lose focus and forget about things, and his misery
is so acute that he finds himself wondering what he has to live for, and
why he keeps getting up in the mornings and carrying on. It seems to
him that it's a habit, nothing more; a routine that he has created because
he can manage it, that's all. He likes Melbourne but while he was away
in Alice most of his friends moved on, and now he finds himself at a
loss. He has been so focused on recovering that he hasn't given much
thought to what is supposed to happen afterwards.

He phones Sandra. He hasn't told her before now about the paintings, and he can tell from her tone of voice that she is surprised to hear
about them now, and perhaps not entirely convinced.

'So I could just, you know, just pay for another car. Get someone in
Alice to drive it out there. Do you know anyone who would do that?'

'Elliot,' she says, 'You know more people in Alice than I do. You
lived there, remember?'

'But I lost all my numbers. On my phone.'

'Then find them again. Write down a list of your friends in CAHS
and the RFDS and start from there. Just ring the offices. It's a small
network. You'll soon get everyone's numbers.'

He nods, glumly, which she can't see. 'Elliot?'

'Yes. Yes. I can do that.'

'Are you sure it's a good idea, though? The whole thing with the car?'

'What else can I do? I lost the paintings and I rolled the troopy. Everything is my fault. I can't just pretend it never happened.'

'They've probably forgotten all about it. Doris will have done loads more paintings. Maybe they even have a car by now?'

'Can you find out?' he asks.

'No more easily than you can,' she said. 'That new nurse moved on a year ago, and I don't know who the new one is. Just like that, all my contact with the place is gone. It's as though I was never there.'

8

He dreams that he is crossing the riverbed and the sand is deep. It fills his shoes and drags at his feet. He is afraid that he will get stuck there, bogged down in all that pain, waiting for all eternity for the river to return.

9

BUT SANDRA IS right about tracking down people in the whitefella community; it isn't hard. He finds the number of the payphone in Nyaru and rings it, but no one picks up. He finds the number of the store and rings that. Eventually, a young person picks up, sounding harassed. She is new, she says, and she doesn't know Luke. She puts him on to her boss, who says he doesn't think Luke is in town and he doesn't have his mobile number. But someone who overhears the conversation does have it and writes it down for the store manager, who reads it out to Elliot.

Elliot dials but he knows it's a long shot. There is no answer. It might be days or even weeks before Luke is in an area where there is coverage. He tries the CAHS office, where they give him a number for Drew. Elliot thinks he, at least, will understand, but he doesn't. 'So you want to give me the money to buy a car and drive it to Nyaru?'

'That's about it, yeah.'

'And how do I get back from Nyaru?'

'I don't know. Get a l-lift in the Hawker, maybe?'

'Oh, right. So you want me to buy a car, drive it out to Nyaru making sure to arrive on the one day in the fortnight that the plane is coming home, and assume it will have a spare non-emergency seat?'

'Or I don't know, Drew. Someone would be driving into town. They always are. It would be an adventure.'

'What, like the one you had? You want to share that kind of adventure with me?'

Elliot laughs despite himself. 'Ah, come on, Drew.'

'And then, just to follow through, you want me to hand it over to an old woman of eighty?

'I think she drove all kinds of things up in the Kimberley. Tractors, trucks, you name it.'

'She wasn't eighty then.'

'Well, it's her granddaughter that's going to be doing the driving anyway. Linda. In fact, I bet Linda would give you a lift back to town herself.'

Drew says, 'Hmm. Is she Linda Kelly?'

'Something like that. Yes, I think so. She has four kids. Do you know her?'

'Yes, I know her. I remember you had a bit of a thing about her.'

Elliot says, 'What?' but Drew doesn't elaborate.

'She's not living in Nyaru now. She's here in town. I saw her the other day. She's working on a new language project; some kind of video series for the little kids. She's staying in Morris Soak, I think. Has a new baby. Brought her to me with an eye infection. Are you sure she's going back to Nyaru?'

Elliot says nothing. He is trying to remember whether he confided in Drew about his feelings for Linda, or whether they had just been obvious to everyone. Either way, he is paralysed by embarrassment, and Drew gives him space. Eventually, he says, 'You know, you should come back here sometime. Even if it's just for a visit. If you need to sort things out, you should be doing it yourself.'

Elliot says, 'You think so?'

'It's like getting back on the horse. You shouldn't let that rollover be your last experience of this place.' Again Drew waits while Elliot gathers his thoughts. Then he says, 'Is there more you want to tell me, Elliot? I'm guessing this has something to do with those paintings you were trying to sell. Did it work out, in the end?'

Elliot explains about the robbery in the house. 'If someone wanted to hide a bunch of paintings like that, or to pass them on quietly, how would they go about it?'

'Don't ask me. But if you want my professional advice, I think you should let go of this and forget about it. It's not your fault you were robbed. No one is going to blame you for that. I guarantee you Doris has forgotten it ever happened. You're the only one left in the world who is still worried about it.'

Elliot says nothing. It is the second time within a few hours that he has been given the same advice, but he isn't ready to take it. Drew says, 'I tried to ring you a couple of times, after the accident. Some young fella answered. Did they give your old number to someone else?'

10

WHAT WAS MORE LIKELY, Elliot thought, was that someone had fossicked his phone after the accident. His SIM card was Pre-paid, so it was possible someone was still using it. Out of curiosity, Elliot phones to find out. A voice at the other end says, 'Hello.'

Elliot says, 'This is Elliot Fielding. Who is that?' There is no reply, and Elliot finds himself listening to dead air. He is not particularly concerned and is turning his attention to something else when his phone rings. He answers it.

'Elliot?'

'Yes. Who is this?'

'Eric. You don't sound like Elliot. Are you drunk?'

'Eric!' Elliot is ridiculously pleased to hear him. 'How you going? I'm not drunk, no. I just sound like this because of the accident'

'Your brain get damage, they said.'

'That's right. But I'm OK now. How about you?'

'I'm good, Elliot.' He sounds older, more distant. 'I'm in Adelaide.'

'Adelaide? Doing what?'

'Staying with my mother's people here.'

'Oh, that's good. I suppose. How come you have my phone?'

'Just your SIM card,' says Eric. 'I got a new phone.'

'And how about Luke, do you ever see him?'

'I don't know where he is. Nyaru, might be. Where you living, Elliot?'

'I'm back in Melbourne.'

'Melbourne. Where you living in Melbourne? Might be I come and see you, eh?'

Elliot says. 'Why would you be coming to Melbourne?'

'What street? What number?'

Elliot tells him. 'Do you have a phone number for Luke?' he says. 'Did you ever get back to the jila? Did you open it up?'

'Not me. Might be Luke went. I don't know.'

'Are you really coming to Melbourne?'

'Some time. If I get the money. I don't like this place. No good for me, Elliot. Can you send me money? Then I can come and see you in Melbourne.'

'I don't know, Eric. I don't think so.'

The line goes dead again, and Elliot stands and looks at the phone for a long time. When it doesn't ring he calls back, but there is no answer. It has only been half a conversation; not even that. He wants to open a proper channel of communication. He didn't even get round to asking about Tommy. He feels cheated. Later he tries the number again, and after work the next day, three times, but it's clear that Eric doesn't have anything more to say to him.

11

AT HIS NEXT check-up in Caulfield, Elliot asks the consultant whether he will be able to drive again, and is told there is no reason why not, but it might be an idea to get a few lessons first, just to make sure. She sends him a letter for the Driver Licensing Authority. It lifts his spirits; gives him more impetus to work. He tells people he is in training to be his old self again, and he is getting there. As the months go by he notices that he gets fewer worried looks from new patients and has to explain less often that he isn't drunk, just has a speech impediment. He can walk further and faster. One day he forgets to take his stick when he goes out and he finds he no longer needs it. And he has a bit of energy for more than work. He goes to Adelaide for a weekend to watch a cricket match with Sandra. He tries Eric's number again, on the off chance that they could meet up there, but Eric doesn't answer. In the weeks that follow, he starts meeting up with friends and going for a meal or to an early evening showing at the cinema. He doesn't fully realise how ill he has been until he finds he is well enough to start living again.

He doesn't talk much about his accident, but people are curious about him and his story. Rumours go round, and he is sometimes asked what he was doing out there in the desert, and he is always left with the impression that his explanation, 'just visiting country', isn't a good enough answer. He thinks that, in the end, he came to understand why it was so important to Luke to see the jila, and there was no doubt about the effect the trip had on the teenagers, no matter how short-lived that effect might have been. But Elliot doesn't want to go into any of that with the kind of people who ask him about it. He doesn't trust the reasons behind their interest. He doesn't trust their guilty curiosity, their desire to hear about the anthropological or the political, the mystical or the spiritual, their need to share his experience, however vicariously. Nor does he trust himself to answer without being drawn into the anthropological or the political, the mystical or the spiritual, and because the reason he was there had nothing to do with any of those things. He is more inclined to tell them about the little trip with Doris: the men's site and the picnic. And one day, when he is doing that, he gets a vision, clear as daylight, of one of the paintings. It is the one that Nicholson pointed out, the one with the flowing dune lines and the off-centre action.

It sends him straight back to the computer. He visits the Five Tree Gallery website again. The painting he remembers isn't there, but he studies the other Doris works again and again, blowing them up as big as they will go, hoping that he will recognise other features from his paintings, now that the lid is off. He racks his tired brain for clear images from before, visualises himself with Nicholson, and with Sally Cameron too, looking down on the paintings, one by one. But he hadn't really been looking at them; he understands that now. Apart from the one that had been brought to his attention, he hadn't really seen them at all.

He keeps going; searches for the painting everywhere, revisiting every website that is linked in any way to Doris. He doesn't find it, but he can't give up. He searches more assiduously, looking up all the Aboriginal art websites he can find and combing their inventories for Doris. Some of the searches bring him to pages with biographical details. There isn't much information on Doris herself, but one specialist gallery, which once staged an exhibition from the old Nyaru art centre, has fairly comprehensive biographies of most of the desert artists. There he finds that:

"Doris Banks was born in a remote part of the Tanami Desert. She doesn't know exactly when, and she doesn't know exactly how old she is, but she lived with her family in the traditional nomadic style until she was somewhere around ten or eleven years old. After that, the family moved on to a station in the Kimberley, where Doris worked at a whole range of occupations, from housekeeper to stockwoman. She was married twice, the second time to stockman Jimmy Banks. In 1967, when Aboriginal workers became entitled to equal wages, Doris and her family, along with thousands of their compatriots across the north of Australia, were evicted from their homes, since it was considered uneconomical to pay them a living wage. For a year or two, the family lived in a makeshift camp on the outskirts of Tennant Creek, before finally moving to Doris' mother's country at Nyaru, along with two of their four surviving children.

Doris is a senior law woman for her people, and she speaks at least five languages, including Warlpiri, Walmajarri and Pintupi. Although Nyaru was not involved in the very outset of the western desert painting movement, her husband Jimmy Banks began to paint soon after they moved there and eventually came to be recognised as one of the great desert artists. Doris learnt to paint by working on the infill of his bigger works and did not begin painting in her own right until after his death. She didn't become known as an artist until the Nyaru art centre opened in 2004. Despite its closure in 2008, she continues to paint, and her work can be found in many major galleries and important private collections.

OUT OF CURIOSITY, Elliot googles Jimmy Banks. He finds more information on him, but still not a huge amount. In a set of biographical notes on a different art website, he reads that Jimmy was among a group of artists who went to Europe with one of the first international exhibitions of desert art and, before the opening in London, was introduced to the queen.

Suddenly he wants to see Doris. He wants to apologise to her for his assumptions and preconceptions and lack of proper respect. He would like to see Linda as well, and he is aware, out of the blue, that the complication of his crush on her has gone. It is a thing of the past. He knows that if he was invited again, he could sit around Doris' fire and listen to her talking, in whatever language she chose, for as long as she would let him. The same with Luke. He can hardly believe those things really happened; that he was out on that land with those people; that such a culture still existed in the same country as Melbourne, with its café society and its liberal arts scene and its rapidly burgeoning economy.

And yet, Elliot sees Aboriginal art everywhere, as though spending so much time looking at it has attuned him to it in some way. Stylised representations appear as corporate logos and backgrounds for council flyers. Actual artworks appear on TV shows nearly every day, on the sets of middle-class houses and the walls of government offices. Elliot finds that he can even identify some of the artists. He can pick out the broad colourful brush strokes of Minnie Pwerle, the spare ochre maps of Rover Thomas, the wild, eccentric roundels of Nyurapayia Nampitjinpa, the perplexing scribbles of Emily Kame. Where he can't name the artist, he can often identify regional styles, the energetic representations of country coming out of the APY Lands or the bush medicine designs from Utopia. But their presence in these shiny places disturbs him. They are too remote from their origins, too oblivious to the conditions in those places. There is something hypocritical about their presence on those walls. They are a nod to the existence of Aboriginal culture that is almost insulting, given the ongoing policy of assimilation pursued by the federal government. It helps him understand Doris' need to create something that isn't on offer to whitefella culture, neither for sale nor for evaluation, and he catches himself in thinking that is bordering on the political.

At times he loses it; is unable to make sense of all the rushing around that constitutes modern existence, all the acquisition and the accumulation and the homage paid to those who do it best. If those people accumulated toilet paper the way they accumulated money, it would be seen as pathology and they would be referred for psychiatric treatment. He knows the kinship system in Aboriginal communities leaves room for abuse, but he finds he can't argue with the basic premise, that resources should be shared and used, not hoarded for personal aggrandisement. For the first time, he finds himself in sympathy with the marchers on Australia Day, watches the TV footage of their procession down Swanston Street with their Aboriginal sunrise flags and Invasion Day placards. He can almost, but not quite, envisage himself among them.

12

He wants to go back. He has the money to buy another car or to pay Doris outright for the paintings; he has so much money that it wouldn't even be painful. But he finds he isn't ready yet. He isn't physically ready, not quite, and nor does he feel mentally prepared. He needs to build up a bit more stamina and take a few day trips; stretch himself a bit more than he has been doing. He takes longer walks, and books himself a series of driving lessons. He isn't at all sure he will feel safe behind the wheel and is delighted to find he can drive as well as he ever could.

In the evenings, he continues to pore over images of Doris' work, on new websites that he finds and on images pulled up on google from exhibitions all over the world. He searches through the online archives of the state galleries, finds a couple of images there, but none of them is currently on show in Melbourne. He begins to recognise individual images and remember the websites where he first saw them. He is getting nowhere, apart from becoming an expert on the web representation of Doris Banks' work. When a gallery lists a painting but doesn't have an image, he phones or emails. Some never answer. Others are pleased to talk, and most are happy to describe the paintings, send him photos by email, even tell him when and where they sourced the works. Others are more cagey and say they always deal directly with the artists, or that they get their art 'through the proper channels', though what those proper channels might be they are not willing to discuss.

One website he visits gives no address, only a mobile phone number. Doris isn't mentioned there, but Elliot calls and asks his usual questions anyway. The man on the other end says he has paintings by Doris, and when Elliot asks how they are sourced, he says, 'Are you one of these art code enthusiasts? Have you been listening to a lot of rubbish about protecting the artists and their reputation, keeping out the carpetbaggers? I tell you, mate, these people out here don't care about their reputation or making a big name for themselves and being "protected" by some big agent or ethics committee who are going to tell them what is good for them. If they want to sell lots of paintings for small amounts of money, why shouldn't they? Why should some fat gallery owner from Toorak or Bondi Beach have a monopoly on what's good for Aboriginal people? Do you see them around here? Giving Annie Mac a lift to her sister's place so she doesn't get beaten up by her boyfriend? Taking Charlie Dean for his dialysis because his brother forgot what day it is?'

Elliot cut across the diatribe. 'Where's here?' he said. 'Where are you based?'

'Alice Springs, mate. Right at the coalface, you know? Not flying in and out on Qantas like these gallery owners from Sydney and Melbourne. But they want to dictate the terms, those people. As if they weren't dealers, just the same as we are and all the other small players around the town, around the country. I'm not saying no one was ever exploited. People were and they still are. But if they are happy to come in and paint for me, and get a few hundred or a few thousand dollars to help out their families, who has the right to tell them they can't?'

There is no sign of the lecture abating, and Elliot moves onto the sofa in the sitting room. He ought to hang up, but he has an idea who it is he is talking to, and he holds on, only half listening.

'The big players don't like it because it devalues their investment. If you can get a Tommy Giles from me for two thousand dollars instead of one off them for ten thousand, they aren't going to like it, are they? We're here, mate. We live out here, not back in Melbourne having cocktail party openings for the Fitzroy set. We're dealing with the artists every day of the week, looking after them, giving them handouts and advances. Sometimes they never even do the paintings they get paid for, and then what? I'll show you my books any time you like. I got nothing to hide. Some of the top artists there, they owe me thousands. I flew one old fella to Adelaide to get his rotten teeth sorted out. His face was like a balloon, poor bugger. Went with him too, stayed there for three days, cos his useless family only care about him when his pockets are full of cash. Where do I get compensated for that, eh? Where do I get compensated for the days I lost sitting beside old Aggie Bates when she was dying in the hospital, eh? No one else there, you know? Her own mob off arguing about who owned the last of her paintings. Humbugging some other old aunt or uncle to start painting and keep them all in grog.'

Elliot said, 'Are you Gary Cameron?'

That stopped him. 'Do I know you?'

'No. I met your daughter once, though. In your gallery in Alice.'

'Right. So you reckon you know a bit about art?'

'Not really.'

'I tell you, mate, you don't know the half of it. Tell me this, eh? When the government sets it up and pays the staff they call it an art centre. When I set it up and pay all the expenses, they call it a sweatshop. Where's the logic in that? They just don't like us, all those uni-educated mob. They look down their noses at us. But we're the ones dealing with the day-to-day reality, you know?'

Elliot says, 'Will you send me some photos of the paintings you have? The Doris Banks ones?'

'No worries. Give me your email.'

Elliot does, and rings off before Cameron gets up a new head of steam. The conversation has disturbed him, dragged him back into the turmoil of contradictions that he remembers as Alice Springs. He liked Sally when he met her. She had given him that length of water pipe to protect the paintings, and the end caps as well. Those things weren't cheap to buy. He remembers Dougie Nicholson opening one end, sliding out the contents. He doesn't know why this image of the white tube is so disturbing to him, but it is. There is something, has always been something wrong with his story, and this has somehow brought him closer.

It occurs to him that it could have been Cameron, or someone employed by him that broke into the house and took the paintings. He waits eagerly for the images to come through on his email, but they don't come that day, or the next. He sends Cameron a text to remind him, gets one back saying he is heading out bush and will get to it next week. Elliot wonders whether he has hit on something. If Cameron did take the paintings, it makes sense that he wouldn't be in any rush to send pictures of them to Elliot. Impatient and frustrated, Elliot can do nothing but wait.

The days pass and still Cameron doesn't send them, and the longer it goes on, the more convinced Elliot becomes that he has stumbled upon something very significant indeed.

13

HE DREAMS that he is trying to sell Doris herself, dragging her around from door to door in dusty, paint-spattered clothes. He dreams that he is trying to sell her country, in the form of huge rolled-up maps. Dreams like these are heavy with humiliation and often end with him discovering he is wearing no pants or being arrested for murder or fraud, or theft.

EVERY NOW AND then he tries calling Eric again, but Eric never answers. He sends a couple of texts, but they don't have any effect either. He worries about him; wishes he would make contact. He feels an affinity with him, maybe because of the position they once shared of uninitiated men, and he remembers his quick intelligence, and the way his bad dreams woke him in the night. The realisation that he is so close, relatively, somehow makes it worse, and he tries, without much success, to picture Eric in Adelaide. He doesn't even fully understand why he wants to see him, but he is aware that it isn't purely personal. It isn't just contact with Eric that he wants. It's that country, those people, his engagement with it all. His old life.

14

ELLIOT BROWSES thousands of listings for Aboriginal art on eBay. Some of them are rip-offs by people with fantasy names. Some are mass-produced, gaudy things described as Aboriginal 'style'. But most of them are by artists from the central desert region, being sold with the promise of a Certificate of Authenticity by people who name the artist, but don't reveal their own identities. These people, Elliot assumes, are the carpetbaggers. Some of the asking prices are so low that the painters themselves must get next to nothing for their work, and the promised certificates will never be accepted by collectors or auction houses if and when the paintings come to be resold.

Almost every listing has a photograph of the artist painting or holding the artwork. Elliot finds the photographs deeply disturbing. They objectify and dehumanise the artists who, with very rare exceptions, look stressed and unhappy. More than anything else he has seen, these listings make him aware of the reason for the code of ethics that most of the bigger dealers and galleries have now signed. But the code, for all its aspirations, does little to dispel the mistrust he has developed for all the dealers out there, big or small. He is perpetually reminded of what Luke said to him that day, out in the desert, about the endless meetings where yapa were invited to contribute, then had their suggestions ignored. He encountered the same set of assumptions everywhere he looked. White people were the ones who knew what was best for Aboriginal people.

15

HE DREAMS he is driving with Luke, out of some dusty war-torn land-scape, towards a major conurbation. There is a border post with armed guards, and they have to stop. The guards demand provenance. Elliot hands over his passport, but Luke is carrying no ID. Elliot is sure there must be a certificate for him somewhere in the car, and he is still searching for it when he wakes up, fearful and sweating.

HE LOOKS AT MAPS, trying to trace the journey he made with Luke and the boys. The part between Nyaru and the salt lakes is easy, but after that, he has no idea. He realises he has forgotten, or perhaps he never asked, which tribal group Luke belonged to. It could have been Ngardi, Walmajarri, Kukatja; he has no idea, and it bothers him that he doesn't know.

16

HE KEEPS SEARCHING for the paintings, and he is gratified to discover that he can now spot a Doris Banks from a mile off, or pick one of her works out of a whole page of similar thumbnails. He finds that a number of galleries have stockroom pages, and when he searches them he finds more Doris paintings on offer, two of them right there in Melbourne. On his day off, he goes to see them. Both the galleries are on tram routes and are easy enough for him to get to, but one of them has nothing to show him. The 'stockroom' turns out to be a warehouse in Coburg North and they need forty-eight hours' notice to get paintings out for viewing. The other one is more promising. An assistant is sent off to an upstairs stock room to hunt out the painting, and while they wait, Elliot and the proprietor have the talk about Aboriginal art.

'Nearly all our backroom stock is left over from exhibitions,' she tells him. 'The desert art still sells to the casual buyer, but the key collectors are looking for what's next, and that can come from anywhere.'

She is a tall woman, all cheekbones and elbows, and her eyes are bloodshot with livid shadows under them. She looks like a textbook case of ankylosing scoliosis and Elliot has to work at switching off his professional interest as he follows her round her current exhibition. It is the work of two urban artists; very modern, completely unlike anything Elliot has seen before. One of the artists uses old black-and-white photographs of Aboriginal people and superimposes them on the cityscapes that now stand on their country. The other uses papercuts. Some of the symbols she uses are familiar, but most of the work is incomprehensible to Elliot. There are plenty of sold stickers in evidence, but they are the only red dots and Elliot finds the whole exhibition colourless, bloodless, stark against the stark white walls of the gallery. It is more likely to smother than encourage the germinating seeds of his political interest. He nods and says, 'Hmm.'

'We do solo shows occasionally. Doris is someone we might consider. She is one of the last remaining first contact artists. I'm not sure what she's up to these days, though. I haven't heard anything about her for a while.'

'And where would you source her paintings, if you did put on an exhibition?'

The owner sits down beside a long table covered by a white cloth. There are a couple of typewritten handouts on it with the names and prices of the current artworks, but nothing else. He can imagine it at launches, covered with glasses of wine and mineral water.

'We would generally set it up with the artist a year or two ahead of time and have them paint with the exhibition in mind. Ideally, we like to go out and meet with them; come to a proper arrangement, but it isn't always possible with the older people. If there was an art centre in her community we might work through that, but as far as I know, they still haven't reopened it.'

'Do you ever work with dealers?'

'We occasionally work through agents. One or two of the top artists paint exclusively for an agent. So if we want to show them we have no option. But dealers? No.'

'Someone like Dougie Nicholson?'

She seems shocked by the suggestion. 'No. I don't have any dealings with Dougie Nicholson.'

'Or… people like him.'

'There aren't many people like Dougie Nicholson,' she says. 'In any case, I think he sells most of his important paintings directly to collectors. Most of them overseas.'

Elliot nods. It would make sense, of course it would. Just ship the stolen paintings off to collectors in other parts of the world. No need to ever promote them in Australia. No need for them ever to be seen here.

When the painting he has come to see appears from the stock room, Elliot is momentarily taken aback. It is huge, nearly two metres wide by one and a half. The blaze of colour in the monochrome space, and those colours in particular, create an emotional reaction that he hasn't expected. He has a vertiginous sense of looking down from a great height, and a strange and terrifying sense that all his dreams, those longings and memories and visions are all in convergence here in this painting, in this essence of Doris and her country and the ancient laws of her people. He looks away, gathers his scattered wits, remembers that it is just dots on canvas, and when he looks back, that is what he sees. Dots and smudges.

'She doesn't come to openings,' the owner says. 'As far as I know, she has never appeared at one. Happy out there on her country, I suppose.'

'I know her,' Elliot says. He is focussing on the dots, following the lines and circles. 'I used to work out that way.'

'Really? Doing what?'

He tells her, but he can see she isn't really interested. She just wants to sell him the painting, and he is wasting her time. He looks at it again. It could be one of his, but it probably isn't. Seeing the painting—an actual painting as opposed to an online image—has brought the truth home to him. With one possible exception, he wouldn't recognise the canvases Doris gave him if he saw them. There is no way he could ever identify them.

'It's a good price,' the proprietor is saying. 'If we do a solo exhibition in a couple of years it will be double that.'

'Did you say forty?' he asks.

'Forty-five,' she says. 'But if you were to make a firm offer...'

'I'll think about it,' he says, and declines, as politely as he can, her invitation to leave his details for her mailing list.

17

ELLIOT'S SEARCH for the paintings has become an addiction. It has taken on a life of its own, almost without regard to its outcome. He begins to look at galleries that deal in Aboriginal art overseas. He finds one in Singapore, one in London, a couple in the USA, one in Canada. He sends emails to them all, aware even as he does it that he is wasting their time. But he can't stop himself. It is a compulsion.

He works on his coordination and his speech, he rides his exercise bike until he sweats, he goes to work, he meets a financial consultant and discusses what to do with all his money. One of the suggestions she has is that he invest some of it in art, and he can't explain to her why the idea makes him laugh. He gets a trickle of emails back from the overseas galleries. They have or they haven't got pictures by Doris. They could source them for him, if he likes. He doesn't answer any of them, and it makes him feel grubby.

But he is getting better. He is still improving. At his regular check-up in Caulfield, he is told he only needs to come in once a year, provided he doesn't develop any new symptoms. He should have been pleased. It is a good outcome; far better than he had initially expected. The trouble is he doesn't feel he has come back to himself. He doesn't feel anything like the person he was before the injury, and when he tries to explain this he gets nowhere. It is common in cases of head injury. He is referred to a psychologist, and together they spend a couple of sessions examining the concept of self. She gives him books to read, but if anything, they make things worse. He is not ready for Jungian theories of soul. The books contain answers to questions he has not asked. What he wants is to find the connection between who he is now and the person he used to be, but it is too hard. There's a thread that was broken in the period of unconsciousness. His old self died on the Tanami road and this new self is a poor reconstruction. A fake.

18

He goes to an auction of Aboriginal art in Sotheby's. Some of the artists whose work is represented there are still alive, but none of the works on offer is a new one. They are from collections, mostly private collections, up for resale. There is no one there that Elliot recognises, but he is sure the auction room is full of people like Miles, or Miles' uncle Roly; maybe people like Dougie Nicholson, hunting down treasures for distant clients. As far as he can see, there are no Aboriginal people there at all.

Very few of the paintings sell for less than the price of a good toyota.

19

ELLIOT DREAMS that his old self is frozen into a glacier in high, white mountains. He tries to dig it out with a pickaxe, but it is impossible. He can't do it without hacking himself to pieces. But when he wakes up, he is compelled to go and have a look at his history. In the corner of the front bedroom is a pile of boxes. They contain everything that came down from his unit in Alice after the robbery. He went through them once with Sandra, very early on, removing the best of his clothes and any important documents. The rest has been sitting there for the intervening three years or so, unregarded.

In some ways, the boxes are disappointing. There are a lot of books that he will never read again; there are bank statements and utility bills and legal documents relating to his mother's death, all neatly filed and labelled. There are flyers from fast food outlets, old copies of The Centralian Advocate, which he often bought when he was living there but seldom read. He finds an unopened rego reminder for the station wagon, and for a moment he forgets that he did eventually sell it; practically gave it away in the end, to the dealer where he had left it all those years ago. He puts it aside and finds, underneath, a sheaf of papers, stapled together and bearing the imprints of several coffee mugs. On the top page it reads:

'Indigenous peoples have the right of self-determination. By virtue of that right they freely determine their political status and freely pursue their economic, social and cultural development'. - UN Declaration on the Rights of Indigenous Peoples

ELLIOT TURNS OVER THE PAGES; finds what he knows he will find. Not one single signature. Not even his own. He drops it back into its box. A memory stirs, of the political upheaval around then: the coup against Rudd, the take-over by Gillard. But the excuse won't wash. That isn't why he did nothing with the petition. And he sees that going through all this stuff is doing nothing for his spirits, and he piles it all back where it came from until there is nothing left on the floor except for one thing. He didn't notice it when he was going through the boxes, but it must have fallen out from between the pages of a book or a journal. It is the feather, still ablaze with colour, of the red-tailed black cockatoo.

20

WHEN HE TURNS on the computer after breakfast, there is the email he has been waiting for, from Gary Cameron. There are two attachments, photographs of paintings by Doris. He opens them, convinced that at last he has tracked down the stolen paintings, but he is shocked by what he sees. These images are nothing like the ones he has been studying so assiduously over the preceding years. These are like bad copies, the dot-work sloppy and sparse, with nothing of the fine detail that Doris is renowned for. They are her work, though. He knows that because she is in some of the photos as well, holding the canvases by their top corners. She looks small and very frail, and absolutely furious.

Elliot is badly rattled. He returns to the email again and again, staring at the photographs, unable to work out what to think or what to do. He phones Drew, but Drew's patience with him has run out.

'I'm a doctor, mate, not a social worker.'

Elliot said, 'Right. Not your problem, then.'

'For fuck's sake, Elliot. You'd need to be God to sort out all the social injustices going on in Alice Springs. And, in fact, even he can't seem to manage it.'

Elliot said, 'I'm not asking—' but Drew wasn't there any more.

He tries Luke's number again, but it is, as always, out of range. There is no one else he can ask about what is going on, and whether there is anything he can do about it. Or at least, there is one person. Eventually, he swallows his pride and phones. Nicholson's mobile goes to message and when Elliot tries the gallery, they tell him Nicholson is out bush and can't be contacted. He leaves a message and waits.

21

LATE THAT EVENING, when he is watching TV, his front doorbell rings. He doesn't have drop-in relationships with friends or neighbours, and it is too late for hawkers or people selling utilities deals. He takes his stick, for psychological more than physical support, and opens the door. For a moment he doesn't recognise the young man on the doorstep, but when he smiles and says 'Hello, Elliot,' he recognises him. The colour in his hair has gone and so has the child-like appearance, but it is unmistakably Eric.

Elliot stands back, ushers him into the sitting room, turns off the TV. He says, 'Good to see you, Eric. What are you doing here?'

'Told you I might come to Melbourne,' Eric says. 'This your house?'

'It is.'

'Like, you own it? Or paying rent?'

'I own it.'

There is an awkward moment, when both of them stand and look at each other, full of uncertainty, then Elliot says, 'Go and have a look around. I'll put on a kettle.'

Eric takes himself on a tour, upstairs and down. When he gets to the kitchen, Elliot offers him a Coke, and he cracks it.

'You better now, Elliot?' he says.

'Yes. I am. And even better for seeing you.'

Eric grins. 'My Japanangka dad, eh?'

'Did I agree to that? I don't think I did.'

'Doesn't matter. Agree or not. You a Japanangka man. Everybody can see it.'

Elliot knows it is nonsense, but he glows anyway. Eric sits at the table, then stands up and tries the armchair, then stands up again, and Elliot realises he is too restless; there is something wrong.

'Have you taken something?' he says. 'Are you OK?'

'I'm good,' Eric says. 'My friends coming soon.'

'Coming here?'

'My cousin and his girlfriend. Some other brothers.'

Elliot opens the cupboard, sets out bread, butter, cheese and pickle, takes another loaf out of the freezer. He says, 'Have you seen the others? Been out to Nyaru?'

Eric shakes his head. His hair is black now, but still long, still curly. 'Never been there again. I seen Luke, though. Seen him in town. He told me he still got your toyota.'

'What?'

'Good car that one.'

Elliot says, 'Gammon?'

Eric laughs, and Elliot notices that he now has a tooth, or perhaps a bridge, where the gap used to be. 'True. That mechanic from Balgo, he pull it back there with his big truck. Fix it up. Luke driving it now, but only out on country. He can't get rego for going to town. I ask him why you never came for it. He said when you ready you can go to Nyaru and get it.'

'Fuck.'

Eric laughs. 'Fuck. Yes.'

'I thought it was finished.'

Eric helps himself to bread and pickle. Elliot says,

'So how long have you been in Melbourne? Where are you staying?'

'Been here a few days. Staying with family.' He gestures, in a direction that Elliot knows to be perfectly accurate, but which is meaningless to him. 'I don't like it there. Can I stop in that room? East one?' He gestures towards the front of the house.

'Well, I suppose…'

'I'm getting a job.'

'Really? What kind of job?'

'Any kind. Can you help me find one?'

'I don't know about that, Eric. Have you just come here on spec?'

'On spec?'

There is the sound of car doors slamming and feet scuffling on the street, and then on the doorstep. Elliot heads for the front door but Eric is there first. There are more young people there, in hoodies and scarves, wrapped up against the cold. Elliot turns back, leading the way, as he thinks, to the warm kitchen and the sandwiches. But the others don't follow. From the front door, he sees them standing in the street, in a close huddle, speaking in Warlpiri, their breath rising like steam in the cold Melbourne night. Then, without looking back, they walk away and begin to pile back into the car they came in.

Elliot calls out after them. Eric waves, but he doesn't wait. They are young people with somewhere to go, and Elliot is an irrelevance.

22

———

THAT NIGHT he finds it hard to sleep. The experience has rattled him deeply. Eric's brief visit somehow holds far more significance than the simple sum of its parts. Elliot has put his years of working in the desert communities behind him, as though they were related to the accident, as though they were one and the same thing. He is angry at Eric for leaving so soon, and he finds there is nothing he wants more than to have another chance; to let Eric have that room at the front of the house for as long as he needs it. He wants to be a Japanangka man, father for Eric. But could he handle it, in reality? Maybe it wasn't fair, but the truth was that he didn't have any confidence in Eric's ability to find a job and hold on to it. And having a young man and his friends hanging around the house was probably more than his temperament, still not entirely stable, could stand.

But he sees another possibility; that he could be a doctor again, back there in the desert communities. He is nearly well enough now, he thinks, to get back in the saddle again. He'll never be a missionary and he is far too wealthy to be a mercenary, but maybe, despite his conservative upbringing and conventional views, he is a bit of a misfit after all.

· · ·

WHEN HE DOES, eventually, fall asleep, he dreams about the car, a battered wreck now, limping along on oval wheels, creaking and juddering. When he wakes up he laughs at the dream, knowing it might not be too far off the truth.

BUT HE HOPES it has earned its keep, that toyota, and that it has taken Luke out on country, and his family maybe, and the troubled youngsters of Nyaru. The glacial wastes of Elliot's life are melting fast now, and it seems to him that everything is suddenly happening at once; memories streaming through, coincidences piling in, one upon the next. He puts the cockatoo feather in the spout of a teapot he doesn't use, up on the shelf, and the minute he takes his hand off it, the phone rings. It is Nicholson, returning his call. He doesn't need to see the photographs to know what it's all about. Doris has started doing 'quick ones' for small money. He has already seen them coming up on eBay. He doesn't know what is behind it.

'Sometimes, with the old people, it's not too hard to persuade them.'

'I can't imagine anyone applying persuasion to Doris,' Elliot says. 'She's tough as nails.'

'She's old, though. She hasn't been painting for a while. Not for me, anyway. Maybe somebody is leaning on her.'

Elliot finds the idea hard to swallow. The photos are up on his screen. He can hardly bear to look at them. Nicholson goes on, 'You ever turn up those other paintings, Elliot?'

'No.'

'You know I didn't take them?'

'I don't know anything, Dougie. But I've given up hope of every finding them.'

'Yeah. You're right. I would have heard about it if they turned up on the market. They're in a creek somewhere, mate. Take my word for it.'

23

So Elliot does, finally. He admits defeat, and in a symbolic gesture of resignation, he goes through his browser and deletes all the book-marked web pages of dealers and galleries and museums and articles. But it turns out that Nicholson is wrong about the paintings. They aren't in a creek. And they were never stolen, either.

24

THE FOLLOWING AFTERNOON, after his morning clinic, Elliot returns to the spare room and looks at the unpacked boxes. He should throw the whole lot out, he knows that, but there is some little part of him that resists. He thinks of the sessions with the psychologist and the book about Jung. He listens to that small resisting piece of himself. It is the same personality complex that made him keep all those things in the first place, all those bills and receipts, all the records of his life, for tax purposes perhaps, or just for the sake of being orderly and organised. And that is how it comes to him, finally—the missing piece of the jigsaw—the thing that has been disturbing him since he found out about the break-in. He would never have left the paintings in a place with such shoddy security. It just wasn't in his character.

He races downstairs. He still has no memory of what he did, but there is a very obvious place to begin. He makes a phone call.

That is all it takes.

25

THE PAINTINGS TURN up on Elliot's doorstep a few days later, still in their water pipe with all its crossings out and stickering. The label with his address on it and the courier company sticker represent the beginning of a new layer, but underneath them, protruding from each side, is his name in red marker, exactly as he now remembers writing it, the day after he bought the car and visited Dougie Nicholson, the day he left the paintings in the RFDS control room, for safe keeping, on his way out to take his last-but-one clinic. The tube had been put out of the way, propped up in a dark corner behind the filing cabinets, and had been there ever since, unconsidered by anyone in the busy office, where there were always more urgent priorities.

Elliot is prepared this time for the powerful emotional reaction the paintings create in him. He can feel their energy even before he opens the tube and slides the roll out. He takes his time looking through them, laying them out flat on his kitchen floor, one by one. And finally, at long last, he sees beyond the dots. When he comes to the strange one that Nicholson had remarked upon, he knows straight away that he will never again be without it, wherever he ends up living. Provenance or no provenance, Elliot intends to buy this painting from the woman who created it. It isn't just because of the things Nicholson said about it: that it might be a representation of an ancient dreamtime story or something that happened last year, or even that there was an outside chance it could have been an image of his own little trip out on country with her and Linda. It is the waves, the huge area of flowing lines conjoining from several different directions, which he now sees are dunes, just like the ones he crossed with Luke and the others. He sees waterholes in there as well, he sees Eric drawing in the sand, how those marks were not a map, not a story, but both: they were jukurrpa. He understands the way the land speaks through the artist, creating the symbols of the culture that once looked after it, still looks after it, where it is given the chance. The painting brings him right in there. The painting is country.

The other ones he will return to her. What she does with them, or with the money he pays her, is none of his business. His fight, if he has one left in him, is not with Dougie Nicholson or Gary Cameron, or with any of the dealers in Aboriginal art across Australia. His fight is with diabetes and otitis media and rheumatic fever and all the other endemic problems that are the business of doctors in remote Aboriginal communities.

The way things have come together over the last few days has lost the power to surprise him now. He is not of that land, but he still has a love for it, and he can't deny that it is calling him back. As soon as he can organise a locum, he will be booking tickets and heading for the red centre, to finally tie up his longstanding business with Doris, and to meet up with Luke again and maybe, if what Eric told him is true, to get back behind the wheel of that old toyota.

He thinks that old self that he has been trying so hard to find might be waiting there after all, still roaming with the dingoes on the other side of the dog fence.

ACKNOWLEDGMENTS

Thanks to the *Arts' Council of Ireland* for the travel and training award which kickstarted this book, to *Varuna, The Writers' House* in New South Wales, where some early ideas were hatched, and to *The Tyrone Guthrie Centre in Annaghmakerrig*, who facilitated the exchange.

Thanks also to the residents, yapa and kardiya, of the Warlpiri community of Yuendumu, who were so generous with their time and knowledge.

And finally, thanks to these people, who took the time to read drafts of this book at various stages and give invaluable suggestions: Sara Jane Kingston, Dervla Murphy, Michael McCaughan, Leonie Norrington, Jo Dutton, Wendy Baarda and Sam McKell.

ABOUT THE AUTHOR

Kate Thompson is an award-winning author of literary fiction for readers of all ages. She lives in the West of Ireland.

ALSO BY KATE THOMPSON

Lightning Source UK Ltd.
Milton Keynes UK
UKHW010616311019
352616UK00004B/277/P